Neptune's War

Neptune's War

Broken Cosmos Volume Three

Ian Kennedy

Copyright Notice

Special Thanks

Beta Readers:
Geoff Kwitko
Jenna Harper
Hannah Climas
Janina Kennedy

Cover Art:
Courtney Egan (Eucafox)

Chapter 1

The *Old Monarch* and the *Iron Bastion* were at the forefront of the Collective Zone fleet as it forged into Solar Solutions space. The crews had been woken up. Everyone was at battle stations as the ships moved in practised formation. They took up a blockading pattern around Europa and the other colonies and stations that hovered around Jupiter. The ships stayed outside the weapon range of the colonies and stations, but they set up a cordon around the planet preventing ships entering and leaving the area.

Uxus stood on the bridge of the *Old Monarch* and watched as his ships branched out and took up a holding pattern around the planet.

"CEO Sir, there's a signal from a shuttle. It's faint, but it is our security code..." the Communications Officer said with precision from her holo-terminal on the bridge.

"Pick it up. I want to know what it is." Uxus had an idea, but he needed to be sure.

"Yes, sir! It'll be in the docking bay in about thirty minutes as our craft have scrambled already," the officer said.

Uxus smiled and headed towards the docking bay. He got there and waited, his personal guard fanning out around the observation chamber. After a short time, the shuttle was brought onboard by a salvage craft and the medical and salvage teams began investigating the person who contained within.

The shuttle was squat and lozenge shaped. It had one view port that stretched across the tapered front and at the

1

back it had a couple of small engines. It sat on four small landing skids

"CEO Sir," the radio crackled into the observation room. "It's a Trader, a priest...he seems to be alive. Do we wake him up?"

Uxus smiled, he was right. "Yes, wake him up. I'll be there to talk to him in a minute." He left the observation room and headed down to the docking bay down a flight of metal stairs, his Guard not far behind.

Uxus got to the shuttle just as the occupant was coughing and spluttering to consciousness. "So, Virtus, what news?" he snapped at the man in priest robes who staggered from the pod.

"Master!" Virtus grovelled and grabbed the CEO's right hand, which looked smoother since the longevity surgery.

Uxus shook the man free and watched him grovel with disgust. "Stand up, man!" he barked.

"Sir, Master, CEO! I, I have failed you. The Europa Colony's computer is not free. They set up firewalls and blocks on me...I couldn't..." Virtus seemed to be crying.

"I know the Europa Colony is still there. I've blockaded it! I know you failed!" Uxus towered over the snivelling man.

"Our dream of freeing the computer is over..." cried the priest.

"Dream? You think I care about your stupid little cult?" snapped Uxus.

"Sir?" Virtus paused, his face contorted.

"I. Don't. Care. About. Your. Cult or Sect. Or whatever you want to call it!" said Uxus in staccato chatter, labouring each word. "I never have. I just wanted the armed bastions in my way removed so that I could invade without hassle. When I contacted you years ago, when you were just setting up on *Florida Station*, I knew you'd fall for anything that made you feel special. And you've screwed it up! I have no further use for you." Uxus turned and began to leave the docking bay.

"B-but?" mewled Virtus, "but, CEO Sir! Our plan! You said..."

"All I needed was your devotion and it did not pay off. Oh well, I made a mistake. Do as you wish, I have no more need of your services," snapped Uxus and he left the docking bay and the broken Virtus collapsed in a heap on the floor.

Uxus smiled. That had gone well.

***

Virtus felt lost. His great benefactor and supporter who he had based much of his life's work on had proved to be a lie. Everything he had worked for and killed for was a lie. Anger rose in him. He felt cheated.

The salvage crews and medical teams had left him alone in the docking bay with his small spacecraft. He had no purpose left on the *Old Monarch*. And it was evident that his CEO did not care for him anymore.

Virtus got back in the shuttle and set the cryo-pod for an indefinite length of time. He launched the craft out of the *Old Monarch* and prepped for an infinite sleep. No one paid him any attention.

Someday, someone might pick him up. A cryo-pod could sustain someone in suspended animation for an almost infinite time, provided it did not fail. He just wanted oblivion. His world was gone, and his purpose was over.

As Virtus climbed into the cryo-pod aboard his little craft, he felt somehow serene. He knew that he would never see life again. He would drift around Jupiter forever. Perhaps that was a fitting end to his folly.

The cryo-pod closed around him, and he fell asleep. His soul was gone, yet he smiled as darkness overcame him. He did not dream. He drifted through the void.

Chapter 2

The Europa Colony was in crisis. Draz and Artisius had been called to the command centre. Alfred was already there, still working on fixing Virtus' planned insurrection. Draz looked over at him and wondered whether Alfred had been given a chance to sleep.

The Collective Zone fleet had arrived sooner than expected; weeks sooner. Somehow they had navigated the Mazine Pass in the asteroid belt nearest Jupiter instead of going the long route around it and they had shaved weeks off their travel time.

Artisius was livid. Draz saw him raging at Anya for keeping them on Europa. Draz saw that he had changed his tunic to a new, unbloodied, undamaged one of the same kind after he was treated for the wound on his arm.

"It wasn't my decision," Anya replied. "I merely wanted Alfred to fix the problems; you were free to go..."

At this Draz saw Artisius rage even harder. He yelled and swore, and Draz smiled to herself in seeing him exhibit emotion in these circumstances. She realised that he was a normal human being after all, and that he did care for his crew, not just himself.

"How am I meant to get my crew and passengers off Europa now?" Artisius yelled at Anya, he flailed his arms for emphasis.

Draz smile widened. He did care for her and Alfred; who Draz assumed were the mentioned 'passengers'.

Draz turned her gaze to the observation dome above her. There were ships hanging in the space above them. They were the large, angular craft of the Collective Zone, with white, silver and blue hull plates. They had set up a blockade around Jupiter and had blocked any flight in or out of the planet's vicinity.

According to the Scanning Operator's barked responses to Anya's repeated questions, the Collective Zone fleet was spread out around Europa, blocking all traffic.

It seemed strange to Draz that such a body of craft could almost sneak up on a collection of colonies and stations. However, this was not the case, they had detected the Collective Zone ships a week ago, but it was assumed they were a month away. But suddenly after a week, they were on the Solar Solutions' doorstep.

"Can we fight them?" asked Draz in the middle of one of Anya's rants at her subordinates.

Anya paused mid rant. She had forgotten about Artisius and was busy dressing down the Scanning Officer for not planning for the enemy fleet's arrival so soon.

"Fight? FIGHT? The entire Collective Zone fleet is on our doorstep, and you want to fight them?" Anya bellowed, fixing her icy gaze on Draz, who shifted uneasily in the spotlight.

"Well, we have weapons don't we?" Draz said.

"Yes, but," Anya said, slumping, "it's only a few auto-turrets and some missile pods. We'd be eradicated. We're a trading outpost and a research centre, not a military base."

"Eradicated like Mars..." Draz mumbled. Anya did not hear; she had turned her attention to someone else.

Artisius came over to Draz and drew her aside for a moment. "Do you want to escape? We could flee amongst some refugee ships if they try to break the blockade. We have a cloaking device..." he said.

Draz looked at him with calculating eyes. "And Alfred?" she said.

"Well, if we could get him then he could come with us..." Artisius looked over at the zetter.

The response did not please Draz and she shook her head. "No, I'm not leaving without him!" Draz shook her head again.

Artisius sighed. "All right then...I hope we make it through this..." He stood next to Draz as Anya raged around the colony's command centre.

Suddenly a voice came crackling over the radio and the entire command centre went silent. They knew who it was, and could not believe it. It even put an end to Anya's raging. Draz saw Artisius turn a rather lighter shade as he heard the syllables unfold over the frequency.

"Solar Solutions, Europa Colony," the voice spoke, "and all other stations and colonies around Jupiter, you will submit without a fight to the glory of the Collective Zone..."

"It can't be," said Draz, not believing her ears. She knew the voice from back on Earth, from the broadcasts over the holo-terminals and radio stations. It was her former ruler. It was Uxus! His voice sounded a little younger than Draz remembered, but it was the CEO of the entire Collective Zone on a ship invading Solar Solutions space. Draz could not believe that he would risk himself like this.

"If you submit," the voice continued, "then you will be welcomed into our great corporate empire. If you resist, you will be expunged from the face of history, you have my firm promise!" The communication paused. "And Europa Colony specifically, I know you're harbouring the fugitives on the *Green Dragon*. For this reason, you must be punished, please broadcast your submission to my troops and this will be as painless as possible. To the *Green Dragon* crew: I want that certain hard drive that you stole with my special plans. Turn yourself in. If you resist in any way, the colony will be turned into molten slag. I await your compliance." The communication went dead.

Draz stared at Artisius who looked back in horror.

Anya had reappeared in their faces again. She yelled something about them bringing doom to her colony. Draz did not quite understand her shrill voice. It had assumed a dialect that was foreign to Draz's Earth understanding of language.

"You'll have to evacuate the colony," said Artisius.

"Evacuate!?" Anya yelled. "I'm turning you over to Uxus, we're not evacuating!"

Draz dashed from Artisius' side to Alfred's who had just finished his zet and was regaining consciousness. He stood but was unsteady on his feet.

"Zet complete...can I rest now?..." Alfred staggered, holding his head. He was unaware of the current events transpiring around him.

Draz explained the situation, but it was plain to see that, in his exhaustion, Alfred did not quite understand.

"Please, Anya," Artisius begged. "You know what's right. Evacuate the colony; you know that's the best action. Some ships will get through the blockade..."

"Ma'am!" shouted the Scanning Officer. "We have reinforcements!"

All their attention was directed at the young soldier crewing the terminal.

"What is it?" asked Anya, moving to the terminal.

Artisius smiled. Draz saw on his face that he knew what it was.

"It's the Solar Solutions Fleet!" whispered Artisius. He looked at Draz and smiled. "We might be saved!"

"People of Jupiter!" came the transmission from the incoming ships. "This is the Solar Solutions Fleet led by the *Silver Ark*. We have come to your aid and will defend you. Do not be afraid. The Collective Zone fleet will be turned back!"

"It's the Solar Solutions Fleet! They're a few days away!" shouted Anya with joy and relief. She spun on her heel and glared at Artisius. "You wanted to evacuate, then go. Just. Go!" She pointed her finger at the command centre door and then snapped around on her heel and continued to bark orders to the command centre staff.

Artisius followed her. "The Solar Solutions fleet," he said. "This changes everything. They're here Anya! They're here!" He paused as she turned to face him. "I...we'll stay. It's safer for everyone that way, now that the Solar Solutions fleet is here! If the *Green Dragon* runs then the Collective Zone will see us running to the Solar Solutions fleet and will punish Europa. Remember what happened to Mars!" Artisius tried to make Anya see.

"So now you want to stay?!" asked Anya. "Why shouldn't I just hand you over to the Collective Zone? Wouldn't that solve everyone's problems?"

"Don't do that...please. Just trust me. If you hand us over, many more will die," Artisius said. "We'll stay here for now. We'll be ready to leave if things go badly with the Solar Solutions Fleet..."

Draz could just hear Artisius explaining this at a distance.

"Take the zetter to rest, but I'll need him later," Anya said, waving her arms in exasperation. "I never understand you, Artisius."

Artisius smiled. "I always understand you..."

Draz and Alfred stood together in the chaos. Alfred was almost passing out from exhaustion. Draz was joined by Artisius, and they helped him back to the assigned quarters they had on Europa.

***

When they left Alfred sleeping off his exhaustion, Draz and Artisius then headed to one of the large, open, observation platforms dotted around Europa's colony in an effort to see more of the fleets that were massing around Jupiter. They joined a throng of people who had the same idea and had heard that the Solar Solutions fleet was on its way. Everyone in the colony seemed to have stopped work and come out to look from the observation platforms at the massing fleets.

"I hope staying is the right thing to do..." said Draz.

She looked at Artisius with concern in her face. He was looking skywards at the large and angular Collective Zone ships that had taken up a position near Europa, and were totally visible in the dull light from the Sun.

"So do I..." whispered Artisius. "So do I, but you see my reasoning? Don't you? If we leave now the Collective Zone fleet will destroy everything here. They cannot risk bombarding Europa while we're here. We have to see what the Solar Solutions fleet does, too. If they lose, we run. If they win, we don't need to run..."

Draz nodded her understanding. It seemed sensible reasoning. "What about our cloaking device? Can't we use that to get away?" She craned her neck up to see the spectacle above her as the Collective Zone ships moved and spread out.

"You know Uxus better than I do. You were born on Earth and lived there under his reign." Artisius paused. "Do you think he would just let Europa go if we did that?"

Draz knew what he meant, and she knew he was right. Uxus would punish all of Jupiter if his prey slipped away unnoticed. Uxus wanted a quick victory against the Solar Solutions fleet and then the *Green Dragon* would be his.

Draz and Artisius stood looking up, like many of the other people around them. They watched with bated breath.

"So...it looks like war is inevitable," Draz said with a sigh. "I wish, I just wish I could fight...somehow."

Chapter 3

CEO Gunter stood on the bridge of the *Silver Ark*. He saw Jupiter in front of them and he had ordered his ships to adopt a broad formation so that the fleet could observe all of what the Collective Zone fleet was doing.

Gunter watched from the observation dome at the top of the bridge. He was silent and pensive. He, as he kept reasoning with himself, did not want conflict; but that seemed inevitable now. He felt angry. The Collective Zone fleet had the audacity to cross into his territory and threaten the peace and stability of his corporation. He was more than angry, he was enraged. Somehow he had hoped that the reports that had reached him years ago on Neptune had been fake; a lie. But now it was clear that all the reports were true.

As Gunter watched the bridge around him, he saw Cranmere fussing over something with one of the Scanning Officer crew at a holo-terminal. Gunter overheard something about Cranmere protesting that the enemy fleet was too large, and the sensors must be wrong. Gunter smiled.

An aide stood next to him, looking attentively at his master. It was apparent that the aide believed absolutely in the word of his master in the way he was standing and staring at Gunter waiting to carry out any order.

The aide was young, late teens perhaps; Gunter was only in his mid forties, but he felt ancient. The aide seemed too young to be about to go to war.

Gunter's mechanical leg protested as he turned to the aide, who stiffened as his master turned attention to him.

"What's your name, son?" asked Gunter.

"AlphaGammaDelta95, CEO Sir!" reported the aide with precision.

"No, I mean your actual name," Gunter asked, as if the aide was the only person in the world around them and they were not in a hectic command centre of a ship leading a fleet to battle.

Gunter knew that the aide might not see tomorrow. Gunter knew that he might not see tomorrow.

"Uh..." the aide stuttered. It was evident that he was not expecting this line of questioning, and that he was honoured by his master's frank question. Only important people in the Solar Solutions Corporation knew the person's real name. The aide blushed. "Simon, CEO Sir..." His voice was quiet and uncertain.

"Well Simon, I hope we see the end of this day." Gunter smiled at the aide, who smiled back. "Prepare a comms channel; I want to talk to that bastard in the lead ship, broadcast widest band; unencrypted. I need everyone to hear this!"

The aide scurried away to make his master's command come true.

After a short wait, the aide returned giving the nod that the communication channels were open. Gunter steeled himself for what might be his last announcement.

"People of Jupiter, your CEO is here to protect you. Do not be afraid. The Solar Solutions fleet is here to drive these bastards from our space." He paused to add emphasis. After a short gap, Gunter continued. "Invaders of the Collective Zone fleet, turn back now. I give you this one and only warning. We are prepared to fight for our territory and will not tolerate any infringement of our sovereignty. We trade with you, but we will not submit to you. Turn back, I say, or face the consequences." Gunter fell silent and made the signal to cut communications. The aide ran off to oblige, returning seconds later.

"How was that, Simon?" Gunter asked looking at the young man next to him.

"Magnificent, CEO Sir!" The aide beamed. It was clear he had no idea the CEO would honour him so much.

"Good, I'm glad." Gunter looked sadly out at Jupiter. "Now, prepare the bombers for launch and power up the auto-turrets and missile pods across the fleet..." he trailed off in thought.

The aide lingered a little in case there was something more said, but when it was obvious that the CEO had finished his order the aide rushed off to make things happen.

Gunter paced the bridge. He had never been to war before, but this moment had been building for years, and all his crew were looking to him for guidance. He may be able to motivate people through speech, that was one thing; it was totally different to be able to command people tactically in battle.

He stared out the observation dome of the *Silver Ark* at the rotating form of Jupiter ahead of him. He hoped for good fortune. He knew he must prevail. He did not want this, but his hand was forced. He knew he must prevail.

***

"...Turn back, I say, or face the consequences."

CEO Uxus paced the bridge of the *Old Monarch*, the insolent words of Gunter ringing in his ears. He was restless. He wanted to get into the fight as soon as possible and smash the Solar Solutions fleet that had appeared from the shadow of Jupiter's bulk.

"Damn their better engines, I thought I had time..." Uxus swore. The bulk of Jupiter's mass had shielded the arriving Solar Solutions ships from his fleet's scanners. "Well, if they want to fight, then who am I to deny them?"

The bridge was a flurry of activity. Missile pod launchers and auto-turrets were being powered up across the Collective Zone fleet that had blockaded Jupiter's stations and colonies.

The communications of the bridge crackled on a secured line. "CEO, what would you have us do?" The voice was Boltha's. Although she may have disapproved of some of Uxus' methods, she would have her battle and her glory.

"Boltha, I need all ships on war footing as soon as possible. You are in command for this battle. My ship will hang back and observe. Don't disappoint me!" Uxus replied.

"As you wish, CEO." Uxus could almost hear the smile in Boltha's voice as she replied to his command.

"I need comms, wide band, unencrypted." Uxus snapped to the Communications Officer.

"Sir!" the woman replied with military precision and indicated that the communications channels were now open.

"To all the colonies and stations around Jupiter, this is CEO Uxus of the Collective Zone. Stay put and you will be unharmed. I have no quarrel with you. Hand over the *Green Dragon* and her crew or else." Uxus paused, then continued. "As for the Solar Solutions fleet and CEO Gunter, don't play at war, boy. I address you directly. I know you; I knew your father. Do you think you can stand up to me in a military engagement? Don't test me." Uxus spat the last words and indicated for the communications channels outside the fleet to be shut down.

"CEO Sir," chimed the Energy Officer on the bridge. "The Solar Solutions fleet are powering up their weapons and moving to battle formation..."

"So, he wants war, does he?" snarled Uxus. "Well, we have crossed the Rubicon...as an old general once said." He smiled to himself before raising his voice to a shout so that all the bridge could hear, and it gave no doubt as to what to do. "Prepare for battle!"

Chapter 4

The *Silver Ark*'s fleet of Triton class heavy bombers sat in the landing bay with arming crews rushing around to prepare the craft for the coming battle. The bombers were large and angular; painted black to make sure that they were harder to see against the blackness of space, as they closed with their targets.

The Solar Solutions method of war was one of sending in bombers first, to soften up the targets and break up the enemy fleet, and then to send the war ships in to finish the job. This jarred with the Collective Zone's tactics of sending in their capital ships and blasting apart the enemy fleet with close range fire from the main ships' guns.

The map crews of the *Silver Ark* were working hard. They had the task of assessing the makeup of the Collective Zone fleet and interpreting the scanner details handed to them.

***

Gunter stood on the bridge and looked at the projection of his fleet and the fleet of the Collective Zone on the Scanning Officer's holo-screen. He pursed his lips. Beads of sweat were forming on his brow and the business suit he wore felt altogether too hot and awkward for him at the moment. Uxus had called his bluff and was mustering for war. Gunter had hoped that his bold intervention would somehow scare off the invading CEO, but it had failed.

"CEO Sir," said an orderly. "Sir, the bombers are waiting for your orders..." the small man said with a grace that belied the fact that he, also, would have felt terribly anxious about the coming engagement.

Gunter swallowed hard. He did not want this. Once the bombers launched there was no going back. Perhaps he could reason with Uxus? No; that was impossible. There was no time for that. The moment for peace had passed. Gunter's stomach churned.

Gunter opened his mouth, but no words came out. He knew that he had to put on a brave face for the common soldier. He knew morale was key. He tried again, after swallowing a large lump in his throat.

"Load the torpedoes on the Tritons and get the crews to their bombers. Launch as soon as they are ready. Follow our standard plan of attack. Cripple the enemy ships and the rest will follow..." he trailed off.

The sweat down Gunter's brow worsened. He had just declared war. Even though he knew it was Uxus who was the aggressor, the fact that the Solar Solutions fleet would strike first sent a shiver down his spine. He would lead his corporation to war, and he had no idea of the outcome.

***

The arming crews bustled around the angular craft in the landing bay. They only armed the craft when they were about to go to war. In the meantime, the weapons they loaded were stored safely inside an armoured compartment in the centre of the *Silver Ark*. The crews drove on bulky transport vehicles that towed the large, capital ship destroying torpedoes that were to be loaded onto the exterior of the Triton bombers.

Each torpedo weighed a number of tonnes and was winched into place with delicate precision that somehow belied their purpose.

The arming crews then inserted the detonators and primed the warheads ready for combat. This marked a turning point in the bombers' existence: before this, they were impotent; after this, they were machines of death.

If an attack were to fall on the *Silver Ark*, or any other Solar Solutions carrier craft after the torpedoes were armed, there was a great risk that the warheads could detonate inside their carrier craft and wreak utter havoc. Therefore, the crews had to work fast, and it had to be clear that there was no incoming enemy attack.

The torpedoes were simply solid fuel rockets that had a small nuclear warhead on each. They were launched at close proximity to the target enemy ship and the solid fuel rocket was ignited and sent the warhead, hopefully, deep into the hull of the enemy ship and then the warhead, on a sensor or timer, would detonate, tearing a hole in the enemy ship.

While the bomb crews were arming the torpedoes and loading them on the bombers, the other arming crew loaded and made ready the defensive machine guns on each of the bombers' hard points. The bombers were too small and lacked the reactor for auto-turret lasers or missile pods that larger capital ships used to defend themselves. Therefore, each bomber was fitted with a crude and old-fashioned pair of large calibre machine guns in the tail and on the upper and lower sides of the craft. The arming crews made sure these guns were functional and loaded with as many bullets as could be fitted into the cramped confines of the bomber.

As the bombers were armed and made ready, their crews braced themselves for the upcoming task and were briefed on what their mission was to come.

Each bomber was crewed by two humans: a pilot and a co-pilot who also doubled as a torpedo aimer and releaser. In addition to the two humans, there were three tech-slaves who operated the gun turrets in the tail and above and below the hull.

***

Bomber pilot OmegaEpsilon15, or OE15, filed into the briefing room with his co-pilot and torpedo aimer GammaDeltaEpsilon78. GDE78 was one of the best practiced torpedo aimers in the fleet. She could hit a fast moving enemy ship from above with ease.

They saw the other pilot and co-pilot teams at the surrounding tables. They sat at a table near the front. OE15 could tell that everyone was apprehensive. It was a collective nervousness that all soldiers get when they are about to go into combat. They knew their training would serve them well, but they did not know whether they would make it back alive.

The commanding officer of the bomber group, AlphaDelta08 walked in and all the pairs jumped to their feet in salute.

"At ease," the commander said. He was a grizzled old man who had seen war before. They all trusted him absolutely. They sat down and got out their tablets and maps ready for taking notes on the upcoming mission.

"Well, this is it. As you probably know," he said. He was the only calm person in the room. "The target is the Collective Zone blockade ships. The Collective Zone has invaded our space and we are the first line of defence..." He paused as a computer generation of the enemy fleet was displayed on a screen on the wall behind him.

A murmur went up amongst the pairs. "...So many of them..."

The commander raised his hand and the murmur died down. "Yes, there are lots of them. Thirty plus in fact, but that will make it easier for our torpedoes to hit a target!" He smiled.

OE15 and GDE78 made notes as the briefing unfolded and it became apparent that the objective was not to hit the main capital ships the *Iron Bastion* and the *Old Monarch*, they would be too well defended with fighter cover and flak batteries on their hulls. The aim of the bomber group was to target the smaller guarding ships that were blockading Europa and clear the path for the Solar Solutions fleet to attack the larger ships when the bombers got back.

"...You'll have to climb for altitude well before beginning your attack on the enemy ships. Their armour is weaker on top and there should be fewer flak cannons pointed at you. They've amassed Octhos Pattern, which means they're a staggered formation that defends in depth..." The briefing went on. "...Flight time to target is approximately four hours. We believe the enemy will stay put so there should be no change in time. They want to draw us in and attack us in their blockade of Europa and the Jupiter stations. They have no need to move. It is our turn to press the attack..."

"Should be easy..." said OE15 to himself.

GDE78 chuckled a little.

"Yes?" snapped the commander. He was suddenly standing in front of OE15.

"Uh, piece of cake, sir!" snapped OE15. His face went red.

"Indeed? Well, don't get cocky. You'll have to fly through flak, and enemy fighter cover. They know our tactics, but we also know theirs. Good luck! Dismissed!" The commander saluted the pilots.

They all jumped to their feet and saluted him back. After a slight pause, they all filed out of the briefing room and made their way to getting dressed for the flight.

***

OE15 and GDE78 filed into the crew preparation room. It was a large room with many different lockers around the walls. All the other pilot and co-pilot pairs were getting ready for their mission.

As OE15 moved to his locker, he heard the various conversations between the pilots and co-pilots. All of them had never seen action before; the last war was before their time. Technically the last war was before his time too, but they had all trained very hard for this moment and it would not be long before they took off.

He was tense, but excited. His mind raced through the pre-flight checks that he would have to go through in a short time. He knew his Triton heavy bomber like no other.

He had trained for both fighter and bomber squadrons, and in the end he had been picked for bomber duty. He did not regret this. He enjoyed the camaraderie of a bomber pilot and co-pilot. But he wondered what it was really like to soar in a fighter into battle, not just in a simulator.

OE15 and GDE78 reached their lockers in the crush of the prep room and used their assigned keys to open them. Inside were the vacuum resistant flight suits and breathing apparatus that they would have to wear on the flight.

"I can never get used to these suits," said GDE78, she turned up her nose as she pulled the plastic and synthetic rubber suit from its hanger.

"But we need them," said OE15. "The inside of the bomber is equalised pressure to space so any flak shrapnel or bullets that pierce the hull don't decompress the whole thing. We need these to breathe and survive!" He knew that GDE78 knew this, but he smiled as he said this.

GDE78 rolled her eyes. "I know that, you fool."

"Well, before every practice run you seem to comment on the horrid nature of these suits...and I have to reply. It's like a ritual we have..." OE15 trailed off. It was clear GDE78 was not listening to him. She was busy donning her flight suit and her eyes told him she was a million kilometres away; probably going through the torpedo release and attack sequence, he reasoned.

They dressed in silence from then on. OE15 slipped the plastic and synthetic rubber airtight suit over his standard issue jump suit and considered what he was about to do. He was about to strike the first action in the next solar war. It may be his torpedo that caused the first deaths.

He shook his head. The Collective Zone started this with their invasion and blockade of Europa. They started this, it was his and his flight's job to stop them here and now so that there did not progress further into Solar Solutions space. He was actually promoting peace with this bombing run, he reasoned. If the Collective Zone broke through their defensive lines then there was no telling how much havoc they would wreak in Solar Solutions space.

He finished dressing. The suit felt uncomfortable. He and the rest of the squadron carried their helmets that would link up with the breathable oxygen canisters in the bombers. They did not put them on too early as they stank of synthetic rubber and plastic and were rather unpleasant. They also restricted some of their vision.

The squadron filed out towards their bombers in the landing bay at the bottom of the *Silver Ark*. Each pilot and co-pilot team split off, with confident but skittish glances to each other, some wished each other luck, and headed towards their respective bombers, which were now fuelled, bombed up and armed in their positions arrayed in a grid pattern on the flight deck.

OE15 and GDE78 came to their bomber and stopped. The ground crew were making the final checks to the systems and the torpedo that was slung underneath the bulk of the angular craft.

Three tech-slaves clomped past them as they stood on the outside of the bomber. OE15 shivered. He did not like those things. But they were necessary. They operated the guns. They had been equipped with vacuum suits so as they could survive the vacuum of space inside the bomber in flight; and they were very good at targeting as their eyes and senses had been upgraded substantially from a normal human's.

Also, if a bomber went down, only two proper humans were lost. It took a while to train a pilot and co-pilot team. Out in space where life was precious and people lived in space stations, there were not as many available humans as in the Collective Zone planets. Every life counted. If a tech-slave died, it did not really matter.

The tech-slaves boarded the bomber from a hole in the side and the ladder that led up to it. OE15 looked over at GDE78 and he saw the same look of disgust on her face that he assumed was on his. No one liked tech-slaves. It was something about their blank eyes, skull mesh and exposed spinal column that made them very inhuman. They felt pain just like a human, and they could be killed, but they were regarded as second-class creatures: cattle to be used and discarded when necessary, even though they were human too, once.

The gunnery stations in each bomber had no escape hatches. If a bomber was destroyed, then the tech-slaves died. The pilot and co-pilot could eject if they had time. And their emergency supply of oxygen would last a few hours if someone came to rescue them on their homing beacons.

After the tech-slaves had been loaded into the craft, the pilot and co-pilot teams boarded their respective craft.

OE15 and GDE78 climbed aboard, up the ladder, through the tight opening in the side of the bomber. They made their way along the interior of the bomber towards the cockpit at the front. They climbed over the wires and

24

cables and equipment that were exposed in the centre of the bomber.

Reaching the cockpit, OE15 sat down heavily in the pilot seat. He began to strap himself in with the assistance of GDE78. He connected up his helmet with the oxygen supplies that had been put there by the ground crews and were located below the cockpit and the two pilot and co-pilot chairs. He had to be strapped in tightly as when the craft decompressed he did not want to be injured or dislodged. He affixed his helmet over his head to his flight suit.

After OE15 was strapped in and connected to the oxygen, it was GDE78's turn to strap herself into her seat next to the pilot and put her helmet and breathing apparatus on. She was not strapped in as tightly, somewhat dangerously for the decompression, but she had to get out of her seat and drop down into the nose of the craft to guide the torpedo to its target in the middle of the battle. This was the most dangerous time for the bomber crew, as they had to fly level and guide the torpedo to the target. But all the crews knew this, and they were all trained to do it.

OE15 went through some of the pre-flight checks he had to do before the bomber took off. He checked the fuel and engine pressures and made sure his oxygen was flowing smoothly.

He looked out the cockpit at the landing bay around him. All around him the crews were doing the same thing, and trying to choke down their nerves.

He saw the ground crews scurrying out of the way of the bombers and the crews began to leave the docking bay, as the bombers waited for the decompression. He hated that part.

He looked over at GDE78. She seemed calm in her seat, but he could not really tell with her helmet on obscuring her face and eyes. She was too busy conducting pre-flight checks to pay attention to him.

OE15 breathed deeply. He smelled the synthetic rubber and plastic smell of the suit he was in. He felt sick, partly because of the smell, partly because he was going to war. But he had a job to do, and he was going to do it.

He looked out the front windows of the bomber and past the entrance to the docking bay ahead of them and into the darkness of space. The docking bay was slung under the *Silver Ark* and from where he was sitting he could see a good view of Jupiter and space out in front of the *Silver Ark*. He tried to calm himself.

The pre-flight checks were completed, and the ground crews had cleared the landing bay.

"Prepare for decompression and removal of gravity in the landing bay..." came the crackled command over all the crews' radios within their helmets.

OE15 braced himself and he sensed his co-pilot do the same as the magnetic fields on the docking bay opening in front of them was switched off and all the atmosphere was sucked out. There was a whooshing rushing noise and sensation and OE15 hoped that his helmet was fixed on properly.

After a minute, there was silence; pure silence; the silence of the vacuum of space. He felt even sicker, thanks to the lack of gravity. The bombers did not have any gravity well generators themselves, so the crew needed to be strongly strapped in.

Then came another radio command that broke the silence, "Begin engine start up!"

OE15 pressed the ignition switches and the four engines, two on each side of the bomber, kicked to life. He felt the rumble of the engines through his seat rather than hearing them, as there was no sound transmitted in the vacuum. He watched as the readouts on his control panel indicated that all four engines were operating optimally.

OE15 looked over at GDE78 and she gave him the thumbs up. He smiled. He looked out over the landing bay and saw blue glows coming from all the engines of the bombers around him. He did not hear them, but he knew they were all feeling what he felt.

"Launch!" The command was crisp and clear in the headphones of all the crews.

OE15 angled his engines through his controls and his craft began to rise off the landing bay without gravity. Then with a smooth movement, he angled his bomber's engines to face behind and he increased the throttle to maximum and he guided his bomber, with the others, out of the hole in the front of the *Silver Ark*'s docking bay.

OE15 formed up with the rest of his flight and climbed for altitude, as did the rest of the bombers to attack the enemy from above. He prepared for the four hour flight to his target. He looked out the windows at the black painted craft around him. They appeared as instruments of darkness, the predators of mechanised war. They were on their way to kill. But it was their job, OE15 reasoned. And their cause was a righteous one.

***

OE15 settled into his seat. He had trained in the simulators for these long flights. He felt the low rumble of the bomber's engines through the control column in his hands and through the seat he was sitting on. He felt calmer. The nerves of the pre-flight action had receded, and he was ready to achieve his mission. He knew he would feel nervous again when he got within flak and fighter range of the enemy fleet, but for now, their journey was peaceful.

He studied his instruments. Speed? Optimal. Targets? Highlighted on the computer screen in the middle of the command console. His target was assigned and lit up green amongst the swarm of red possible targets. His bomber's target was a medium sized cruiser that was blockading the nearest flight path to Europa. Other bombers in the flight would have the same target; there would be a saturation of damage so that it was sure that that particular target was destroyed; but he felt the weight of necessity pressing down on his mind: if he failed to destroy this target, Europa would still be blockaded. He took it personally that he had to achieve his mission, for the Solar Solutions Corporation.

OE15 scanned his other instruments. Fuel? Fine. Bombers were too small to have fusion drives or plasma drives that were capable of taking ships between planets. Bombers were simple intra-planetary craft that had to refuel after every mission. They had an endurance of about 12 hours maximum. This journey was supposed to be approximately eight hours round trip. To increase speed the ground crews only loaded the required amount of fuel into each bomber, so OE15 knew that he could not delay over the target, and he would have to head home after releasing his torpedo.

The Solar Solutions fleet would be making its way closer to the enemy fleet, OE15 thought, as they would have to engage them eventually after the bombers made their runs. Therefore, it would be a faster return than approach, but that was expected. They did not want to linger over the target or within flak range.

OE15 finished checking his instruments and looked up and out of the transparent windscreen that surrounded his pilot's seat. Filling one side of his vision was the unmistakable and gigantic mass that was Jupiter. It was huge. It defied all description.

OE15 felt a lump in his throat. He knew this was the limit of his Corporation's territory and that the Collective Zone had no reason to be here. They had brought war to the Solar System, and he, personally, felt that he was going to drive them back. With all the beauty of the Solar System, with all the wondrous things that were in it, both in the Solar Solutions territory and Collective Zone territory, they had to make war. How dare they, he thought, how dare they...

He scanned the space around him. There were stars, stars beyond imagining. He never got tired of that. He wondered if there were creatures out there. He assumed there were, but if there were, were they at peace? He hoped one day to see another star. He chuckled; he had never really seen his own star. He had never been out of Solar Solutions space, and here he was wanting to visit other stars.

He knew his views were not uncommon amongst the people of the Solar System. Many wanted to know about the other stars around their system, but he kept his views to himself anyway. He wondered if his very own CEO, who was back on the ship they had come from, wondered about the stars. OE15 wondered if Gunter ever stared into space and wondered what was out there. He pondered if the leader of the Collective Zone ever did the same...

Blanking his view of some of the stars around him were the silhouettes of the other bombers in the flight. He did not so much as see them, as they were painted black to make them hard to see with the naked eye, but he saw the blank spot where the stars should be behind them. Some blue glow from their engines was also visible. His nerves returned at the sight of his fellow pilots moving in towards their goals. Of course, the enemy ships and fighters had electronic scanning so the bombers would show up on that, but they tried to make themselves as invisible as possible.

Suddenly he was aware of the nasty plastic and synthetic rubber smell within his helmet and suit as he took some deep breaths to calm himself. He hated the fact that the whole ship was decompressed and all that was between him, and the vacuum of space was a suit of thin plastic and synthetic rubber that was sealed around the edges. He understood that it was necessary, as if the ship was punctured and it had an atmosphere in it, then the decompression would kill everyone. This way the bomber was much sturdier, but he still hated it.

"What's up?" came the chatter over the radio. It was from GDE78. She was looking at him. Her ghoulish helmet and oxygen tube and plastic suit were staring at him.

"Oh, nothing," he replied. "Just nerves..." he lied. He knew that she was not party to his views about visiting other stars and the beauty of the Solar System that they were in now.

GDE78 was a very practical woman; she knew her job as a co-pilot and torpedo aimer, and she was excellent at both of those, but she viewed OE15's opinions about the beauty of the Solar System as irrelevant. She basically viewed the universe through her job goals. GDE78 was an excellent soldier, but that was all.

OE15 saw the hood of the helmet and suit nod and GDE78 said nothing. She returned to her task of making sure the engines were operating correctly and monitoring fuel use. Every so often she would check the torpedo controls and make sure the warhead was armed.

OE15 could tell that she was jumpy too. She did not say anything, but the repeated checks indicated to him that she was nervous.

They settled into the journey. The low rumble of the vibrations of the engines made a sort of mesmeric thrumming. OE15 gripped the control column gently. The enemy fleet was still hours away, but they would be crossing into the flak zone and fighter cover as the enemy fleet would defend itself against their attacks. The bombers were still beyond visual range to the enemy fleet, but it would detect them on its scanners soon, and then they would be in combat.

Time went by. OE15 checked the chronometer on the instrument panel. They had been flying for two hours thirty minutes approximately. Suddenly a bright flash happened off the port side of his cockpit. It was silent, and there was no shock wave, but he knew what it meant. They were within flak range, and they had been detected.

More and more flashes dotted the space around the bombers. None very accurate, but their purpose was to discourage movement within the formation as much as damage the bombers and so that the enemy fighters could intercept the bombers that were kept on course.

The bombers did not have their own fighter support due to the range involved. The fighters would only have the range for half the trip. Fighters were made for short-ranged interceptions. Although the capital ships would get closer to each other and then the fighters would be used, the bombers would have no initial cover and would have to brave the enemy alone.

Flashes came left and right, some close, some far. OE15 gripped the control column tighter. He held his course.

The glinting of the enemy fleet was at the limits of visible range now. He saw the scout ships of the Collective Zone fleet dotted against the outline of Jupiter. They were harsh and angular, but still very hard to see. OE15 smiled. Their time was coming.

There was a large flash off to starboard and OE15 snapped his head around to the right to see a nearby bomber take a direct hit from the flak shell. He swallowed hard as he saw the craft buckle and burst apart as the shrapnel from the shell scythed through the thin metal case of the bomber and caused the fuel to ignite. There was another flash as the engines detonated and the crew screamed over the radio and were cut off as they were killed in an instant. The nuclear warhead on the torpedo did not explode, luckily for the fleet of bombers around it.

OE15 swallowed hard. He saw GDE78 looking out the window after the stricken bomber that was destroyed. He knew what she was feeling. She looked back out the front window. She checked the torpedo and bombing equipment again. OE15 held a steady course.

Chapter 5

CEO Gunter stood on the bridge of the *Silver Ark*. He had been there for hours. Although he did not believe in the conflict unfolding around him, he would rather have been partying, it was the right thing to do to remain on the bridge and wait until the bombers had delivered their payloads and returned safely. He was their commanding officer, and he, just as they did, had a job to do. It was what his father would have done.

He stood, staring out the bridge observation dome. Gunter's mind wandered. All they had to do was wait. He stared at the stars. He stared at the revolving form of Jupiter that swallowed up a large portion of the vision of the dome. He wondered if there were other creatures out there who were doing the same as he was. He wondered if there were other alien leaders, leading their forces to war, and whether they looked out at the stars and wondered the same thing. He wondered if any of the bomber crews, on the way to their targets, regarded the celestial bodies in such a way or whether they were simply practical people who were concerned with their targets.

Gunter was torn. He knew his duty, but he did not want to perform it, yet he knew he had to. They were all looking to him to lead them. They were all looking to him for guidance. They were all looking to him for hope. And all he wanted to do was go back to *Neptune Prime*.

Gunter paced back and forth along the command dais. His palms were sweaty, and his heart pounded. His fleet was moving towards the Collective Zone fleet, under orders, so as to make the return journey of the bombers a little shorter; and because the two fleets would have to engage each other in order for the Solar Solutions fleet to drive out the Collective Zone forces. He dreaded the moment that the two fleets would engage.

His officers were looking to him for commands and directions and they believed in him absolutely; but he had no real idea what to do. He was not a fighter. He had been instructed on fleet tactics in his youth by his father, but he knew that Uxus and his commanders were much better instructed in the art of war.

The terrible thing was, that Gunter's inferior officers looked to him for all their commands. They believed that he was their guide and saviour. They trusted in him absolutely, even though he had a sense of crushing self-doubt. Normally he would talk his way out of such a terrifying situation and that would be enough. But now, there was no time for words. Now, it was the time for leadership and action, and the only actions that he enjoyed were the embrace of a woman and the soft burn of some brandy down his throat.

"Sir, CEO Sir." The attendant was at his elbow. "The bombers have been gone hours now. And the fleet is set on its course to engage the enemy. You can relax..." the boy's voice trailed off. He was obviously uneasy about almost giving his CEO an order to leave the bridge.

"No son, I cannot relax. They're out there risking their lives, I have to be here, no matter how little I can do," he paused, "my job is here. I must be on duty as long as they are." Gunter knew this was the right thing to say.

The attendant skittered away into the shadows after bowing. Gunter wanted to reassure him that he had said nothing wrong, but the boy was gone before Gunter had realised.

Gunter saw Cranmere hanging around the edge of the bridge. He seemed just as nervous as Gunter felt. He was looking anxiously out towards Jupiter.

"Cranmere? You don't have to be here," Gunter said with a smile.

"Oh, but I must! You are here; I must be here! It is my duty!" replied the man with a tremor in his voice.

Gunter smiled and stared at his feet. Duty, he pondered the meaning of the word. Everyone in the fleet was doing things because it was their duty to do so. Did anyone actually want to be here?

Then Gunter looked wistfully out the observation dome. He could not see the bombers or the Collective Zone fleet, but he could picture them closing on each other, and he wished them all the best luck he could. He knew that they would need it. All that he could do now, was wait.

***

Fleet Commander Boltha glared out of the front bridge windows on the *Iron Bastion*. The bridge was a hive of activity. The officers crewing the terminals were performing their tasks and barking orders to the ships in the fleet not to break formation and to prepare for the Solar Solutions bomber attack.

Boltha knew that the Solar Solutions forces would initiate the offensive with a bombing raid, and she had to be sure that her ships would withstand the offensive. They should; it was unlikely that the bombers would do too much damage, but they could break up the fleet a little and allow some ships to break free from Europa if the siege was lifted.

"Prepare the flak teams. Their bombers will be here soon. Launch the fighter screen. Keep up the scanning. We'll be ready for them," Boltha ordered. She knew that her crews were the best in the Solar System and that they

35

would prevail. She had a job to do for her CEO and she would not disappoint Uxus. He had trusted her to conduct these operations and she would do so to the best of her ability.

An hour went by, and the waiting was difficult. They could not abandon the blockade of Europa, that was Uxus' express order. They had to hold their ground, and wait.

"Ma'am, enemy bombers incoming," came the cry from the Scanning Officer.

"Open up with the flak batteries. Send the fighters to intercept. We will withstand their assault!" Boltha said. A grin crossed her face. This was what she lived for.

Chapter 6

Artisius and Draz stood in the crowd of people on one of the civilian observation platforms on the surface of Europa. They had watched the Collective Zone fleet mass and then fan out to a blockade pattern.

"...And then they'll launch their fighters," Artisius continued. He was explaining to Draz the fleet procedure of the Collective Zone fleet.

"But I can't see the Solar Solutions fleet?" Draz sounded uncertain.

"That's because they're hours away at full speed travel. They've launched their bombers and they'll be here soon enough." Artisius pointed. "There, they're launching their fighters."

Tiny bright specs shot out of the one of the nearest Collective Zone ships that was large enough to have a fighter contingent. They looked like angry insects that buzzed around their mothership.

"And they're to protect the capital ship from the bombers?" Draz asked.

"Indeed. And they have flak batteries too." Artisius nodded

"Like the large anti aircraft guns back on Earth on Atraxa Prime?" Draz related it back to something she understood.

Artisius smiled. "Yeah something like that, but for space, and with a much longer range. Their flak shells, on time delay, reach far beyond visual range and they are actually fired by rail gun technology, so they accelerate to massive speeds meaning that even though the ranges are extreme, the accuracy is reasonably high."

Draz nodded while still staring up at the starry sky.

Artisius looked down and around him. He was surrounded by people who were doing exactly what Draz was doing: craning their necks up and around to get a glimpse of the enemy ships. He shook his head a little. What they did not know, that he did, was why the Collective Zone ships had arrived. It was his fault that the war had started. He and he alone bore the weight of the lives that would be lost. If he had not helped Draz and Alfred, if he had simply fallen in line and obeyed the Collective Zone then, he reasoned against reason with himself, the war that had just started would not have happened.

But he was kidding himself; Artisius continued thinking. The Collective Zone would have had the cloaking technology if he had fallen in line and the war would have happened anyway. At least this way only his ship had the technology. Why did it always end in war?

He did not blame Draz or Alfred; they had been caught up in the circumstances just as he was. But they had had no choice. He had had a choice, and he had made it. He had sided with those who had hoped for a better world. He regretted it only a little.

Artisius looked around and some people in the crowd were looking at him in a strange way. He realised that he was still wearing his dress uniform of navy blue, with gold trim and braid, and red epaulettes. He looked every inch a ship's captain; and the way that he was describing the unfolding situation above them, made the people around him feel rather apprehensive at his role in the whole thing, it was evident.

He smiled at the suspicious glances, who turned away quickly, obviously embarrassed that they had been discovered gawping. This made Artisius smile more.

He chuckled to himself. Then he paused. Why was he laughing? It was very likely that his actions would result in the deaths of a large number of people. That was the thing with war: you never knew what would happen in the end.

"Hey, what's up?" He heard Draz's voice muscling in on his consciousness. He felt her hands tug on his arm.

Artisius drifted out of his reverie, not really wanting to leave it. "Oh, just thinking; about what will happen now..." he said with a smile. It was a hollow smile. His eyes did not smile.

"The Solar Solutions fleet will kick the Collective Zone out!" Draz laughed.

"Do you really believe that? After all your training and indoctrination into the power of the Collective Zone? Do you really think they'd come all this way to be driven out? They have both the *Old Monarch* and the *Iron Bastion*." Artisius paused for effect.

Draz looked down, and then back at Artisius.

"You know what they did to Mars..." Artisius said. "You weren't on the bridge when we left it, but you know..." Artisius finished and trailed off. The words caught in his throat. He thought of Lady Hangara and looked up and away from Draz's gaze.

"Maybe you're right...I watched Mars for a while through a window..." is all Draz could say.

Artisius composed himself. "When the bombers strike, they'll probably try to break up the fleet around Europa as it will mean the blockade will be temporarily lifted and some refugees can get out. They won't go for the *Iron Bastion* or *Old Monarch* on their own; they have too many flak batteries. Only the Solar Solutions fleet with massed fire can break those two ships. But there are plenty of smaller ships that can be targeted."

"How long until the bombers get here?" Draz asked.

"Hours yet..." Artisius said.

Draz changed the subject. "You talk as if this colony needs to be evacuated...You said to Anya too..." Draz looked up again at the buzzing hive of fighters that surrounded their mothership.

"Trust me, I wouldn't mention it if I didn't think it necessary. Remember Mars..." Artisius stopped, not from emotion this time, but for thought.

"So, we just run, and keep running?" Draz snapped.

"You might have to. I..." Again, Artisius paused.

Draz looked at him for a moment, and then blurted, "You're not going to leave us?"

"Not now...not yet. But the time might come, when I have to face my demons and finish what I seem to have started." Artisius paused and pursed his lips.

"But where will we go? What will we do? Alfred and I that is, we're part of your crew now!" Draz sounded rather anxious.

"And for that I thank you, and as I said, I'm not leaving you yet, but there might be a day coming where you two will have to make your own way. Don't be angry." Artisius tried to calm Draz with a hand on her shoulder.

Draz looked at the floor. "Not yet?"

"Not yet," Artisius said, mirroring her question as a statement.

Just then, a siren sounded and many of the people in the dome grumbled and started to walk down the shafts away from the observation dome.

"What's that?" asked Draz.

"Night work cycle two starts in thirty minutes," said one of the shambling station civilians. "We need to get to work now; playtime's over."

Draz nodded and the man filed past her and on to some unknown and unsung job within the vast system than was the Europa Colony.

Artisius and Draz were left virtually alone in the dome. Artisius was staring out at the starry sky, his mouth open and eyes wide. Draz stood next to him.

"Why did you become a ship's captain," Draz asked.

"Isn't it magnificent?" Artisius responded. He waved his arms at the stars. He looked back down at Draz who had a confused expression on her face. "Stars, Draz. For the stars. I wanted to see space and so I joined the Solar Solutions military all those years ago--"

"That's how you know their tactics..." Draz said.

Artisius nodded with a smile. "Yes, that's how. And so, I know all about the military engagements between the two corporations and I know both of their tactics. Then after my stint in the military I got hold of a ship and then I became a trader or smuggler..." he paused and watched Draz's face carefully. She was processing the information.

"Have you seen military action?" she asked.

"I have. In ship-to-ship engagements I'm well versed in tactics. I have seen combat, if that's what you mean."

"That's what I meant." She nodded, looking up at the stars again. "But I do agree, out there looks magnificent."

Artisius smiled to himself and watched her. "Indeed it is," he said at last.

"You might wonder why I fuss...over Alfred, and you," Draz said in an unsure way. "The reason that I get upset when Alfred zets, and you want to leave...I've never known true friends. The life of a Collective Zone scavenger is a lonely one; brief relationships." She paused and stared at the sky. "You two really are my rock; my stable people I can rely on. So that's why I fuss. That's why I complain. Because I don't want to lose you. Because I need you. Under all the hard-arse...I need you." She looked deeply into his eyes.

Artisius felt bad that he had hinted that he might have to leave Draz and Alfred at some point in the future, but they surely knew it too. They could not expect to be on the *Green Dragon* forever, given the circumstances. He kept looking at her.

"What are you looking at?" Draz's words cut into Artisius' concentration. He shook his head and realised he had been staring at her. She smiled as it became clear that he had been looking at her in a certain way.

"I uh..." he said.

She laughed. "Remember what I said, I'm not interested..."

"No, it wasn't that..." Artisius stuttered. He was caught. He had been thinking about how much he wanted Draz to be his daughter, and how nice it would have been to have a daughter. However, she had thought he was attracted to her. He did not want to reveal his true intentions.

"What then?" she asked, a fire in her eyes.

"Never mind, I'm going for a walk...alone..." is all he said.

"Fine then, I'll go check on Alfred. He'll probably be sound asleep, but I can see." Draz walked out of the observation dome.

Artisius watched her go. He sighed. Maybe he should just say that she was like a daughter to him, he thought. Maybe that would be easier. Maybe it would not be.

He looked up again. "Why does it always have to be so complicated," he said to the stars.

He walked out of the dome and went for a walk to clear his head. The Colony was in transition mode. Even though there was the blockade, the workers were changing from day to night shifts. The Colony's life went on, even with the impending war. What else could they do? Artisius mused.

***

Artisius walked. He walked to clear his head. He walked to think things through. He knew that tough times were coming. The Solar Solutions bombers would be on their targets in a few hours. And then the two fleets would meet in an engagement.

Artisius knew that the Solar Solutions fleet would be no match for the Collective Zone fleet if they met in a pitched battle engagement. The Collective Zone had better warships with more armament. The Solar Solutions ships relied on their bombers and range to win the day, by tying down the slower Collective Zone ships and then picking them off.

The Collective Zone had the advantage of being able to pick the terrain of the battlefield. They had blockaded Jupiter and could choose around which satellites to hold the battle.

Nevertheless, the Solar Solutions fleet could, if skilfully commanded, out manoeuvre the blockading forces and force them into situations that would render their guns less effective.

The guns of a warship were positioned on turrets that could circle and rotate, whether they were auto-turret lasers or missile pods, or the smaller flak turrets. This aside, they still had most firepower facing forward and sideways, from the bow or sides of the ship. If a warship could get around the back of another ship, the firepower of the rear of the ship was much less than the front or sides. The necessity to

43

place engines and the reactors meant that there was less room for turrets of any kind. This was the fatal flaw of both Collective Zone and Solar Solutions ships: they were vulnerable from the back. However, usually fleet deployment protected this vulnerability.

Artisius walked. The people milling around him as he walked went about their tasks and the change from day to night cycle and shifts in a semi mechanical way. They all knew that war was imminent and that things would turn bad very soon. Artisius could tell this from their faces, and the whispered conversations that he overheard as he walked. They were all frightened about what was going to happen. Artisius could sense it in the air. There was a tension building in the Europa Colony and he knew that when it broke the outcome would not be good. But people still went about their work and lives as normal.

He walked through a makeshift park. There were a number of these dotted across the surface of Europa. He wondered if Draz had seen one. He wondered if she would want to. Would she understand the majesty of the trees having grown up on a planet where there were no natural trees? The irony of the idea of a tree being preserved on an ice moon a long way from their original point of Earth was not lost on Artisius.

The parks were created under large domes and had trees and grass placed in the fake soil that had been created to grow them. It was all false, the trees and grass were real enough, but the whole idea of a park on Europa jarred with the order of the universe. How the trees grew, Artisius was not sure, the light from the Sun was too weak for them here, but there must have been some sort of artificial light beamed down from above. But now it was night-time, officially, and the fake Sun was turned off and replaced by a sky full of stars; and warships.

Artisius stopped to watch a family playing. There was a young woman playing with a young child while the father looked on adoringly. The child was full of hope of its new life; full of promise; full of joy. The mother was paying full attention to her child. The child was all the world to her, it was apparent from her expression. The father looked on, and then looked up, and his expression changed to worry as he saw the menacing shapes take form above them. The mother looked over to the father to see what he was doing, and then she herself looked up. The child kept playing, oblivious to the threats taking shape around it.

Artisius stopped watching. He could not watch any more. He walked on. He walked out of the park to one of the commercial districts on Europa. People were shopping and going about their lives, but again there was an atmosphere of dread. People did not know what was going to happen to them, and so they were nervous. But they went on with their lives. They went on.

Artisius remembered himself as once a boisterous man. He would crack jokes and act raucously. But that had changed. Recently he had become more serious and concerned about people. He reasoned that it was because of the war that was coming. Joviality only sustained one so long. Soon there would be a time when he had to choose a path. He had already chosen a path.

Artisius walked on and found himself wondering about what he would do. He did not like being tied to a planet. He wanted to leave and just escape, keep running. But he knew that he could not keep running forever. He would have to make a stand somewhere, somehow. Their original plan was to link up with the Solar Solutions command and give them the red hard drive, his insurance. But it would have taken years for the technology to be implemented and the war happened sooner than he had planned. He would have to fight, sometime, somehow.

What about Draz and Alfred? He had drawn them along with him all this time. Would he bring them to war? It seemed inevitable. But was it right? Did he have the right to bring them all this way and further? He did not believe in gods or fate, but Artisius knew, that it could not end peacefully for him; and he did not want to bring Draz and Alfred into that ending.

Artisius smiled to himself. Draz was making gains again. She seemed to be overcoming the withdrawals reasonably well. She had not mentioned them a little while earlier under the observation dome.

What to do with Draz? He wondered. What to tell her? Of course, he wanted her around, but... He grimaced.

His thoughts turned to Alfred. He was more enigmatic, Artisius thought. He seemed fine on the surface. He just kept on functioning whatever was thrown at him. He just kept going. Even though his implant was failing and that he was definitely experiencing memory problems resulting from that. But he just kept his head down and played his part. Artisius felt feelings of friendship towards him. He felt somehow responsible for the strange young man. Not quite the father relationship that he felt for Draz, but still a protective feeling.

They had ended up in his care all those years ago and now the time was approaching that he might have to let them both go. So as to save them one more time.

Artisius kept walking. He walked for an hour. He thought about his friends, his life, and his ship.

He wondered whether he was a good man, or could be a good man; it was the question that had haunted him for a long time.

***

Alfred tossed and turned in his sleep. He was having fitful dreams. He kept having the same dream: a strange woman leaping off some coolant pipes. She always smiled sadly at him. He did not quite know who she was.

The dream was foggy, as if it was crisper in the past, but now it was foxed around the edges and there was a strange blurriness to it. Alfred did not quite know why. He knew that this woman was important to him, he still felt that, but it was infuriating that he did not quite know who she was.

The dream changed. Then he was strapped to a slab in some horrific environment. His brains were being ripped from his skull by a terrifying and huge man. Alfred recognised this as his encounter with the pirates. The torture went on. His brains were being drawn out the side of his skull and into a computer, which proceeded to chew them up and spit them out onto the floor.

The dream shifted and morphed again. This time it changed to him navigating some strange computer network. He was zetting. He was being chased by something. It clawed its malevolent way through the system behind him. No matter how fast he rushed through the circuits, this thing kept following him. He zetted as fast as he could, but it kept following. He started to panic. The dread permeated his being as the path in the zet that he followed ran out of space and the thing that was following him devoured him.

Something went bang as he was consumed by the thing and Alfred woke up with a gasp. His head hurt. He regained his senses and came to terms with his surroundings. He was in his assigned quarters; on his bed; in his clothes. Someone was knocking on his door. He remembered that he had been zetting madly for Anya. He wondered if it was one of her staff that was going to summon him back to zetting.

The dreams he had been having retreated into the darkness and he could not quite remember what his brain had conjured up. That was the nature of dreams.

The knocking paused and he heard a voice on the other side of the door. "Alfred, you okay?" It was Draz!

Alfred swung his legs stiffly over the edge of the bed. He mumbled something about he was coming. He triggered the lights with a command and the room was flooded with light. It hurt his eyes.

The room was sparsely decorated with a bed and a small table. It had a metal floor, walls, and ceiling. The room was lit by one strip of light in the centre of the ceiling. It cast a harsh, unforgiving light to all the corners of the room. It was not the special guest assigned quarters, but just general staff quarters. Anya had given Alfred standard colony quarters as he was basically working for the colony.

The knocking came again. "All right, I'm coming..." Alfred made his way to the door. He pressed the activation switch and it slid aside.

Draz was standing there in the passageway. She looked at him with a worried expression. He realised that he had a pained expression on his face. He changed it to a smile.

"You all right? Were you sleeping? I don't want to..." Draz said.

"No, no, that's all right. My sleep is full of demons anyway. I don't like sleeping. What's up?" Alfred smiled wider; it came out as some kind of ghoulish grin. He realised and his face went back to neutral again.

"Oh, I was just talking to Artisius, and I thought I'd check on you..." she trailed off.

"Should we go somewhere? These quarters are not so great. They remind me of..." Alfred paused, he searched his faulty memory. He knew that he had been in quarters like this before. "Damn it, I knew that there was something..." he whispered to himself. "*Florida*!"

Draz's concerned expression deepened. "You couldn't remember *Florida Station*?" she raised an eyebrow. "You should seek--"

"Treatment? There is no treatment," Alfred said. "Yes, I forgot *Florida Station*, but then I remembered it. Shall we go?" he said a little harsher than he intended. "Look," he said, seeing Draz's face, "I welcome your concern. I really do, but there's nothing that can be done, so there's no need to worry. Come on, my dreams a full of nightmares anyway, let's go somewhere."

They started to walk to some unknown place, and they talked. They walked to one of the commercial districts and found a bar. There were a number of 'night time' activities and businesses going on around the station as in slipped into night mode.

They made their way into the bar and noticed it was mostly empty, except for the bartender and the rather too loud music.

"Most people are either at home, working, or watching the unfolding scene in space from an observation dome," said the bartender when they asked why there were so few people. "They know war's coming," the bartender said.

"But you're still open?" asked Draz. She looked around the empty seats.

"Business goes on." The bartender smiled at them. "And people still need intoxicating oblivion, perhaps more so in war...So, what'll it be then?"

Draz and Alfred both chose some nondescript beer from the taps on offer and sat at the bar. They sipped at their drinks not really tasting them.

There was silence, apart from the music, for a while as they both considered their own thoughts. Alfred broke the silence. "What now? You said you talked to Artisius?"

Draz nodded. "Yeah, he thinks that we might have to go our separate ways sometime in the future." She stared at her beer.

"Why's that?" Alfred said. There was concern in his voice.

"He thinks he'll have to do 'something'. It's as if he wants to fight, but is torn between going to war, and protecting us..." Draz paused. "He seems to think that he...oh I don't know." There was silence again, except for the music that seemed to invade every thought.

"We'll survive, regardless of what he does. I'm sure we'll survive." Alfred shrugged.

"You're so sure?" Draz said calmly, but a hint of annoyance in her voice. She turned to look at him.

"Yeah, I mean, I've survived a lot and I'm still here," he said with a smile. It was not reciprocated. "I'm sure you've survived a lot too, being the scavenger on Earth and all."

"You mean you just want to exist through life, just survive? What about friendship and loyalty?" Draz asked.

"Well, it's all you can do in life really, survive that is..." Alfred finished his beer and ordered another.

"I see, so it's just survival no matter the cost?" Draz sipped her first beer; it was still half-full.

"I suppose," Alfred shrugged again, "living moment to moment with survival is all I can do with this..." He tapped the implant in the side of his head.

Draz sighed. "I'm sorry, Alfred. I know you're suffering but I just believe that we owe Artisius more than just a 'thanks, no thanks, goodbye'."

They fell silent again, and then there was the annoying music. It bored into Alfred's brain like a zetting needle.

"How are you going?" Alfred asked. He tapped his nose.

"Oh, all right...I guess," Draz said. "The gnawing withdrawal is still there...but I get by..."

"Survival, there it is. You do it because you must...to survive." Alfred nodded.

Draz was silent for a while

"It'll be only a short time until the war breaks out," Draz said.

"Why's that?" Alfred said. He had been zetting and asleep all through the build up.

Draz, realising this, explained the build up of ships and that the bombers of the Solar Solutions fleet would be approaching soon.

"We'd better finish up here then and head back to the command centre. They might need me." Alfred finished his second beer.

Draz grimaced it was apparent that she was unconvinced with the prospect of them 'needing' Alfred. She finished her beer and they headed out of the bar.

As they left Alfred smiled at Draz. "Since when did you have friends?" he said with a laugh.

Draz looked at him, puzzled. "What do you mean?" she asked.

"Well, one thing I do remember, is when I met you, back on the Earth Moon, you didn't want friends. Now you seem to care for both Artisius and me like friends..."Alfred fell silent, his point made.

Draz paused for a second. She looked at the ground and then back at Alfred. "Sometimes to survive, we need others...I've learnt that...recently..." She paused a little. "Since when did you drink beer?"

"I don't know," replied Alfred. He laughed. "I just felt like it..." he said with a grimace.

"I see..." said Draz; her face indicated she was thinking.

Alfred nodded. He said no more on the matter, and they walked on. They walked for a while in silence and then headed back to the command centre on one of the many hover trains. It was evident from the people they passed in the street that there was a tension in the air.

Chapter 7

OE15 gripped the controls tightly. Flak burst around his bomber. GDE78 kept checking the instruments and had checked the torpedo's arming for the third time now.

They were approaching the dive point. This was where all the bombers moved from a parallel course to their target to a perpendicular one. This was so that they could deliver their payloads onto the top surface of the enemy ships where they were less armoured and supposedly less defended.

The Heads Up Display or HUD on OE15's side of the cockpit highlighted the course he had to take and below him his target was approaching. It also told him the operating level of the three tech-slaves that operated the guns in the rear of the craft. They were all green, indicating that their life signs were good.

A number of the bombers around his had been hit by flak and had suffered damage. He could see out his starboard window that a bomber had lost one of its port engines to a blast and was limping along. The pilot would have had to throttle down on the other engines and the craft was at risk of breaking formation.

Suddenly there was a bright flash of fire from a flak burst on the starboard side of his craft. OE15 heard a muffled and cut off scream over the intercom and felt his bomber lurch as the shrapnel from the blast cut into the rear fuselage and one of his tech-slave indicators went dark. The one from the upper hull. He swore as he tried to compensate for the damage that the flak had done.

He looked over at GDE78 and she was busy scanning the surrounding space on her instruments for incoming fighters. There was nothing yet. It was strange; they were within fighter range now, yet there were no enemy fighters. What were they waiting for, OE15 wondered. But any reprieve from an enemy attack was welcome. OE15 went back to concentrating on the dive point. That was when the danger really would start.

Thirteen minutes went by, and the HUD indicated that he had to pitch the bomber over and initiate a dive on the target. "Here we go..." he said to himself in the sweaty, synthetic rubber and plastic suit and helmet he was wearing. He looked at GDE78 and nodded. She nodded back. He applied pressure to the controls and as if as one, all the bombers did the same and pitched forward to initiate the twenty-minute attack run on the ships below.

The flak intensified. It burst around them like angry stars detonating and fading in the black of night. OE15 knew he had to hold a steady course and line up on his target so that his co-pilot could launch a well-guided torpedo.

More bombers were hit and damaged. There was a scream over the radio as a bomber to the port of OE15 was hit full in the cockpit. The blast shattered the glass and obliterated the pilot duo in an instant. The bomber careened off course and spiralled out of OE15's sight.

OE15 gritted his teeth. They had to make it through the flak. They had to. And then all of a sudden, the flak subsided, and they were flying through clear space.

"Keep scanning for enemy fighters. They'll attack now the flak's gone..." OE15 ordered his crew over the intercom. He knew that all other crews would be scanning just as his were.

"Incoming, four interceptors from underneath, and six from above," barked GDE78.

OE15 knew that the fighters would launch all their missiles first from beyond visual range and then close with their guns. If the bombers dropped their countermeasures, the missiles should streak by.

On cue, the bombers began to drop countermeasures and he saw missile after missile fly past with glowing rocket tubes. The countermeasures actually worked, OE15 thought with a smile.

After what seemed like an age, the missiles stopped, and the enemy fighters closed in to use their deadly cannons.

OE15 saw them highlighted on his scanner. He felt the dull thud and slight course correction as his rear and bottom gunners opened up on the incoming craft. Other bombers around him were shooting at them as well. They created a web of death for any enemy craft brave or stupid enough to cross into it.

One of the lights on the scanner went dark and OE15 assumed that the combined fire cones of the bombers had destroyed the fighter.

Suddenly there was a burst of fire past the port window and a Collective Zone fighter screamed silently past while emptying its guns into the bomber above and slightly ahead of OE15's.

The Triton class heavy bomber could take a lot of punishment, but not that much. The point blank fire into the bomber's engines caused a detonation that sent debris and shrapnel scything through the surrounding space. Small parts ricocheted off OE15's bomber and he winced as he saw the fireball fade and choke away in the vacuum of space.

The other bombers around him targeted the lone fighter and raked it with bullets as retribution for killing one of their own. The fighter jerked up and then began to spiral slowly away into the blackness of space. The pilot had probably been killed, OE15 reasoned. Good.

There were still many other fighters buzzing around the bombers. Some stayed at a distance, waiting for an opportunity to attack, while others braved the criss-crossed fire and moved in on the bombers.

The bombers were far from helpless, given their gun defences. Fighter after fighter tried to breach the web of death and fighter after fighter met a poor end. But a number of bombers also fell, and the fewer bombers there were, the fewer torpedoes would land on target.

They had to get through, OE15 thought to himself. He had never experience combat before. He was well trained, but he had never felt this degree of terror combined with the desire to complete his mission. In the simulator it was always okay to have another go. Here, it was different. There was no other go; there was no second try.

The bombers were reaching their torpedo launch points. The formation started to break up as they each zeroed in on their respective targets. This left them more vulnerable to the enemy fighters, which had a much less concentrated field of fire to fly through.

OE15 selected his target in front of him and on the scanner. It was a largish cruiser type craft that was hanging in space near Europa. If his torpedo hit its mark, it should be enough to cripple it. The ship was still a long way away, but he had to prepare for the run up and remain steady for GDE78 to guide the torpedo to its target.

Suddenly there was a flash, and an enemy fighter flew over the cockpit canopy. He felt the shudder as its guns bored holes into the bomber. He checked his instruments:

nothing vital was hit. An auxiliary fuel tank was punctured, and he gave orders to GDE78 to transfer the remaining fuel into the other tanks.

The enemy fighter did a flat turn in front of the bomber and came back head on. This is it, OE15 thought. We're dead.

But somehow the fighter missed its target that was closing too fast and as it took evasive action and dived under the bomber, the two remaining tech-slaves opened up with their guns on it and OE15 saw the fighter's symbol on his scanner go dark. OE15 smiled.

OE15 nodded to GDE78. "It's time to start release sequence," he said. He was suddenly surprisingly calm now that their mission was going to be complete. They had almost done it.

GDE78 nodded back and, without a word, she unstrapped herself from her seat and pushed herself in the lack of gravity into the nose of the bomber and began the final release procedure of the torpedo.

The target was dead ahead. OE15 could see it now, visually. This was it. This was the moment!

"Steady," came the command from GDE78. She had checked the release switches and was lining the torpedoes targeting systems up with the enemy ship dead ahead. "Steady..." she said again.

Damn it, I cannot go any steadier, thought OE15. However, he said nothing; he knew GDE78 needed all the concentration she had.

"Steady...target almost locked," she said. Then she barked suddenly, "Torpedo away!"

OE15 felt the bomber buck under him as the torpedo flew away from it. He pulled back hard on the controls as GDE78 clambered back into the co-pilot seat. The bomber's structure strained as the G-forces nearly tore it apart, but it held, and they were on their way away from the combat zone. Now all they had to do was brave the fighters and flak on the way home, and they were done!

OE15 turned and rolled the bomber so that he could see the enemy ship they had targeted out of the top of the cockpit.

The torpedo was slow but determined. It hit the target amidships. There was a moment of bated breath as both OE15 and GDE78 watched as the torpedo ploughed into the top of the cruiser and then, in silence, there was a huge detonation. The fire leapt up and blossomed in a nuclear blast that tore the ship apart. Its reactor, open to space and now devoid of coolant, split asunder and the stricken ship detonated again in an even larger explosion. They had destroyed their target. The war had begun.

Other bombers were releasing their payloads and banking away from their targets. They were all now making a straight line to their host craft. They still had to run the gauntlet of fighters and flak, but they had achieved their goal. A number of Collective Zone ships rolled and burned as they were hit by torpedoes.

OE15 looked at GDE78. He smiled beneath his helmet. She could not see it, but he imagined that she smiled back. Now they had to get home.

***

OE15 knew that he did not need to make the same trip back to the *Silver Ark*. The Solar Solutions fleet was making its way towards the Collective Zone fleet and as such, his time to landing was reduced; but he still had to make it through the fighters and the flak. He needed to make it home.

The formation of bombers had fragmented as the bombers had delivered their payloads to the targets and now the bombers were spread out in their return to their host carriers. This was the most dangerous time. The enemy fighters could pounce on them, and they would not have the full benefit of their machine gun arcs of fire.

Some of the bombers formed up together and made the journey home in groups of three or four. OE15 saw on his scanner that a couple of bombers had formed up in formation on either side of him.

"Now we need to make it home," he radioed to the other two bombers and his crew. GDE78 turned to him and nodded.

"Should I man the turret with the dead tech-slave? You don't need me to aim the torpedo anymore..." she radioed to him.

OE15 considered a moment and then replied, "All right, just be careful back there, don't puncture your suit on the torn metal."

GDE78 saluted and moved awkwardly back down the passageway of the bomber taking her oxygen supply with her. It was made a little easier with the lack of gravity as she floated down the length of the bomber.

The gun turrets were not built for human use, but they could perfectly be used by human crew if the tech-slave was taken out of action.

OE15 gritted his teeth. GDE78 was brave, he knew that, but they needed to get home.

He checked the fuel. The holed tank was now empty, and the fuel transferred to the other tanks, but it would still be touch and go for them getting home. He predicted they had about two hours fuel left, and he hoped that the *Silver Ark* had moved within that range in its approach to Jupiter.

There was a red flash on his scanner. "Incoming fighter!" he yelled over the intercom. He felt the lurch of the bomber as the gun turrets opened up and filled the space around the bomber with bullets. He craned his neck, looked out the cockpit window, and saw the other bombers around him shooting too.

Tracer bullets looking like short laser bursts shot past his canopy and he felt the dull clang of them hitting the outer hull of his bomber. Suddenly the canopy of the cockpit shattered, and bullets slammed into this control console. The Collective Zone fighter streaked overhead and flew out in front of the bomber before banking around and circling out of sight.

OE15 was stunned. He checked his suit integrity and oxygen level. They were all stable. No bullets had hit anything vital. He breathed rapidly. He checked his instruments. They were wrecked. He had to fly blind now. He tried the controls; they worked. He breathed a sigh of relief. He was okay, the bomber was okay, it was just the cockpit instruments that were destroyed.

He knew what he had to do, he could not guide the bomber home without the instruments, he would need guidance from the *Silver Ark*, and the bombers off his flanks.

There were more judders from the bomber as the gun turrets opened up on enemy fighters.

"How is it back there?" he asked GDE78 over the intercom.

"Messy, and busy, how are you?" came the reply.

"Pretty much the same..." He smiled, but GDE78 could not have seen it. "*Silver Ark* this is OmegaEpsilon15 from your bomber group, we have damaged instruments. Could you please guide us home?" OE15 radioed for assistance.

There was silence for a while as the message was beamed through space and interpreted. "Copy your report OmegaEpsilon15. We'll vent some plasma and that should light up the sky for you. Be prepared," came the reply.

OE15 knew what that meant: the *Silver Ark* would open some of its reactor vents to space and the bright flash from the plasma would light up like a flare in the darkness and so serve as a guide to where they had to go. All he had to do was see it, aim in that direction, and lock the control so he did not deviate from that course.

"OE15 standby..." came the call from the *Silver Ark*. "Venting in 10 seconds...5, 4, 3, 2, 1, venting"

There was a bright flash slightly off centre of the cockpit's shredded window. It burned in space like the brightest star. It lingered for a while as OE15 realigned the bomber and locked the controls to that position. And then, the flare was gone. The retinal burn lingered for a while on OE15's sight as a brown smudge but soon enough that was gone too.

OE15 hoped that he would not have to take any evasive manoeuvres and have to unlock the controls.

"Do a good job," he whispered to himself. He referred to the gunners in the bombers. Only they could scare off the enemy fighters until they got out of range of their endurance.

A dozen or so minutes passed, OE15 was unsure as his instruments were shattered, and no fighter attacks came. It would be soon that the bombers would pass beyond the range of the enemy fighters. They were almost safe.

Even though his controls were locked, he still held them so he could, if necessary, heave the craft into a turn to avoid an enemy's bullets. He gripped them tightly. They were almost home.

***

GDE78 operated the dorsal gun turret. It was shredded from enemy flak and shrapnel, and she had had to scrape out the remains of the tech-slave that had crewed it. It floated in the body of the bomber, stone dead.

She gripped the gun turret's controls. They were slick with the tech-slave's blood. Despite the fact that there were holes in the turret, the guns seemed to function perfectly well and the targeting system for them worked fine.

Suddenly a red flash appeared on her guidance controls and GDE78 swung the guns to bear and let fly with the twin barrels of the large calibre machine guns. The enemy fighter tore in and let fly at her with its guns. For an instant, it seemed that the tracer rounds would meet and hang in the air together, but then they ripped past each other. The fighter's bullets missed their mark and streaked past the body of the bomber with centimetres to spare.

The enemy fighter rushed past, smoke and flames gushing into the vacuum from its engines. It was hit! It spiralled out of control over the top of the bomber and detonated as its fuel exploded inside it.

GDE78 smiled, she liked this.

There was little action for a while. GDE78 wondered if they had passed beyond the fighter screen's fuel reserves. And then there was another flash on her sensors. Another fighter was incoming!

GDE78 spun the turret to face the foe on her scanner and thumbed the trigger. The guns bucked and kicked silently in the void. She did not actually see the fighter until too late. It approached under her guns' trajectory. It let off a short burst that slammed into the turret and the bullets ripped through her seating position. And then it was gone.

GDE78 breathed heavily. She tried to see what the enemy's bullets had done. She suddenly felt weird and started to choke. She checked her suit. She noticed a slight tear in the suit on her left shoulder. It was venting atmosphere rapidly. She stared at it in blind panic.

GDE78 knew she only had a short time to live. "OE15," she gasped as the oxygen poured from her suit. "OE15, they hit me. Good luck, my friend, and goodbye..."

GDE78 felt her blood begin to boil as the atmosphere fled her flimsy suit. The pain was enormous. She tried to jam her hand over the tear, but the atmosphere shot out around her fingers. Her vision started to turn red. She felt short of breath. Her oxygen was almost gone. She knew she had done her task. The enemy fighters had retreated due to their limited fuel. The Solar Solutions fleet would be victorious; she knew it. She breathed her last as the vacuum stole her life from her.

***

OE15 gritted his teeth. He had heard the last transmission of GDE78 and felt nothing but rage. There was no time to be sad. He felt anger boiling up inside him. She had been one of the best torpedo aimers in the fleet and their torpedo had destroyed the target that they aimed for. Now she was dead.

"Dead..." he said. He realised how lucky he was that the bullets that had shredded his instruments had not punctured his suit too.

He wondered what it was like to die in a vacuum. He knew your blood boiled due to the zero pressure of space. But he wondered what it felt like.

OE15 gripped the controls tightly, despite the autopilot. He snapped himself out of his reverie because he had to be totally concentrated on getting the damaged bomber home.

He checked his fuel. The gauge seemed to work. There was about an hour's flight time left. He could start to see the *Silver Ark* in the centre of his damaged cockpit windscreen. He was glad he had kept an accurate course thanks to the plasma burst from the *Silver Ark*'s engines.

"*Silver Ark*, this is OE15, do you read me?" he radioed.

63

After a short time came the response, "Bomber pilot OmegaEpsilon15, we read you. What is your status?"

"Low on fuel. One hour left. My Triton has sustained damage. Some crew dead." He kept the transmission as succinct as possible.

"Due to our current movement towards the battle zone, we should intercept your flight path in about one hour. Hold firm. There will be medical crews on standby." There were no more transmissions.

OE15 had heard what he needed to hear. He looked at the stars so far away. "This will be cutting it fine..." he said.

The threat of the fighters had passed. They had returned to their Collective Zone ships due to their fuel restrictions.

OE15 could not see any other bombers on his ruined scanner. He looked around out of the damaged cockpit. He hoped to see the black silhouettes of other bombers around him. But he saw nothing but stars, and, over his shoulder, the large form of Jupiter sitting smugly in position.

***

After about half an hour the rest of the Solar Solutions fleet appeared. The *Silver Ark* was flying proudly in the middle of the formation, but the rest of the craft looked no less impressive.

OE15 smiled. He would be home soon. And his job was done. Then it would be up to the gunnery crews and boarding teams in the coming fight. He and his crew had done their duty.

After another twenty-five minutes, OE15's bomber was right near the *Silver Ark*. He disengaged autopilot and angled the controls to pass under it and into the landing bay. This was the hardest part of the whole trip: guiding a damaged bomber home safely and landing it in the landing bay.

As he cleared the lip of the entrance to the landing bay, he lowered his landing gear. OE15 felt the tug of gravity overcome him. When the bombers took off the landing crews disabled gravity so that the bombers could wrestle their torpedoes into space; when the bombers landed, they had to turn gravity on, or the bombers would simply bounce off the bottom of the landing bay.

With landing gear lowered, he guided his bomber skilfully by turning the engines of the bomber so that he almost hung in mid air, resisting the pull of gravity but also not shooting into the ceiling of the landing bay.

He throttled down, and the bomber came to rest gracefully on the landing bay floor. He felt a dull clunk through the craft as the landing skids touched the metal floor of the landing bay.

OE15 checked the fuel counter, it was reading empty. He had cut it fine.

OE15 breathed a sigh of relief. He was home. His job was done. The sour taste of the synthetic rubber made him cough a little. He still relied on his oxygen as the landing bay was still without atmosphere and the bomber crews all had to make the long trek to the airlocks on the edges of the landing bay before they could take off their helmets and suits.

The landing bay would only be refilled with atmosphere when all the bombers returned, so that maintenance crews could perform repair and salvage tasks. But until then, the landing bay was a vacuum. This also prevented any fires breaking out on damaged bombers.

OE15 looked out of the shattered cockpit. He saw quite a number of bombers had already returned. Some looked damaged; others were like new. He snarled to himself, why had his been so badly damaged?

OE15 extricated himself from the seat he had been strapped into for the last eight or so hours. It was harder without the assistance of a co-pilot. He grimaced.

As he moved, he felt a snag in his oxygen line. He froze. He looked down and saw the tube caught on a jagged piece of metal that had been torn due to the fighter attack. He reached down carefully and disentangled the tube from the sharp metal, before moving on.

"Hah, to do all that and die here," he said to himself.

OE15 clambered down the length of the bomber to the exit door. On the way he saw the mangled form of the tech-slave that GDE78 had shoved into the body of the craft as she had taken its position.

He looked up and saw her corpse. Or, more truthfully, he saw her crumpled suit. It was not his place to remove her body, the tech-slaves would do that, and if he snagged his suit on the jagged metal of the gun turret, his life would be over too. So, he left her there, gripping the guns. He did not see her face, but he imagined it all swollen and bloated. He shuddered.

He reached the door of the bomber and climbed down the ladder that had deployed on the outside of the craft. The tech-slaves from the rear and bottom gun turrets followed him automatically. They knew their place was after the human. On the way they collected the body of their own fallen and the body of the human co-pilot.

Around the stricken bomber there were vacuum prepared tech-slaves already rushing to attend to the machine that brought him home.

OE15 did not look back. He made his way through the airlock to the preparation room. He had to get to the debriefing.

As he passed through the airlock, he removed his helmet. The rush of air that greeted him as it peeled away was wondrous. He breathed deeply. Great gulps of air entered his lungs. He felt so alive. He felt so ashamed.

Stripping off the plastic and synthetic rubber suit, he handed all his kit into the tech-slave crew that came around to his locker so that they could check any of it for damage before it had to be used again.

"Now. You. Must. Debrief. Sir." fizzed one of the tech-slaves.

"I know..." OE15 mumbled. He looked at the locker next to his. It was GDE78's. He paused a minute.

He made his way from the crew preparation room to the debriefing chamber. A number of bomber pilot and co-pilot teams were in there sitting at tables and being debriefed by flight crew personnel.

OE15 made his way to the master table and received instructions to go to one of the tables in the room. He followed the instructions.

He got to the table and sat down. Opposite him was a sympathetic looking woman who asked him gently about a number of things.

"Did the torpedo go off all right? Did it hit the target? Was it destroyed? How was the fighter danger? Was the flak bad? Was anything damaged?..." The questioning went on and on.

OE15's stomach churned. He should be here with GDE78, but he was alone. But he answered all the questions truthfully and as accurately as possible. He knew this woman was only doing her job as he did his, and as GDE78 had done hers.

Then came the question that set his nerves on edge. "What happened to your co-pilot?"

"She died. She guided the torpedo perfectly and then crewed a gun turret when the tech-slave was killed. She was shot in the turret. She died!" he snapped, instantly regretting it. The woman in front of him was not to blame. "Sorry," he added when she fell silent.

The questions went on. "How was the fuel load? How was the oxygen supply? Did the suits work as intended?"

Finally, they stopped and OE15 was allowed to make his way back to his quarters. His job was done. The ground crews would repair the bombers and maybe they would go out again later, but for now, at least, his job was done; and he felt so alive and yet he felt awful. He felt ashamed.

Chapter 8

Fleet Commander Boltha stood on the bridge of the *Iron Bastion*. She stood rock steady as the bridge was at fever pitch. The crew of the *Iron Bastion*, like all the ships in the Collective Zone fleet, were now at full war alert. The crews of the ships were prepared for military action. They were trained from a young age to cope with the stresses of combat; even so, there was a nervousness that shot through the body of the crew as the wave of bombers broke on the ships of the Collective Zone and their nuclear torpedoes tore holes in some of the capital ships. But Boltha was calm. She seemed almost serene in her confidence and resolve. It was as if she knew the outcome of the battle before it had even been fought. She stood, arms behind her back, dry hands clasped together, totally at peace with her situation. Boltha barked the orders to her crew and to the fleet. She knew exactly what to do.

"Ma'am, the bombers are making their attack runs. They seem to be targeting the smaller ships around Europa. Our fighters are making their attack runs and are inflicting damage, but some bombers are making it through," one of the scanning crew yelled. Sirens sounded throughout the ship as defence turrets whirred into action to defend the ship from any incoming torpedoes.

Boltha smiled. "Of course, they are; they would be blasted apart if they targeted us or the *Old Monarch*. They'll go for the smaller ships and try to break the blockade. It's a distraction. The Fleet must hold together, and we'll be fine. We might lose a few ships, but their bombers only soften us up. Stay strong." She ended with a flourish of her hands to add emphasis and went back to her contemplation with her hands behind her back.

The outside space began flashing with bursts of light as the manned and automated anti missile turrets spat into action and let fly against incoming torpedoes. The *Iron Bastion* and *Old Monarch* need not have feared the torpedoes, as capital ships they were too large, but they were able to lend an anti missile shield for the smaller craft.

After a short time, Boltha spoke again. "I need fleet wide broadcast range!"

After a few seconds, the response came back, "The fleet is waiting Fleet Commander."

Boltha nodded and waited a few more seconds before addressing the Collective Zone fleet. "Ships and ship captains of the Great Fleet, the enemy is bombarding us with nuclear torpedoes. Hold your ships in formation and trust in your defence turrets and fighters and we will come through. Just hold strong and we will prevail. This is only a preliminary attack." Boltha fell silent and the communications were cut off at her movement. Once again she made a matter of fact speech without embellishment.

For all the confidence Boltha had, and she was supremely confident in the ability and training of her forces, she knew that in the end it all came down to the individual ship captains and crews. If they were afraid, if they broke, then the fleet was lost. As powerful and fear inspiring as she was, she was also afraid that, in the cauldron of war, the individual captains of the smaller ships might break and run from the formation and the torpedoes. If the fleet broke up, they were lost. She gripped her hands tighter behind her back. Her palms had begun to sweat.

Suddenly over the radio came the screaming of one of the ship captains. Even in his panic he still managed to identify himself. "Captain Klorx here. They've targeted us! Torpedoes incoming! Our flak is useless! They're too close! I salute you CEO!" And then there was silence.

Boltha looked out the window of the bridge in the direction of Captain Klorx's ship. There was a flash of nuclear fire as a torpedo tore its way into the deep levels of the hull of his ship and detonated amongst the sub levels. The blast was impressive as the nuclear warhead detonated. The blast from the ship's reactor going critical and overloading was even more impressive as the ship burst apart and radioactive debris was spread over a wide area of space.

Boltha gripped her hands even tighter. "I salute you CEO?" she whispered to herself. She snarled a little. She was the commander here. The CEO was sitting back watching how she performed. Boltha was grateful for the opportunity to prove her military worth, not that it really needed proving, but it still galled her that it was the CEO leading this fleet, not her. It was he who would get the glory, not her. It was he who the crews revered, not her. She was simply his attack animal. The CEO was holding the leash.

"Hold steady," she barked. "We'll weather this and then they'll close with us, and we can bring our guns to bear. We will be victorious. Just hold firm. We must hold firm!"

Boltha moved to the front of the bridge and stared out the panoramic windows of the *Iron Bastion* and regarded the fleet around her. The ships were spread out to blockade Jupiter, and particularly Europa.

Small flashes of light peppered the darkness and lit up like miniature stars as flak blasts, fighters, and bombers duelled in a life or death struggle. Boltha scanned the surrounding space. Jupiter hung as an ever-present force, its massive form taking up a large proportion of the sky. But Boltha's keen eyes could pick out her fleet's ships even at a long distance.

The Solar Solutions fleet was not visible yet, but she knew it would be closing within firing distance as soon as the bombers had completed their attack runs.

All of a sudden there was an unintelligible screaming over the radio and off to where Europa hung in the near distance there was a bright flash and double explosion as the ship guarding the entrance and exit from Europa's space was hit by a torpedo and exploded in a reactor overload.

"Damn it!" Boltha swore to herself. "They're trying hard to break the blockade. I knew they'd avoid us, but they want that blockade lifted. And they're succeeding..."

And then, all in an instant, the explosions stopped. The fighters reported that they were running low on fuel and had to return to their ships. The flak died away as the gunners lost contact with the retreating bombers. And there was peace, for the moment.

"Damage report?" snapped Boltha. Even before she asked, she knew they had lost at least two ship and sustained damage to others. She grimaced; the Solar Solutions pilots had done a good job. They were a worthy foe.

"We lost three ships, ma'am. All small destroyers or cruisers. None of the main battle ships were hit, nor were the supply ships targeted. Four more are damaged, but not too seriously," reported the First Officer of the *Iron Bastion*. "But the blockade on Europa is weakened, and we cannot fix that unless we change our whole ship formation..."

"Fleet Commander Boltha?" cut in a male voice. It was CEO Uxus from the *Old Monarch*. "Do you read me?"

"I read you, CEO!" said Boltha.

"Well, how did we fare?" the CEO asked, malevolence in his voice.

"Reasonably well, CEO Sir. We only lost three ships and only four are damaged. They're all--" she was cut off.

"I hope this won't impinge on our operations?" The voice spoke with a hidden threat.

Boltha swallowed hard. "No, CEO Sir, everything is on task. We now wait for the Solar Solutions fleet to try to drive us from Jupiter. And then we win--"

"I hope so Commander. I really do hope so..." the threat was clear in the CEO's voice.

"I'll need to command your ship too, CEO Sir. Am I allowed to give the *Old Monarch* orders?" Boltha tried to sound commanding.

"If that's necessary, then I suppose so. You are the Fleet Commander after all. I am merely your CEO..."The voice sounded like it was a predator toying with its prey.

"Thank you, CEO Sir."

After the conversation, Boltha's face set in a grimace. Boltha barked more orders to the crews of the *Iron Bastion* and the other ships in the fleet.

"Man the guns! Get ready to receive the Solar Solutions fleet! We'll have to relax the Europa and Jupiter blockade in order to mount a good defence. Spread out the ships in Voznor Pattern. We will smash them as they approach!" she yelled over the radio to the ship captains. "Prepare for war!" Although, given what had happened, she was sure they were all prepared for war already.

Chapter 9

Artisius had made his way back to his ship. He sat, alone, on the edge of his command dais on the bridge. The consoles around him were dark. The ship was shut down. He had given the crew time off to enjoy a little rest on Europa; or at least, as much rest as they could get, given the war going on in the skies above.

When he had dismissed them, none had protested or said anything to their captain, except the First Officer. The First Officer had come up to him and asked if everything was okay. Artisius had, of course, reassured him that things were fine, and that he had a plan for the future, but it had been a thinly veiled lie. It was obvious that the First Officer knew this, but he had said nothing more, simply nodding and leaving the bridge to his captain.

Artisius sat. He looked at the floor of the bridge. His mind was numb. There was a flash that illuminated the whole bridge through the observation dome above him. He looked up. Above him the sky boiled with rage. He saw flak bursts and explosions from burning ships as torpedoes hit home. The flash was from a particularly well aimed torpedo hitting the Collective Zone ship that was guarding Europa. The ship split and exploded in a burst of nuclear fire; followed by the overload and detonation of the ships reactor core.

Artisius smiled to himself. There was no one else to smile to. He watched the stricken ship split asunder and fragment in silence as it died. He stopped smiling. The crew of the ship were as human as he was; as human as Draz and Alfred were; and now they were dead. No one could have survived that blast and exposure to the vacuum of space.

Artisius got up, stiffly. He was getting old, he snarled to himself. He walked around the bridge. He walked to every darkened console and touched it with his hand.

One day, perhaps soon, he felt his destiny was approaching.

He shook his head. That was not yet. Not today. He looked up again at the fire boiling away above him. He had a better view than most of those on Europa as the *Green Dragon* was moored at the top of one of the tallest towers, and landing pads, on the ice moon.

He thought of running: grabbing Alfred and Draz and simply running away, as far away as possible. Perhaps to the medical centre on Pluto, and hiding there until it all went away. The war would not last forever, he reasoned. He and his friends could wait it out. The resulting governments would not be much different from the current ones. Humans do not change. Perhaps he could just run? He knew, that if Gunter lost, all the Solar Solutions forces could do, was run.

He also knew he had to get Draz and Alfred to safety. They had to survive. They would be his deliverance. They would be the good that he did in the world.

"I will be a good man..." he said. It was as if to convince himself, yet somehow, he still did not believe it.

Artisius walked out of the bridge. Silence greeted him as he left. He walked down the white corridors, dragging his left hand along the left wall and then moving to the right wall with his right hand. There was no vibration as the engines were not operating. There was still the slight hum of the oxygen scrubbers working to purify the air, but the wonderful thrum of the engines was missing.

Artisius walked in silence. He traced the ship. Its every corridor was known to him. Its every nook and cranny an extension of himself.

"One day, Old Girl, one day, we will have to leave this world..." He spoke to his ship as if it were an old friend. "Don't be angry with me, but I will have a few last things that I want us to do together...We need to keep them safe. We need to keep Draz and Alfred safe."

He came to the storage bay. The special storage bay. The bay that had held Alfred all those years ago. The bay that he kept off limits from most of the crew. The bay that held the slaves.

Many of the slaves had been offloaded onto Mars as payment for the repairs and installation of the cloaking device on his ship. However, there were still some remaining: about a dozen.

Artisius moved amongst the cryo-pods. He studied the faces of those frozen for so many years. They were simply cattle to him. He felt little for them, but that was more than he used to feel. He considered setting them free, here and now, on Europa. But he had a bad feeling about what the Collective Zone would do to Europa, given what he saw on Mars.

"Not yet." He passed a hand over the porthole in the nearest pod. "You might still be useful..."

He moved through more of the ship. He went down to the exercise bay. He thought he heard punching and kicking of a target dummy, but when he approached the sound faded and it was simply an hallucination. There was no one there.

He headed back to the bridge after completing a loop of the ship and visiting every corridor and room that was not private quarters for the crew.

He wanted to fly. He watched the flashes and fire above him again. He wanted to escape. His ship was one of the fastest and he was one of the best captains. He could just run!

But no, he had been over this with himself before. He shook his head. He had duties. If he ran, not only would Draz and Alfred be left alone, the whole of Europa would be a target for the Collective Zone. They had attacked Mars; there would be no quarter for Europa. He had to wait for the Solar Solutions fleet to come and try to break the blockade; then he could take Draz and Alfred and escape with the Solar Solutions fleet. Then they would all have a chance.

He hoped that the Solar Solutions fleet would break the blockade and drive the Collective Zone fleet back into their own space. He hoped. But he knew Uxus, and he knew Gunter, and Gunter was nowhere near as good a tactician as Uxus, and Uxus had Fleet Commander Boltha, perhaps the finest tactician in the Solar System.

Gunter had his work cut out for him, Artisius knew that. But perhaps, just perhaps, things would work out? Artisius smirked to himself; he doubted it. Gunter was good with women and wine, but poor on war.

Artisius stared upwards again. He lost himself in the spiralling, boiling sky. Soon the Solar Solutions ships would approach and there would be much more killing.

"Why does it always end in killing for humans?" he whispered. "That and breeding are our greatest skills..."

He passed the time watching the turmoil. He wanted to get involved, but he knew he could not. He had to wait. He hated waiting. But he had to wait until the blockade was cleared from Europa otherwise it would be a very short journey.

Chapter 10

Alfred and Draz walked into the command centre. By now, the guards knew to let them pass. Word had obviously got around amongst the security staff that they were valuable people to the colony.

Anya was rushing around, giving orders like a mad woman. Alfred could see her on an upper tier of the command centre. She was discernible not for herself, but from the mob of attendants and aides that rushed around her and away from her. They carried her instructions to various parts of the colony and the command centre. There seemed to be no end to them.

Alfred smiled. He wanted to zet. He always wanted to zet now. It was some sort of mad craving that ate away at his very being. He looked towards the zetting terminal, and his heart sank. There was already some other zetter in it. She was working away, mid zet. Her teeth bared and her eyes wide and popping out of her skull. Alfred stared. He forgot everything and everyone else. All he wanted to do was to replace her at the terminal, but he knew that was impossible. Alfred felt resentment well up inside him.

Alfred also realised something, he realised how horrid the zetter's grin looked. He had never really seen it from the outside before. Sure, he had seen other zetters zetting. However, he had never really looked at them; he had been too busy planning his own entrance into the computer network.

This woman, she had an arched back; poppy eyes; a set and locked jaw with teeth bared from behind peeled back lips. It was horrid.

"Do I look like that?" he said quietly, not sure if he wanted anyone to answer. He felt a hand on his shoulder.

"You do. Do you see now?" It was Draz.

He turned to face her.

Draz looked concerned. "You just want to zet don't you?" she said, and smiled.

"Yeah..." is all Alfred could say for a while. It was the truth. He could not deny it. "It'll kill me, I know it, but I have to," he said.

"I have that feeling about ferkis powder, but I have to stop. Why can't you?" Draz looked deeply into Alfred's eyes.

"I...I...don't know, all I know is, it's my job. People need me," Alfred stammered, slightly unnerved by Draz's gaze.

"Damn other people. I need you. Artisius needs you," Draz paused. "We're your friends! Just stop; just give it up. I did it with my poison, why can't you?"

"Because he must aid the colony!" came a cold voice from behind Alfred. They spun around. It was Anya. She still had the cohort of aides around her, but she was standing calmly in the eye of a storm. "We have a secondary terminal; I would like your assistance!"

"I--" Alfred said.

"He refuses," said Draz. Her face set in a scowl.

"He cannot refuse. He is here to work, and I demand that he work. Come, Alfred, over here..." Anya indicated a short distance away behind some pillars that they had not seen before.

"Come join me" came a voice. Alfred paused. He turned to see if anyone had heard it.

"What are you waiting for?" snapped Anya.

Draz looked at him, anxiously.

Alfred shook his head and continued towards the terminal. His palms became sweaty and his mouth dry.

"Goooooood!" The voice again.

Alfred spun around. "Can anyone hear that?" he blurted out. He was scared now. It was the same voice as in the pirate base. He knew it. And he had heard the voice before, some time, a long time ago, he could not quite remember; somewhere back on *Florida Station* perhaps.

"What are you talking about?" snapped Anya again. "Come on!"

"Don't be scared...I am you; I am everything you ever want to be!"

"Are you hearing voices?" asked Draz. She looked concerned.

Alfred nodded.

"We don't have time for this, you will zet and while the war is going on you will make sure all our systems are at full capacity should something go wrong!" Anya instructed.

Alfred gave in. He sat down in the zetting chair and began the boot up procedure. He had given in, again. He had collapsed under pressure. And now he was hearing that voice again.

"Good, now, I have other things to attend to. Log in when ready!" Anya said and then marched off. She had become much colder with the threat and then advent of war. She knew how to command, that was apparent. But she did not know how to inspire people. All she did was give orders and expect absolute obedience.

As Alfred got ready to zet again, a sense of joy and dread crept over him. He felt a hand on his shoulder again. It was Draz's.

"Take care," she said.

Alfred smiled back. "What do you want?" he asked. Not to Draz but to the voice.

Draz paused and almost answered, but Alfred held up a hand. She seemed to understand that he was not talking to her.

"I don't want anything. I already have you..." came the reply.

Alfred shuddered and then rapidly jammed the zetting needle into his implant. Once more there was nothing but pain, and light.

***

Draz stood by Alfred until it was plain to see that he was not conscious of the world around him anymore. He sat like the woman near him: eyes wide, teeth bared, back arched. Draz thought it was hideous. But then she knew that when she was on drugs, it was hideous too. It was just that Alfred was doing a service while he got high.

"Maybe I should use again..." Draz mused to herself. She looked around. She was not alone in the command centre; there were many computer and holo-terminals that were being used, but the storm that was Anya and her aides had passed by and was on some other tier of the multiple walkways of the centre.

Draz looked up and out of the dome that allowed vision into the space around the colony. There it was, the Collective Zone fleet. It hung and burned in the space around the host planet of Jupiter.

Jupiter's great red eye churned. When they arrived, Draz had thought that the surface of Jupiter, particularly the red spot, was a calming influence, that it was always constant, and somewhat peaceful; but now it was clear to her that the eye churned with a malevolence. Jupiter looked on with one great globe and was laughing as the humans around it dashed themselves to pieces in its shadow.

Draz cursed the great planet. Then she paused. She realised that it was not the planet's fault that the humans were killing each other out there. That was entirely the humans' doing. Humans always found a way of causing misery to themselves in the darkest reaches of the Solar System. Whether it was The War on Earth long ago, or this war now, or just Alfred zetting or her taking drugs, humans always found a way to make a paradise into a misery.

Draz heard the door of the command centre open, and she turned from her thoughts to see who came in. It was Artisius. He saw her from across the room and called out to her. She responded with a wave.

"Good, I've found you. Where's Alfred?" Artisius panted. He seemed short of breath.

Draz stood aside and revealed Alfred zetting away in the chair.

"Damn it, how long's he been there?" Artisius scowled.

"He just got logged in," Draz said. "Why?"

"Ah shit!" Artisius said. "I was going to get us all out of here. It seems the blockade ships for Europa have been hit and the way is open to escape!"

"Oh no you don't," snapped a voice from the eye of a storm. Anya had come down again and seen Artisius.

"Are you arresting me?" snapped Artisius, with the same vitriol.

Draz was taken aback at how Artisius had addressed the woman who he had tried to schmooze earlier.

"No, no, but I forbid you permission to leave. The Collective Zone ship might not be there, but you cannot leave without my permission. The rest of the Collective Zone fleet is still there, and we have to wait until our fleet drives them back to their own space!" Anya retorted. The storm around her had subsided as the aides stopped to watch the conversation.

"What if they aren't driven back? What if they win?" snapped Artisius.

"I don't think that's possible. Our CEO is leading our fleet. He will be victorious!" Anya positively gleamed as she said the words. Her face smiled in a smug grin.

"Look, I know Gunter, and he couldn't--" Artisius bit his tongue.

"Yes? Were you about to insult our CEO?" Anya smiled. "Our CEO can take on the Collective Zone filth and drive them back. Everyone knows that. That's why I have ordered the Europa Colony to behave as normal. We are not evacuating!"

"What's changed, Anya? Why are you so convinced that Gunter will succeed? What happened to the sensible Colony Commander?" Artisius said after her.

Anya paused and turned back. "Because I have to believe. Because my colony depends on us winning. Because we cannot lose! I have not changed; it's the circumstances that have changed. War demands things of people that peace does not!" She continued on and away around the command centre.

Draz watched Artisius. He seemed deflated. He leant against one of the pillars supporting a walkway.

"And so, we have to wait," Artisius said.

Draz watched on. She looked from Artisius to Alfred and back again. "We need just a little luck," she said. "Is Gunter really hopeless?" Draz whispered to Artisius.

Artisius nodded. "He inspires great respect with his ability to speak but as a tactician he's hopeless, and the sycophants," he looked towards Anya, "love him. I do not think this will go well."

"Then perhaps, we need to take things into our own hands?" said Draz.

"What are you thinking?" asked Artisius, his head cocked to one side.

"I don't know," replied Draz. "But somehow I want to take the fight to the Collective Zone. Somehow I want to do...something; rescue some people; fight...somehow. I really don't know how. I don't want to give up! Even escaping would mean not giving up. We have to do something!"

Artisius laughed. "Now there's the old Draz I once knew! What spurred this change?"

Draz looked at Alfred. "He seems just resigned to his fate." She paused. "I refuse to just lie down and die..."

Chapter 11

CEO Gunter stood on his command dais. His fleet had crossed many millions of kilometres of space for this moment. He stood, in his business suit, his mechanical leg whirring under him as he shifted his weight from one foot to the other. He was nervous, but he tried not to show it. He failed a little in this task.

"One third of the fleet will break off and head around the other side of Jupiter. The *Silver Ark* and the main attack wing will proceed straight on and engage the enemy in a head on battle." Gunter paused. He wanted someone to advise him on correct tactics. He was simply going by what he remembered from his academy days and what his father had said.

"As you wish, CEO Sir." COO Cranmere was back at his elbow. He had taken a back seat when the battle was approaching, but now, when he was needed, he reappeared and was ready to assist his CEO. He relayed his CEO's orders to the various aides and attendants that milled around. It was a complex thing controlling a whole fleet at full speed going into a war zone. It required precision and great timing. "Anything else, CEO Sir?" he slurped his words through his teeth.

"Prepare main auto-turret batteries; load the missile tubes; prepare for combat!" Gunter shifted again and his leg protested. "Get all the soldiers to their stations. We must prepare for the Collective Zone's boarding parties. We have our bombers; they have their boarding crews."

"Excellent planning, CEO Sir..." Cranmere responded.

Gunter wished the man would contribute something rather than just praise him. There was only so much praise one could tolerate before it became hollow.

"Battle stations!" Gunter bellowed. "Prepare to engage!" He knew that this might have been one of the last things that he said. He did not want to die a coward.

A klaxon began to sound, and the bridge became even more lively with activity. Sub officers barked orders to technicians and soldiers around the bridge and throughout the ship as weapon systems came online and prepared to fire.

Missile pods rose up across the nose of the *Silver Ark* as their protective covers were wound back and the vicious red tipped ship-to-ship torpedoes protruded from their moorings. Auto-turret lasers were unveiled from their hidden places deep within the hulls of the craft of the Solar Solutions fleet. Their menacing profiles breaking up the clean lines of the ships they were carried on.

"Enemy ships will be in range in thirty seconds, CEO Sir!" Cranmere related the information from an aide who had rushed up to him.

Gunter could now see the outlines of the Collective Zone fleet blockading Jupiter with his own eyes. He could see a couple of ships burning and destroyed due to his bombers. This was it. He knew history would judge him for this moment.

"Orders, CEO Sir?" Cranmere touched his commanding officer on the shoulder. It was clear he was nervous too.

"Fire!" ordered Gunter.

A second passed as the order was relayed to the ships in the fleet and then it looked like the entire Solar System burst into flames. Missiles and lasers streaked from their berths in the hulls of the Solar Solutions fleet.

Gunter's face was illuminated by the fire through the observation dome. He shuddered. "I would not like to be on the end of that!"

***

Fleet Commander Boltha stared out the windows of the bridge of the *Iron Bastion*. She smiled. The Solar Solutions fleet would soon be upon them. She had split half of her fleet up and hidden it behind the mass of Jupiter. She knew that the pathetic Solar Solutions command would try to out flank her there; but she was ready. She had positioned some of her best and fastest missile frigates back there and they would make short work of any Solar Solutions ships.

Both the *Iron Bastion* and *Old Monarch* were visible to the Solar Solutions fleet. And this was intentional. Boltha wanted to scare the Solar Solutions soldiers. What better way to do this than having the two best warships in the Solar System on display and ready for war.

"Boltha," the message came across the radio, it left off her rank which irked her, "I hope you know what you're doing; hiding half the fleet behind Jupiter." It was Uxus' voice over the radio.

"CEO, I have done that deliberately. I know what I'm doing. You left me in command here, so let me do my job!" she snapped a little too forcefully. But going to war was nerve-wracking and she did not like being questioned in her commands. She knew what she was doing.

"Easy now Boltha, I can strip you of your rank if you don't address me properly." Boltha heard a smile in the voice.

"CEO Sir, the enemy will be on us in seconds. I do not have time to teach you tactics. I need my full control of this fleet. You put me in charge, now trust me!" Boltha said. There was silence for a few seconds.

"Very well, proceed," came the reply. Boltha could have sworn it sounded a little hurt. She smiled to herself.

"Prepare all weapon systems! Get the boarding crews to their transports! They'll be on us in thirty seconds. Make sure we do not fire until they do. I don't want any weapons fired until they do!" Boltha barked to her ship crews.

She knew what she was doing. By having the Solar Solutions ships fire first, it would look like the Collective Zone ships were unprepared and would be damaged. But that would be a ruse; she would spring her trap on the Solar Solutions fleet when she was good and ready. The missile frigates and the half of the fleet would cut through their flank around Jupiter and then come around and cut the enemy off from behind. The main battle ships that were in full view could weather a few salvoes of fire before they retaliated. She had faith in her crews. She hoped they had faith in her.

"Enemy fire incoming, ma'am!" shouted the First Officer. The view ports on the bridge lit up as laser and missile fire cut into the Collective Zone fleet.

"Hold!" she shouted. Damage sirens started to sound. She waited as long as she dared. "Now, prepare our guns! Fire!"

***

CEO Uxus paced the bridge of the *Old Monarch*. He was not used to being talked to like the way that Boltha just had. He turned to Acting Commander Tyyz who stood still.

"Is she right? Will the deception work?" he snapped.

"Maybe," replied Tyyz. She tilted her head in a thinking pose.

"Maybe?" Uxus repeated, unimpressed.

"Well, we'll see, won't we? I mean, it's too late to change now..." As Tyyz spoke the space outside the *Old Monarch* lit up with laser and missile fire.

"I hope she's right, for her sake," growled Uxus.

There was a loud explosion as one of the auto-turrets of a Solar Solutions ship bit deeply into the hull of the *Old Monarch*.

In a second, and with a barked word from Boltha over the radio, the crew of the *Old Monarch* leapt to life around Uxus and began organising their defence and firing back at the approaching Solar Solutions ships.

"We'll see," said Tyyz as the fleets exchanged fire. "Anything can happen in war..."

Chapter 12

Trooper Grox of 3rd Platoon on the *Iron Bastion* checked his rifle for the thirteenth time. He knew he should not be nervous; but he was. He checked his rifle again. He was dressed in a vacuum proof uniform of a boarding operation. His helmet sat on top of his bed. 3rd Platoon were in their barracks getting ready.

It was strange; before Mars, Grox had been nervous, but because he had never really seen combat against a true foe before, he had felt somewhat at peace. Now, he knew what combat was like; and he felt anxious about what he was going to experience in a boarding party.

He and his 3rd Platoon were going to be boarding one of the Solar Solutions ships to try to capture it. He did not know which ship they would be aiming for yet as they had not had the briefing. They were in their barracks and preparing for the mission.

He checked his rifle again. It was immaculate. He had cleaned it perfectly and it was loaded and ready to fire. He began loading up on ammunition. He wanted to take extra for this mission as it was unclear how long the battle would last.

Grox felt a hand on his shoulder. He spun around, weapon raised.

"Whoa, whoa!" said Trooper Althar. "It's me, relax!"

Grox lowered his weapon, slowly.

"Sorry, I'm just...," Grox said, shaking his head, and went back to loading up on gear.

"I can see that. How many times have you checked that rifle? Twelve times?" Althar laughed a little.

"Something like that..." Grox said hesitantly. He knew exactly how many times but wanted to seem vague.

"Relax!" said Althar. "We'll be going in against soft ship crew targets. They'll surrender before there's any bloodshed. It'll be easy. We're probably attacking one of the supply ships or something." He waved his hands dismissively. He too went back to loading up on gear and ammunition.

"Soft targets are what I'm scared of. I don't like soft targets." Grox paused and sat on his bed. "Things that shoot back, that's what I want. Clear enemies. Mars had too many soft targets..." he trailed off. His face went blank, and he stared into the distance.

"What about Shakespeare?" Althar said. He could see that his friend was not well.

"What about him?" Grox snapped.

"Well, don't you like to look at that to psych yourself up?" Althar offered a hand to help Grox off the bed and back to his feet.

Grox hesitated a moment and then took the hand and was hauled to his feet. "Yes...but it's different now. Shakespeare obviously never actually went to war. It's all heroic speeches and glory for him."

"Well whatever, I don't know the plays, but don't you want to read some anyway? Read something stirring. Read something that makes the battle righteous. Because what we're doing is righteous. We are on the winning side, my friend." Althar said. "Read something, it might make you feel better."

"Maybe..." Grox whispered. He reached up to his locker and pulled down his copy of *The Collected Works of William Shakespeare*. He flicked open to *Henry V* and landed on a random page.

"He which hath no stomach to this fight / Let him depart; his passport shall be made..." Grox froze. He did not believe in fate or destiny; those were superstitious mumbo jumbo. But this was all too poignant. "Saint Crispin's Day..." he whispered to himself.

"What?" Althar asked with a note of concern in his voice. "Saint Crispies Day?" he sounded confused.

"Saint Crispin's Day," Grox corrected him. "The great war speech from *Henry V*. And I landed on that when I just randomly flicked the pages..."

"Destiny?" Althar smiled.

"Don't joke about that stuff," Grox said.

"You don't honestly believe...?" Althar waved away the notion of a pre-determined fate.

"Of course not. But...it's all too perfect..." Grox paused at the page and read the speech of Act IV Scene iii aloud. He read it with such practiced precision that some of the other soldiers stood around and listened too. They had no idea what it was, but it sounded good and warlike.

Suddenly everyone snapped to attention and the red eye of Lieutenant Vauz could be seen cutting its way through the crowd.

"Get ready men and women of 3rd Platoon," the voice of their commander ripped through the soldiers, "we launch in 15 minutes. Get your gear and head to the docking bay. It's our job to capture the *Silver Ark* with the rest of the *Iron Bastion's* troop contingent. This will be a glorious day." He looked at Grox, who was standing bolt upright, his rifle on his shoulder and the book of Shakespeare in his left hand. "And gentlemen in England now a-bed / shall think themselves accurs'd they were not here, / and hold their manhoods cheap whiles any speaks / that fought with us upon Saint Crispin's day." Vauz smiled as he finished what Grox had started reading. And then Vauz was gone; back out to confer with his commanders.

There was a silence in the barracks. They would be attacking the *Silver Ark*. That was not some supply ship. That was the flagship of the Solar Solutions fleet!

Grox looked down at the copy of Shakespeare in his hand. He closed it gently and placed it reverently back in his locker. This would be his Saint Crispin's Day. He would fight gloriously for his King and CEO. He would not back down from this momentous occasion. They were soldiers and they had a job to do. Yes, they were all scared of what might happen, but it was clear to Grox now that his destiny lay on the battlefield.

"They won't be soft targets on the *Silver Ark*. I think you got your wish!" Althar looked over at Grox. "Come on; time to fall in, in the docking bay."

Grox paused for a moment and then followed his friend and the rest of his platoon out of the barracks and down onto the large and open expanse of the docking bay at the front of the *Iron Bastion*.

Out the magnetically shielded docking bay Grox saw Jupiter and the glittering lights of both the Collective Zone fleet and the Solar Solutions fleet. He swallowed hard. This day would be a momentous one.

They fell in, in ranks in front of their respective landing barges and awaited the orders to board. Fleet Commander Boltha was there. She stood at the head of all the craft on a platform and addressed her soldiers. She gave them the orders to take and hold the *Silver Ark* no matter the cost. They were to take no prisoners.

Grox felt nervous again. He wanted to check his gun, but that would be too obvious on parade. Vauz would have yelled at him for being distracted. Instead, he looked at his helmet under his left arm. The visor was clean.

He was also looking forward to using his stim-unit again. The feeling gnawed at him.

Boltha stopped speaking. She had given them their orders and targets. Then the command was given, and the troops boarded their attack craft.

Each barge was different from the landing craft on Mars. These had their troop entrances or exits in the front inside a large circular drill like object that was used to puncture the hull of the enemy craft and then the Collective Zone soldiers would pour out from the drill bit into the enemy ship.

Grox ducked a little as he climbed through the drill and emerged into the body of the boarding craft. He sat down next to Althar. As they sat down the troops donned their vacuum sealed helmets that locked into their armour and made their uniforms proof against the vacuum of space should any of the docking craft become dislodged and the air be sucked from the enemy ship.

The soldiers filed in and sat down, attaching their helmets as they did. Soon all the seats were full, and the soldiers waited for the word go.

In the middle passageway between the seats was a large welding drill that could be used to cut through any bulkheads they encountered on the enemy ship.

The boarding ramp at the front of the craft shut and they were ready to take off.

Suddenly there was a whining klaxon noise, and the craft began to lift off with a lurch. The engines sounded and the whole landing barge lurched forward and vibrated violently.

The soldiers inside could not see out of the barge. There were no windows in the troop compartment. But the pilot on the top of the craft could see a panoramic view from his or her position.

The barge began to duck and weave as it avoided flak and enemy fire. Grox felt sick. He checked his gun again. It was fine.

After what seemed like an age of ducking and weaving and skidding across space, the pilot spoke, "Twenty seconds to impact! We have to board lower down in the ship due to heavy enemy fire!"

"Everybody up!" bellowed Vauz though his microphone. Every soldier heard the command through his or her suit speakers in the helmet.

The whole barge stood as one and held on to the handholds that provided the standing soldiers with some balance.

"Ten seconds. Good luck!" said the pilot.

Grox thought that it was the longest ten seconds of his life; and then suddenly there was a crash, a lurch, and a grinding noise as the drill on the front of the barge bit deeply into the hull of the *Silver Ark*. After a few seconds screeching, there was another lurch and then the boarding ramp at the front of the barge snapped down and the Collective Zone soldiers could burst out guns firing into the hull of the *Silver Ark*.

Some Collective Zone soldiers fell straight away. Their suits punctured by Solar Solutions' bullets. But 3rd Platoon fought their way out of the landing zone and into the body of the *Silver Ark*. And as the area decompressed, due to the assault of the landing craft, the unprotected Solar Solutions soldiers died or fell back.

Grox, Althar and Vauz along with the other troops burst out into the open space that the drill on the front of the landing barge had torn in the side of the hull. They clambered onto one of the decks and made their way along the winding passageways. They bit down on their stim-units to give them an extra boost of speed and strength.

There were signs that the area had depressurised as the landing barges had made their attack: unprotected bodies were lying around, bloated and red as their blood had boiled in their skins. Grox shuddered; that would be a horrid way to die, he thought.

Red lights had begun flashing in the surrounding area and the large bulkheads that protected against decompression had come down and sealed off the area that the Collective Zone troops were attacking. From behind these barriers the Solar Solutions troops donned their vacuum gear and prepared to resist to the last drop of blood.

"We make for the bridge!" yelled Lieutenant Vauz. A cry went up amongst the soldiers around him and they moved onwards in the direction of the bridge structure that they had seen on the outside of the *Silver Ark*.

"Damn it!" said Grox, after coming up against one of the large bulkhead doors that sealed off the decompressed part of the ship. "We really have no idea of the floor plan of this ship. How do we know the bridge is this way?"

"We don't," shouted Althar. "All we know is their resistance is getting stronger when we go this way, and that's a good enough indicator!"

"Cut us through that!" Vauz said over the radio.

The Collective Zone troops brought up the large welding type drill that was specifically designed to cut through thick plate steel doors like the one in front of them.

As they were cutting through the door, from down the corridor to their left, came bursts of gunfire. Because the area was decompressed and there was no atmosphere, there was no sound. All the Collective Zone soldiers knew of the attack was that one of their number screamed and gurgled his last as his suit was punctured. The soldiers not involved in the operation of the welding drill returned fire.

"How much longer?" snapped Vauz, as he snapped off shots from his pistol.

"Ten, maybe twenty seconds!" shouted Althar who was operating the drill.

"Hurry, man!" said Grox.

After what seemed an age, the door was sliced open and buckled outwards. There was a rush of air as the pressures equalised and the Collective Zone soldiers fought their way into the next compartment.

Inside this compartment was a squad of well prepared Solar Solutions soldiers and they resisted to the last, but they were overwhelmed by the sheer weight of numbers of the Collective Zone. It was a foregone conclusion. A platoon versus a small squad, but the Solar Solutions soldiers sold their lives dearly, accounting for a number of Collective Zone.

As they moved down the corridor, illuminated by their suit torchlights and the flashing red of the decompression warning emergency light, the Collective Zone came to another blast door bulkhead that blocked their path.

"Oh shit...another?" said Grox. He toyed with the drug dispenser in his mouth with his tongue.

"There must be one of these every dozen or so metres," said Vauz. "Don't just stand there; open it up like a tin can!"

Althar and Grox brought up the drill and set it going on the door.

For every door they had to cut through, the Solar Solutions delayed them by precious minutes, which meant the ship was still operational and commanding the Solar Solutions fleet. For every bulkhead, Collective Zone troops died. For every sealed plate door, the Solar Solutions bought themselves time.

Once again, the Solar Solutions soldiers counterattacked as the drill bit into the door. Some soldiers fell on both sides. Their gurgled screams demoralized each of their comrades. No one wanted to die in vacuum.

"Oooookay...Done!" shouted Grox as the next blast door was opened and the pressure equalised as the atmosphere was sucked out into space.

Again came the concentrated fire from squads of Solar Solutions from beyond the bulkhead.

Vauz shouted a battle cry and his platoon surged forward and took the next few rooms and corridors, only to be met by another sealed blast door.

Grox swore again. And he saw that Vauz was visibly demoralised as he slumped a little before giving the order to bring up the drill.

"This may have been a bad idea," Grox whispered to himself.

As the soldiers cut through another door, suddenly there was a change. The door, instead of being slowly cut open and then prised apart and then the atmosphere rushed out, the door buckled outwards when the welding drill only reached half way down one side.

"What the...?" said Grox, and then the entire door structure failed and exploded outwards.

Grox and the soldiers around him were thrown across the passageway and slammed into the opposing wall. Grox felt something snap and then he felt a rush of pain in his left leg and arm. He bit down on his stim-unit. He felt the crushing weight of the door on top of him. He tried lifting it off himself, but it was impossible. The door was too heavy. He heard his fellow soldiers cursing over the radio to each other about the resistance on the other side of the exploded door. It must have been booby trapped, he thought. Then he thought why were they not coming to rescue him.

The pain of whatever was broken in his leg and arm was too much, combined with the crushing weight of the door on top of him. He could hardly breathe. He could not speak. Even with the drugs surging through his system he was losing consciousness and collapsed. As he did so, panic overcame him: would he die in a vacuum? This was not possible. He was not supposed to die here. And then he blacked out.

Chapter 13

CEO Gunter stood at the centre of the bridge on the *Silver Ark*. Attendants rushed around him and the bridge was abuzz with action and noise. The console operators on the sides of the room and walkways around were all doing their part in full war mode.

"CEO Sir?" a voice said at his side. It was Simon's.

Gunter wondered where the boy had come from. "Yes?" Gunter sounded vague and somewhat disconnected from the reality that was war. He saw his ships being damaged and disabled; and the enemy's too.

"They have landed in our sub-quarters, and they're fighting their way through to the bridge." Simon paused as if wanting recognition. Gunter simply waved his hand for the boy to continue. "We've deployed the blast doors as a delaying tactic and that should slow them down as our forces counter attack..."

"Sounds good to me..." Gunter whispered. He was staring out the observation dome at the carnage that was unfolding in front of him. Flashes of light burst across his vision and illuminated the bridge in spasmodic ripples as ships burst and burned in hard vacuum.

"CEO Sir?" said the voice again.

"Uh...yes, yes. Keep resisting. Yes. And send in the fighters...Make sure the fleet stays together..." Gunter mumbled and bumbled his way through the commands. He did not know what to do. He had frozen. His soldiers were fighting the enemy without his commands. They knew what to do. But in his pathetic hopelessness, he had frozen. Gunter felt an icy fear grip his heart.

Simon looked distressed at his commanding officer before rushing off to carry out the orders that Gunter had supposedly given.

Simon ran to the First Officer who was taking up the slack that Gunter had left and was busy commanding the ship.

Gunter stared out of the observation dome. His mind was blank. He saw his fleet around him, fighting, dying. He had to keep his ships together. He had to fight. But his limbs felt like jelly. His heart pounded in his chest and as he turned from left to right, his mechanical leg protested. His mind was a blank. He knew he should be giving orders, but he did not know what orders to give. His soldiers were getting on without him, they were well trained, but without its head, the serpent withers and dies.

***

The call to launch the fighters went up and the pilots rushed to their briefing. OE15 sat in the pilots' mess hall with some of the other bomber pilot teams that had survived the earlier attack. He watched the fighter pilots running out of the mess to their briefing and attack mission. He cursed; he wanted to be with them. He wanted to keep fighting. Now that GDE78 was dead, he wanted to make the Collective Zone pay.

"You look lost? What's up?" said one of the bomber pilots, noticing his wistful looks at the leaving fighter pilots. "You don't want to be with them, do you?"

OE15 nodded. "Yeah...I do..." He looked down at the table and picked at the surface of the metal table.

"Well, they might have a place! Go to it!" the other bomber pilot said, grinning.

OE15 snapped his head up. "Think so?" he said hopefully.

"You can but try!" said the other pilot with a smile. "You can fly a fighter can't you? I heard that you passed the simulator but went with bombers..."

OE15 dashed out of the mess after the fighter pilots leaving the other pilot's words hanging in the air.

OE15 approached the fighter commander in the fighter briefing room who was addressing his pilots. "Sir, sir..." He was panting from the run. "Sir, can I join your attack wing?"

"Oh? And what makes me think you can fly a fighter? You're a bomber pilot aren't you?" snapped the fighter commander, who was annoyed at his briefing being interrupted.

"Yes, sir, but I passed fighter training, too. Just one free fighter, that's all I need!" OE15 was getting his breath back.

"And what does your co-pilot say about this?" asked the fighter commander.

"She's dead, sir. She died on my mission." OE15's voice turned deadly serious.

The fighter commander paused for a second. "Very well, take that one." He pointed at one of the craft on the floor of the docking bay below and through the glass window that separated the docking bay from the fighter briefing room.

OE15 noted that the bombers had been winched away to their hangers and the floor of the docking bay was now full of fighter spacecraft. The hangar bay had also been filled with atmosphere again.

The fighter he was to fly was angular and harsh looking like the Triton heavy bomber, but it was much smaller and not painted black; it was white and red. And it only had two engines in the back.

"Your bomber gear should be sufficient. Go grab that after I instruct the squadron," said the fighter commander.

OE15 beamed. He listened to the briefing. The fighters were instructed to intercept other fighters and protect their carrier craft while attacking the enemy ships.

OE15 then rushed off to get his bomber gear that had been returned to his locker after a tech-slave checked it after his last mission, before he headed out, with his heart pounding, towards his new craft. The fighters, like the bombers, were not pressurised or aerated, that came from the suit the pilot wore inside. This, like the bombers, stopped the small particles or bullets from disabling the entire craft.

OE15 jammed on his space suit and rushed out to his now waiting fighter. He grabbed an oxygen canister on the way. He looked around and saw the other pilots mounting up into their craft. He paused at the bottom of the ladder into his craft's cockpit. He swallowed hard. He had passed the fighter training course with flying colours but had been chosen to fly bombers. He swallowed again.

"Come on!" yelled the flight commander at him over the landing bay. "You said you wanted to fly with us!"

OE15 gripped the ladder tightly and pulled himself into the pilot's seat. He sat down heavily in the low cockpit. He looked over the controls and re-familiarised himself with the computer screen and readouts. A tech-slave removed the ladder from the side of the fighter.

He pulled on his helmet and stashed the oxygen canister behind his seat. He attached the oxygen tube from his helmet to the canister. He made sure this was tightly fastened, as a failure here would result in instant death. He breathed and tasted the metallic taste of long stored atmosphere mixed with the synthetic rubbery smell of the suit and helmet.

Without prompting from anyone, he closed the cockpit canopy and began start up procedure of the fighter. The cockpit lit up with controls and computers. He grabbed the control column and prepared for launch.

OE15 blinked away the fatigue. He had been awake for nearly sixteen hours and had already flown the taxing bombing mission; but he could not pass up this opportunity, his body would just have to deal with it. Already his adrenaline was pumping, and the fatigue was being pushed to the recesses of his brain.

"Flight ready," came the non-question from their flight commander. "Requesting gravity switch-off and vacuum."

After a few seconds, there was a whooshing noise as the atmosphere was sucked out of the landing bay, like before with the bombers, and the gravity was turned off rendering the fighters buoyant.

"Let's go. Throttle up! Stay close, new kid, and follow my orders, let's see what you can do," came the commander's voice over the radio.

OE15 smarted a little. He was far from a new pilot, but he let the matter slide. They were doing him a service by letting him fly.

The fighters lifted off from the floor of the landing bay with their directional thrusters and then rocketed silently out of the landing bay and out into open space.

OE15 felt the whine of the fighter's engines through the vibrations in his seat. The speed at which the fighters took off surprised even him. He was used to bombers that were slow and lumbering. The agility of the fighter craft was liberating, and scary.

"Form up! Prepare to repel enemies," came the commander's voice.

OE15 formed up on his commander's wing along with the other fighters.* He looked around. The space around them was in chaos. There were silent explosions blossoming along the length of all sorts of capital ship craft. Missiles streaked from missile pods to impact voicelessly on both Collective Zone and Solar Solutions ships alike. Auto-turret anti-ship lasers cut swathes through space with their beams and sliced deeply into the superstructure of their targets.

Already there were some burning hulks of ships of both Solar Solutions branding and Collective Zone markings.

"Holy Hell!" exclaimed OE15. He was used to the idea of training missions or even the bombing mission he had taken part in when the fleets were far apart; but here the fleets were close to each other. Their fire cut into each other like razorblades and ripped open the hulls of each other's ships.

"Keep your eyes on your scanners. We need to intercept those enemy fighters," the commander barked.

"Quadrant 3! Here they come! They've locked on!" yelped one of the fighter pilots whose scanner had detected the Collective Zone.

"Break and attack!" yelled the commander.

The flight of twelve fighters split down the middle, OE15 yanked hard on the stick, and the directional thrusters did the rest. He was pinned to his seat as his fighter completed a hard bank to starboard. He kept one eye on the scanner and saw some missiles streak past his wing with a few blips a split second later past his port side.

There was a scream as the missiles detonated on one fighter, which was unable to lose their tracking system.

OE15 looked around. He could not see any friendly or enemy fighters visually. He looked at his scanners. He kept his craft moving so as to prevent a missile lock or any gunfire ripping through him.

His scanners picked up a red blip at maximum range. He aimed for it and selected it through his HUD. The missile lock system sounded in his helmet and after a few seconds, he heard a solid tone and he loosed two of his six missiles. They streaked away. Suddenly there was a puff of an explosion and the red blip disappeared. He let out a cry of joy. He had hit something.

"You'd be dead if I were an enemy!" came the commander's voice over his radio. "Look off your port wing."

OE15 swallowed and saw the shape of the commander's fighter in formation with him. He had not noticed it forming up on his wing. The commander was right, if he were an enemy, he would be dead.

"Keep moving and dodging in a combat zone!" snapped the commander. "Oh...and nice shot." OE15 could hear the smile in the commander's voice.

"What should I call you, sir?" asked OE15. He realised that he had no idea of his current commander's name.

"Call me AA3," came the command.

"AA3. AlphaAlpha3. Yes, sir!" repeated OE15

"And who are you?" came the voice.

"OE15, sir!"

"Good. OE15, well done!"

They had taken up a high angle guarding pattern over the battle that was unfolding below them. Some of the other fighters had rejoined their wing. The carnage was still unfolding below them and OE15 rolled his fighter over so as to get a better view of the battle unfolding underneath them.

He saw the *Silver Ark*, their command ship, in a fierce battle with the *Iron Bastion*. They were both cutting deeply into each other with their turrets, but due to their respective bulk, they were capable of taking vast amounts of punishment.

OE15 saw some of the smaller ships engaging each other. They had less firepower but could take less punishment. He saw a small Solar Solutions frigate blossom with fire and split mutely down the middle as an auto-turret gun cut deeply into it. Then there was a giant explosion, and the ship tore itself apart.

Further in the distance, there were some damaged Collective Zone craft trying to retreat but being pursued by a Solar Solutions cruiser. It chased the Collective Zone ships down and gave them the end they deserved with some swift turret fire. In a short time, that engagement was over, and the cruiser was banking around to return to the main fray.

It looked to OE15 that the Solar Solutions fleet was coming out on top; that it was winning. But he saw the *Old Monarch* sitting out of combat range. It was sitting in space; not shooting; not moving. It was as if it was simply observing and biding its time to see what would happen and then it would react.

"What are you waiting for?" mused OE15 as he rocketed above the combat zone.

Suddenly there was a blip on the scanner again. "AA3, quadrant 1!" he snapped mechanically.

"I see it, follow me!" came the practiced response.

The attack wing dived down through the maelstrom on their commander's orders. There were four of them in the formation.

"There are four of them. Each of us lock on to one. Fire when ready. Two missiles!" snapped AA3's voice.

OE15 swallowed. His mouth was dry from mouth breathing. His heart was beating rapidly. He locked onto one of the targets and fired two missiles.

The eight missiles of the flight rocketed away into the darkness and there were a number of blossoming explosions in the distance.

"Yahoo!" cried out OE15.

"Calm yourself, OE15," ordered the commander.

OE15 felt embarrassed, but elated. That was his second kill! And he had two missiles left and then his guns!

The flight took up escort position above the capital ships again. In the lull, AA3 began radioing with all the other fighters that had started the attack. He was checking whether they were still alive or if they were in another area of the large combat zone. As he called out their names, each pilot did, or did not, reply. There were eight replies. Four call signs had gone silent.

In the brief pause, OE15 looked over the battle zone again. The *Iron Bastion* was pulling back under the attack of the *Silver Ark* and a few other Solar Solutions battleships. This was a momentous occasion, thought OE15. Solar Solutions was winning!

As his heart pounded, OE15 watched as the retro thrusters of the *Iron Bastion* pulled the ship back and slowly tried to extricate it from the combat zone. But the *Silver Ark* and surrounding ships pressed home the attack and followed it with their faster engines.

Further afield, other Collective Zone ships were pulling back into a tighter cordon and the Solar Solutions ships were pressing home the attack.

"We're winning!" said OE15. "Aha!" He kept on his commander's wing and looked at the scanner for more targets.

***

CEO Gunter observed the battle. "Status?" he mumbled to one of the aides next to him.

"CEO Sir, the enemy seem to be suffering casualties. They have lost a number of ships and seem to be retreating!" said Simon.

"Retreating!?" exclaimed Gunter. He could see it too. The core formation of the Collective Zone fleet was slowly pulling back. "We have them!" he paused. "How is our formation on the far side of Jupiter faring?"

"CEO Sir, they will engage the enemy soon. Our scanners cannot scan that side of Jupiter due to its bulk, and our radio transmissions are sketchy, but it seems that they will engage the enemy soon; or so they said before disappearing around the dark side of the planet." The aide grimaced.

"What's wrong? Can't you see we're winning?" Gunter tapped the aide on the shoulder. "We have prevailed!" Gunter looked around the bridge to see Cranmere talking to some other aides. Cranmere seemed rather pleased also that the Collective Zone fleet was retreating.

"CEO...Sir..." said Simon. "Are you sure--?"

"Do you doubt my assessment of the battle?" snapped Gunter, a little too harshly for his own liking.

Gunter had regained some of his nerve since his seizing up at the start of the battle. He had managed to compose himself and start to give orders again. He realised that it was not so hard. The fact that they were winning meant that his commands were working, and that boosted his confidence. He may not have been the best tactician, but, he reasoned, things were going his way! Maybe he was just lucky! He smiled.

Simon shrank back from his commander. "All I meant, CEO Sir, was that it seems too easy..."

Gunter looked out the observation dome at the carnage unfolding around them. "Tell that to those who have already died...What are our losses?"

"So far we have lost four frigates and two cruisers. And the battle ship the *Jewel of Neptune* has been severely damaged and has had to pull back." The aide consulted his portable tablet computer and brought up the statistics. He handed it to Gunter who looked at it vaguely before handing it back.

"Acceptable losses, especially if we're winning," Gunter said. "How are those Collective Zone boarding teams doing on our lower decks?"

Studying the tablet again, the aide brought up a plan of the ship for his CEO and handed the tablet over.

Gunter studied it for a few seconds and then handed it back. "So, they have been stalled by our emergency bulkheads? Good. Continue drip feeding in units to slow them down and seal all emergency doors on that level. Then, when they get to the next level, do the same, et cetera, et cetera. We will bleed them dry..." Gunter's voice had adopted a semi malevolent tone as he said this. He was angry that they had tried to take his ship from under him.

"CEO Sir, the central formation of the Collective Zone is really pulling back! Some of the ships are turning around!" cried out Cranmere.

Gunter's attention snapped to the battle out of the dome. He ran, leg protesting, to the Scanning Officer in charge of mapping out the battle. "Report!" he yelled as he approached. A simple tablet could not convey the information that he needed.

"CEO Sir, they're withdrawing, look!" The officer pointed at her holo-terminal that showed the battle space in three dimensions. It showed the centre of the Collective Zone line buckling under the pressure of the Solar Solutions assault. "You've won!" the woman said in an elated tone.

"I've won!" said Gunter. He did not believe it himself. War was not so hard after all!

"What now, CEO Sir?" asked the First Officer who had appeared by his leader's side.

"Where have you been?" asked Gunter of the First Officer.

"I've been busy dealing with the Collective Zone invasion in the lower decks, CEO. Coordinating the defence is taking up a lot of my time," replied the First Officer. He was clearly a bit put off by his CEO's dismissive attitude. "But my question stands. What do we do now, CEO Sir?"

"We pursue them! I want them driven from this part of the Solar System. We follow them until they are beyond the border of the asteroid belt. I want them gone!" Gunter's eyes flashed as he gave the order. He felt alive! He thought his father would be proud!

"Yes, Sir!" snapped the First Officer with ill restrained enthusiasm. And after a few barked orders, the entire remaining Solar Solutions fleet began moving forward into the space left by the Collective Zone.

Chapter 14

"Commander Boltha, we're retreating as ordered. I hope this works..." said the First Officer to his commander.

"Why wouldn't it? It seems already that they have taken the bait. Look, they're following us!" Boltha exclaimed with glee. She realised that the ancient tactic seemed to be working. They would draw them into an encirclement and then crush them.

"This is Uxus. What are you doing, Boltha?" The question was a demand for answers.

"Something that seems to be working, CEO Sir." She laboured the last words, almost too much.

"And what is that? All I see is you retreating!" snapped Uxus. "Acting Commander Tyyz here says your plan is ill conceived and reckless. We can crush them as they were; why are you retreating?"

"I'm drawing them into a trap, CEO." Boltha rolled her eyes. "It's an ancient tactic, and it seems to be working, as I said--"

"I FORBID you to retreat!" yelled Uxus over the radio.

"Good, because I'm not retreating!" She indicated for the communication to be cut and blocked. She did not have time to explain rudimentary tactical doctrines to political leaders.

"Fleet Commander, our ships from the far side of Jupiter have broken through the flimsy Solar Solutions defence and are rounding the planet now!" cried out the First Officer from near the Scanning Officer's terminal.

Boltha smiled. The plan was coming together. "Good, order them to cut off the Solar Solutions' retreat. Roll up their flank and cut off their escape. We have them!"

Boltha stood, looking out the panoramic view from the bridge of the *Iron Bastion*. She saw the ripples of explosions blossoming across the Solar Solutions fleet from the combined fire from her part of the fleet and the part that had emerged from behind Jupiter. They had fallen for her trap. They had moved into the space she had created and had been caught in a killing zone. She smiled. The field was hers.

***

"CEO Sir! There are ships emerging from behind Jupiter! They're not ours!" yelled the Scanning Officer on the *Silver Ark*.

"What? How?" stuttered Gunter.

"They seem to have swept our forces aside and come out behind us. They're cutting off our escape route!" said the officer.

"Escape route? Why would we need to..." said Gunter, and then he saw it. The truth hit him as hard as a nuclear torpedo. He had been fooled. As he watched, the Collective Zone fleet stopped falling back and began fighting back hard. His forces had been caught in a trap. The Collective Zone never had been retreating; it was all a ruse.

"Sir! Orders!?" said the First Officer.

"I...uh...um..." stammered Gunter. He had frozen again. His name would go down in history as the man who was fooled and threw away the Solar Solutions fleet; he panicked.

Ships began exploding under the combined weight of fire of the two parts of the Collective Zone fleet.

"SIR!" yelled the First Officer. He took the radical action of shaking Gunter where he stood.

Gunter looked over to Cranmere, who looked ashen, and silent.

"Fall back...fall...back..." is all Gunter could manage. His mind had gone blank. He had gone from the elation of fake victory to the crushing realisation that he had been comprehensively outsmarted and defeated. His father would not be proud.

The First Officer nodded solemnly. "Begin the retreat! Fall back to the nearest planet that is," he checked the scanners, "...Neptune." He said the planet's name with reverence and trepidation as it was not only the nearest planet due to planetary rotation times, but it was also their seat of government and home world of the Solar Solutions Corporation. When they fell back to there, there was no further fallback position. That was it.

"Neptune...really?" whispered Gunter. Planetary positions could be cruel at times. He had at least hoped of having Saturn or Uranus as the nearest planets to mount a defence from. But Neptune, that was the end of the line.

"We need to fight our way out of this mess; send the fighters on an escort course. Turn the fleet around. We can out run the slow Collective Zone fleet," ordered the First Officer. "If we survive the withdrawal..."

Gunter was standing in the middle of the bridge again, on his command dais. He was a broken man. His tactical errors had cost many lives and perhaps even cost him his corporation.

"Why?" is all he said as he stared at the explosions around his ship out of the observation dome.

Chapter 15

As OE15 flew above the plane of battle, he noticed a subtle change. All of a sudden the ships of the Collective Zone ceased to propel themselves backwards and began to fight back hard. OE15 looked across the battle zone and noticed that the edges of the Collective Zone fleet now seemed to envelop the Solar Solutions fleet.

OE15's heart froze, he realised what was going on in a split second. "AA3, they've got us in a trap!" he radioed hurriedly. "Sir, do you read me, they've--"

"I see it!" came the snapped reply. "I sure as hell hope the CEO's seen it too..."

The flight rocketed across the battle zone. Suddenly one of the other remaining pilots called out a contact and they all banked their craft to intercept the incoming enemy. "Four enemy fighters incoming..."

OE15 selected his last two missiles and waited for the computer to declare a lock. But before he could, the warning sound of someone locking onto him cut shrilly through his headphones inside his helmet and he cried out. "They're locking on! I have to break combat!"

He jammed the control column into his stomach and felt the crushing G-forces as the directional thrusters on the sides of his craft pushed him into a spiral and he turned away from the engagement and hopefully away from the target lock.

The shrill sound continued however, and after a few seconds it turned into a wailing scream as the enemy fighter had launched its missile at him. OE15's heart was pounding, his palms were sweaty, and his breathing was rapid.

He threw the fighter into all manner of turns and twists and spiralled down through the combat in an effort to throw off the incoming missile.

His scanners picked up the incoming projectile and he noticed the distance closing rapidly. When the missile was close, he triggered his counter-measures in another desperate effort to throw the missile off the scent of his radar or engine emissions.

OE15 banked again and just as he did so he saw the missile streak by his canopy and detonate harmlessly a few hundred metres away from him. He tried to breathe normally again, but his rapid pulse rate demanded lots of oxygen.

He checked his oxygen levels on his dashboard and noted that there was still plenty left in the tank situated behind his seat.

Just as he was regaining his composure, and scanning the space around him, he noticed that he was now in the middle of the combat of the capital ships. His escape from the missile had taken him deep into the combat zone. He knew that he had to get above the combat again.

Angling the nose of his craft upwards, OE15 began to climb back to a safer altitude. Before he could get there though, he saw a flash on his scanner and an enemy fighter was rocketing in on him at break-neck speed. He craned his neck to see and just as he saw it the enemy fighter let loose a burst from its guns that peppered OE15's machine from nose to stern before roaring off silently into the distance.

OE15 was shaken. He checked his systems; everything seemed in order. He had not been hit at least; he breathed a sigh of relief. He tried moving the craft. It was sluggish. They had hit the directional thrusters control.

According to his scanner, the fighter was coming back. OE15 tried to bank to get a shot at it as it came in, but with his thrusters sluggish, it was hard.

He banked slowly around and faced the incoming enemy fighter. He saw it highlighted in his targeting reticle. OE15 knew a head on attack was almost suicide, but he could not enter a turning fight with the enemy with his thrusters sluggish.

He accelerated to emergency combat speed. This pushed the fighter's engines into overdrive for a short period. He was trusting in his aim. He hoped to scare the enemy into breaking off or missing due to the rapid closing speed of the combat.

In a second they were in gun range. The combat was too close and fast to use missiles. OE15 thumbed his trigger and white-hot tracer shells spat from his machine guns in the nose of his fighter.

The enemy fired too and OE15 could feel rather than hear the shells hitting his fighter. He just hoped none hit him.

In another second they had passed each other and OE15 looked back to see the enemy fighter spiralling out of control and venting gasses as it went. Its fuel supplies caught fire and detonated and there was a flash as the craft split asunder in a fiery conflagration.

OE15 smiled. "Kill number three!" he said to himself.

Then he noticed the bullet hole in the canopy just above his head. He reached behind him and felt the hole in the chair he was sitting in just a few centimetres above where his head was. He swallowed hard. "That was too close..."

"OE15 where are you? My scanners say you're alive. Get back to my wing this instant!" It was AA3's voice over the radio.

"Yes, sir! But I've been hit. I'm a bit sluggish," OE15 replied. "Where are you?"

"Quadrant 4, sector gamma 2," came the response.

"I see you. I'm coming!" OE15 throttled down to normal power and began to climb away from the plane of the capital ship combat again. As he did so, he saw the massive anti-ship auto-turrets and missile pods disgorging their payloads into the enemy ships. Both Solar Solutions and Collective Zone ships were suffering large amounts of damage.

OE15 watched the trap enveloping the Solar Solutions fleet. He studied the fleet formations as he climbed back to the fighter wing.

OE15 regained his position on the wing of AA3. There were only he, AA3 and two other fighters left at this point.

"Oh shit..." it was AA3's voice. It was strangely devoid of control. "Look to the scanners on the edge of Jupiter. Missile frigates! Collective Zone missile frigates!"

OE15 looked at his scanner and set it to maximum range and capital ship detection mode. Sure enough, large, bulky enemy missile ships were making their way around the orange planet. They were still out of visual range, but it was obvious: the Solar Solutions fleet was about to be surrounded.

"What do we do, sir?" said OE15 meekly.

"We do our best, son. We keep fighting and make a speedy withdrawal." There was a pause. "Our capital ship commanders have seen it too and are pulling back to try to get out of the trap. At least not all of them are stupid!"

"Orders, sir?" asked OE15. His voice was faint. They had lost. They had fallen for an old trick. The centre of the enemy had pulled back and the Solar Solutions had taken the bait and were being surrounded. Now all they could do was fight an honourable withdrawal.

"Defend the *Silver Ark*! It is our ship and our home! Remaining fighters, follow me!" And with that, the flight leader AA3 put his nose into a dive and went to defend his home ship.

OE15 tried to follow but his controls were heavy and sluggish, and he lagged behind. He would not be much use, but he would try to help any way he could.

OE15 looked to where the missile ships were coming from. He thought that he could see the incoming trails of missiles already streaking towards the Solar Solutions positions.

"Oh shit, indeed," he said to himself.

He watched the slow reactions of the capital ships as they turned around and tried to retreat from the trap. A number were lost in this process but thanks to the Solar Solutions faster engines, the majority of the remaining fleet was able to turn reasonably quickly and start to extricate itself from the closing pincers of the Collective Zone fleet. This, however, exposed their engine systems to enemy fire, and the Solar Solutions ships had fewer guns facing backwards and so could not defend themselves as easily while running away.

"Come on! Come on!" OE15 whispered as the bulk of the *Silver Ark* turned in space, its outer armour scored and pitted by lasers and missiles.

The remaining fighters flew close escort over the remaining capital ships. They waited for the call to land, but in the mean time, they fought as hard as they could.

Chapter 16

Trooper Althar strained as he hefted the welding drill to what seemed like the thousandth bulkhead. He was exhausted. His stim-unit was depleted. His armoured space suit was awash inside with sweat. He breathed hard as he hefted the bulky apparatus to in front of the door.

No matter how heavy the drill was, he would keep going. He would keep going until he was dead. He was enraged. This was due to the fact that he had seen his long-term friend Grox fall doors ago. Althar was unsure whether he was dead or just unconscious, but it was impossible to retrieve him given the Solar Solutions resistance.

"These bastards are putting up quite a fight! And who didn't plan for all these fucking bulkheads?!" Althar swore.

They were under fire again. Lieutenant Vauz was standing by the drill, snapping off shots with his pistol. He seemed fearless to Althar who took cover as bullets raked across the drill.

"Just get the door open!" shouted Vauz.

"Until the next one!" shouted back Althar. But he obeyed. He obeyed without question. The drill started and bit deeply into the outer casing of the door.

The platoon had been severely depleted by now. Many of their number had been incapacitated or killed. They started with around forty soldiers, now they were down to less than twenty; and they had only gone up a few floors. There must have been at least another few before the bridge could be reached.

"Which idiot landed us in the basement?" Althar cursed as the drill powered up.

"Enough of that now. We have a job to do, so do it!" snapped Vauz over the radio.

The rest of the remaining platoon had fanned out around the door again and were defending the drill as the Solar Solutions resistance put up a hard fight and killed some of them before melting away as the door was breached and then the whole process repeated itself over and over.

Althar, and Vauz too this time, took cover after a particularly bad raking of gunfire from the Solar Solutions' positions. Suddenly the drill began to spark and sputter.

"Sir!" shouted Althar. "The drill!"

In a second, the drill tore itself apart as the oxygen and acetylene pipes ruptured and the drill bit melted in the ensuing conflagration. Althar managed to shut off the machine before the entire thing exploded.

"That was our last drill bit...and now the pipes are ruptured..." Althar said to Vauz. They both looked at each other through their helmets. The game was up; and they both knew it.

"We have no more?" Vauz asked, pointing to the mangled drill end.

"No, sir. No more. That was the last." Althar looked at the machine and hefted the large fuel and oxygen pipes pointing to the bullet holes in their armoured segmented carapace. "Armour piercing bullets, sir. We're lucky it didn't explode and kill us all."

"Thanks to your fast work!" Vauz patted Althar on the shoulder. They ducked as more gunfire strafed their position. "This is Lieutenant Vauz," Vauz radioed to the *Iron Bastion* and the landing craft. "Our drill has been compromised. We've lost half our number. There's harsh resistance. Orders?"

As Vauz waited for new orders, taking cover by the defunct drill, Althar looked out the nearest window. He noticed that the stars were changing; that the ship was turning.

"Sir, we're moving," he said tapping Vauz on the shoulder.

"We are indeed. I just received orders from the *Iron Bastion*. We're getting out of here. We cannot continue without a drill and the resistance is too high. But, the Solar Solutions fleet is caught in a trap! Our job is done!" Vauz hauled himself to his feet. "Okay soldiers, let's move. Back to the landing barges, double time!"

Althar heard a collective groan as all the other soldiers realised they had failed and that they were being recalled. Also, the prospect of running all the way back through the ship to the landing barges while being attacked all the way was not a pleasant one, but they did it.

As they passed the place where Grox fell, Althar paused and looked for the body. Strangely, there was none. Althar's heart leapt; maybe he had survived! Maybe he was back on the landing barge already! This hope powered his aching limbs as he ran back to the barges, snapping off shots behind him as he went.

When they reached the barges, the Collective Zone soldiers mounted up under heavy fire from Solar Solutions soldiers who were clearly buoyed by their success at defending their flagship.

Althar searched his barge. Grox was not there. But he knew there were other barges that he could be in.

The remaining Collective Zone soldiers strapped themselves in and the barges fired their thrusters and with a grinding vibration extricated themselves from the hull of the *Silver Ark*.

The barges turned and headed back towards the *Iron Bastion*. Due to the lack of windows in the troop compartment, Althar could not see the Solar Solutions ships being sprung in the trap, but he grinned anyway. He imagined what was happening.

The soldiers sat in silence as they headed home. Each man and woman contemplating their own actions and whether they had lived up to their own expectation of what they would do in combat. They had failed; it was true. They had not reached the bridge and captured the *Silver Ark*. They had lost half their number also, but their fleet had succeeded. They held that in their minds and hearts. They had to; otherwise, they would all be lost in their sorrow.

***

Gunter stood silently on the bridge of the *Silver Ark*. He watched the pitted and scarred outer shell of his flagship as it traversed space and tried to extricate itself from the trap that had been so expertly sprung on them.

He saw other ships of the Solar Solutions fleet dive and climb and turn in an effort to break from the combat space in any way possible. His order had been born of failure. His order had been, "Flee!" And he watched as his once proud fleet of ships, now depleted by a fair number, turned and ran from the combat zone in any way possible.

There were some lead ships that had been too far into the trap to extricate themselves and they were now being pounded into submission by the encroaching Collective Zone ships. Other Solar Solutions ships had been damaged and were listing and trailing atmosphere as they limped free of the enclosing cordon.

The aides had stopped asking him for orders. They knew their commander was now no longer in control. The main person now trying to save what was left of the fleet was the First Officer. He knew his job. He knew he had to save as many of the ships as possible. Even Simon had left

123

Gunter's side and was conferring with the First Officer on what to do.

Gunter could not see Cranmere on the bridge.

Suddenly the First Officer was at Gunter's side. "CEO Sir, the attack on our ship has been repulsed. We have taken a number of prisoners. It is beyond my authority to know what to do with them. What do you command?"

"Are you sure it's beyond your authority? You have basically taken the ship in a bloodless coup. I have no power here," Gunter sighed.

"CEO Sir, you are still my CEO and commander..." pleaded the First Officer.

"Very well. I suppose we should interrogate them. Set the interrogator tech-slaves on them. See what they know." Gunter waved his hand vaguely, as if to shoo off an insect.

The First Officer nodded and retreated to his clique of aides and began giving orders again.

Gunter walked to the edge of the bridge and observation dome. His leg whined. He walked right to the glass shield that separated space from atmosphere. He reached up and touched it with his right hand. It was cold, he noted. In front of him he saw the disfigured form of the front of the *Silver Ark*. It had turned around by now and was beating a hasty retreat out of the pull of Jupiter's gravity. There were some other ships from his fleet that he could see around it.

"How many?" asked Gunter vaguely.

"How many what, CEO Sir?" asked the First Officer.

"How many of our ships made it?" clarified Gunter, still staring out the glass at the expanse of damage ships and harsh space.

"Of the thirty two ships we had before he engagement, we have thirteen totally extricated, six heavily damaged others will probably make it too. So nineteen." snapped the First Officer.

"Nineteen..." repeated Gunter. "And how many enemy ships did we disable or destroy?"

"Of the thirty or so they had, five," said the First Officer. "But the disabled ones will be repaired by them."

"Five..." whispered Gunter still staring out the observation dome. He gently touched his head to the glass and closed his eyes. He had failed...utterly.

Chapter 17

While Artisius had been busy making sure the *Green Dragon* was ready to fly, Draz had been watching the battle unfold. She was under one of the observation domes on Europa.

From the bridge of the *Green Dragon*, Artisius had been watching too, and with his experience in ship manoeuvres, he was communicating with Draz.

They had both seen the disastrous outcome of the trap sprung by the Collective Zone. At the time, even Draz could see the centre of the Collective Zone battle line drawing the Solar Solutions ships in, and Artisius had sworn and cursed something shocking over the radio with Draz at what was going on. He had seen with his practiced eye that the Solar Solutions fleet was caught and would be pummelled into submission.

But that was the past. It had happened. Nothing could reverse the situation they were in, and now their main task was to get off Europa and survive.

"Survive," Draz whispered to herself. She smiled. She felt like she had turned a corner, that the need for her sobriety and sanity had taken root and was growing within her. She still felt the gnawing pain of the withdrawal, but it was getting buried by the need for her to remain sane and collected in the face of the perils and stresses she and her friends faced. "Friends..." she whispered and smiled again as the thought crossed her mind. For the first time in a long time, she felt needed and required in a group of people. Her life on Earth was a solitary one since her parents were killed and then there was her prison experience. Since meeting Alfred, Artisius, and the crew of the *Green Dragon*, she had gotten used to their presence and they, hers. And that made her feel welcome, and not alone.

All this did not mean she would never use drugs again; she could not guarantee that. The pain was always there; the pangs and longing were always just there, ready to burst forth. But through feeling needed and wanted, she reckoned that she could push the cravings to the very back of her soul and bury them there; deep down, where no one and nothing could reach them. If she wanted to survive, she would have to do that, because a relapse would end in disaster.

"We're almost ready here," said the voice of Artisius over the communicator. "The crew's assembled and the ship is restocked. What're you thinking, Draz?"

"Well, given your approval as the expert ship captain," Draz spoke into her communicator and heard Artisius snort and chuckle at his end. "I was thinking that we gather up as many people as we can, to help the refugees escape, and then we blast out of here."

"That sounds plausible," Artisius said. "But why the refugees? We're not equipped for that."

"I don't want to leave people here to be treated like Mars, Artisius. I really don't. If we can help a few people get off this rock then that will be good," Draz said.

Then Draz heard over the communicator a mumbled line about being a good man.

"All right," said Artisius after a short time. "But I won't have my ship compromised by too many people. Ten families, max."

"Thank you," said Draz.

Draz looked up at the boiling sky above her. The sky was still on fire from shots and missiles racing back and forth between the warring fleets. But the Solar Solutions fleet was breaking out of the trap.

"Now. Now's the time!" Draz said into her communicator. "They're too busy with the Solar Solutions fleet to worry about us, yet. But the Solar Solutions fleet is escaping. We have to move now!"

"I agree," said Artisius. "We'll make a ship captain of you yet!" He laughed. "Are you going to get Alfred or should I?"

"We should both go; strength in numbers. I'm not sure I can deal with Anya alone. She really has her claws into Alfred," Draz was already moving towards the command centre, which was near the dome she was under.

***

After a short travel, Draz arrived outside the command centre doors and found Artisius waiting for her.

"That was fast," she said.

"We need to move fast. The battle space is changing rapidly. They could start an invasion any minute."

"Do you think they would? I mean, could they risk it with the Solar Solutions fleet?" Draz asked.

"They could do anything. The Solar Solutions fleet has been routed, and is now outnumbered by the Collective Zone. They now own Jupiter..." Artisius trailed off in thought.

"Right, let's get to it!" Draz said with a nod.

They both burst into the command centre to see it a flurry of action and chaos. Aides were running everywhere, and the walkways were abuzz with colony personnel trying to make sense of what was going on in the skies above.

Suddenly there was a flash of bright light from outside the dome over the command centre. Then there was a loud vibration followed by a roar. The entire command centre shook from the impact.

"Oh shit, that's early..." said Artisius.

"What the hell was that?" yelled Draz. The entire command centre had gone silent and seemed to be in suspended animation as people tried to make sense of what had just happened.

"That...was the start of the orbital bombardment," said Artisius. "That's what happens when an auto-turret laser lands nearby. We've got to move, now!"

The pair looked around for Anya and saw her on an upper tier staring out on the colony. They rushed up to her and, still short of breath, demanded Alfred be set free. She was still surrounded by aides trying to get her to respond to their demands.

"How?" whispered Anya.

"What do you mean how? We need Alfred, now! And we need your word for the evacuation procedure!" yelled Artisius.

There was another blinding flash from space and another rushing roar as the energy of an auto-turret dissipated as it hit the surface.

"How...did he lose? It was a trap?" mumbled Anya again.

Draz grabbed the base commander and shook her. "Snap out of it! They're bombarding the moon! We need clearance to leave! Sound the evacuation," she shouted at the commander.

Anya seemed to wake up for a second. "Evacuate? Now? I suppose." As one the aides rushed away and took the order to evacuate to their required stations.

In seconds a klaxon siren was sounding and if Draz and Artisius had thought the command centre was a hive of activity before, now it was a veritable mess of people running back and forth. Holo-terminal operators were trying to radio the message of the evacuation around the colony, while destroying their equipment so that it did not fall into the hands of the Collective Zone.

"So, we have the word to evacuate?" yelled Draz above the din.

"Why not?" said Anya. "He failed...Gunter, my CEO, he failed..." She was staring out over the colony as now beam after beam of boiling energy slammed into the moon's surface. This caused the lights to flicker in the command centre. "Why are they doing this?" A pleading tone came into her voice.

Artisius put a hand on her shoulder. "Because they are. Now, we must escape. Come with us, we can accommodate you on the *Green Dragon*."

"This is all your fault! If it weren't for you, we'd be safe; we'd be fine," Anya snapped and shook off the hand.

"Whatever the case, they'll shell this moon into oblivion. You must escape, now!" snapped Artisius back at her.

A pained expression crossed Artisius' face and Draz realised that the commander's accusations had hit a raw nerve.

Outside the dome, another blast happened further out in the colony and then, as they all watched, as if in slow motion, the ice that the part of the colony was built on, slipped silently into the ocean beneath.

"Holy shit!" said Draz.

"Indeed," said Artisius. "The bombardment will destroy the ice surface!" Artisius turned to Anya again. "Last chance. We're leaving..."

Anya paused and turned to Artisius. She looked as though she was processing his demand and offer. She turned back to the carnage outside the dome. "I won't be leaving." She said it with such certainty and conviction that

Artisius stepped back and saluted before heading down to where Alfred was still plugged into the network.

Draz paused and looked after him. She then turned to Anya, who was again looking out of the dome onto her destroyed colony. Anya waved her away, and after a slight delay of comprehension, Draz too dashed down the stairways to find Artisius standing next to Alfred's zetting terminal.

"So, how do we get him out of here?" asked Draz. The command centre was still abuzz with activity as messages were relayed around the colony and ships were being co-ordinated as they left, and refugee shuttles were being prepared to evacuate as many of the people as could be saved as possible.

Artisius searched the console in front of their friend. He was still sitting, oblivious to them, with his jaw locked and teeth bared while sitting bolt upright. He found a switch that read "emergency disengage."

"This might work?" he said, pointing to the switch.

"I hope you're right!" said Draz above the noise of the room.

Suddenly another blast happened, nearby this time. The command centre rocked, and they felt vibrations as some of the ice nearby slid into the ocean beneath the icy surface of the moon.

Draz swore and cursed the Collective Zone.

Artisius looked at her with his hand over the switch. Draz nodded and Artisius pressed the switch.

***

Alfred was guiding himself through the system. He had lost count of the number of times he had had to fix the Europa system. It may have been his fifth; it may have been his fiftieth. He had no idea.

Things were not going well. The sides of his vision were coloured and fuzzy; his display and vision were exhibiting numerous artefacts and errors, which made navigating the system precarious. He could misjudge one of the pathways and fall off the system into oblivion.

Furthermore, the computer itself was resisting his touch. This was new to him. He was used to computers being very receptive to his zetting; but now, this computer was resisting him. It put up barriers across his path. It dimmed pathways so they were difficult to see and navigate. It established blocks and obstructions to his manoeuvring.

"Why are you doing this?" he thought.

Alfred pressed on with the zet. He had a job to do, and nothing would stop him from accomplishing it. He found the dead pathways and re-energised them. He unblocked the blocked paths. He fixed errors.

Even with Virtus gone, the system was still exhibiting problems brought about by the Head Trader. It was obvious that his corruption of the system went deep.

Alfred swore. He encountered another block on the system that he had to go around, but the pathways here were faint and the artefacts on his vision made the journey precarious. He navigated around the blockage and then, when he turned around to clear it, he lost his balance. Suddenly he felt that he was falling. He was falling off the system's pathways.

Alfred began to panic. He lashed out with his mind in an attempt to latch onto the faint pathway. He managed to grab it and hang on. He pulled himself up and avoided a fall into oblivion and mindless nothingness.

He floated a time just in one place, just on one pathway. He had never almost fallen into oblivion while zetting before, not even when he was learning. Things were not going well, but he still had so much more to do.

Suddenly the system froze; nothing moved. In that instant, Alfred's vision began to dissolve. It melted as if it were some kind of ice exposed to heat. His vision bled different colours. His mind locked up. His jaw seized up and he bared his teeth. He felt his back arch. Something was seriously wrong. Something was very, very wrong.

"You stupid fool!"

Alfred had never felt anything like this before. He heard the voice. He knew the voice. It was the voice in his head from the pirate base. It was the voice in his head from back when *Florida Station* was still there. It was the voice of his madness.

"Oh, I'm here all right. Waiting; watching. You will be mine..."

"But you're just in my head!" thought Alfred. The thought was a scream in his mind as his entire zetting universe that he was in slowly disassembled itself and melted around him. His mind tried to contain itself and stop itself running out of his ears.

"Oh yes, I'm in your mind. I am your mind. You cannot escape me! The more you zet, the closer I come..."

"But I have to zet!" Alfred caught himself. He was arguing with his own consciousness; his own mind; but it seemed like the sensible thing to do when his own mind was rebelling against him.

"Oh yes. You do. You really do. And I welcome every time you do..."

Alfred saw more of the world decay around him. "What's happening?"

"You're coming out of a zet..."

"But...it's never been like this. I didn't trigger any form of exit procedure..." Alfred was puzzled. He could not get a grip of what was going on.

"Look, he's coming around!" said another voice. It was not Alfred subconscious. It was not Alfred's voice. It was someone he knew, he could tell, but he did not recognise it.

"They're waiting for you..."

"Who?" Alfred had forgotten what was going on outside the zet. His whole world had been consumed in the last few moments.

"Your...friends..."

"Quick, should I pull the needle out?" came a voice from outside the zet.

Alfred suddenly realised what this was. The melting world; the errors; the artefacts. He was being shunted out of the system. Someone had pressed the emergency disengage button. He had never felt what an emergency disengage was like. Now he knew. It was unpleasant to say the least.

Alfred felt the backwash as the needle was drawn from his skull. There was a ripple of energy that flooded through his body as the connection to the system was severed without his express permission. His vision of the system faded and disappeared in a flash of colours.

Alfred had, back on *Florida Station*, he vaguely remembered, once disengaged a zet by pulling the needle out, but that was of his own choice, his body was partially ready for it. This was different.

"I..." he stuttered, "I can't see..."

"He's alive, he's here!" gasped a voice. Alfred could not quite recognise who it was. He knew the voice though. He knew it, once.

"It seems your friends need you. I'll be waiting...Whenever you zet, I'll be close..."

134

"It's...in my head..." Alfred clawed at the side of his skull and tried to pull out the implant. He scrabbled and scraped at his flesh.

"Quick, stop him! He'll kill himself. Alfred, are you okay? Can you hear me? Shit, I don't think he's quite with us." It was a female voice. He knew the sound.

"I...can hear it!" Alfred stammered. His vision had not returned. All he could see were flashes of colour and ghost circuits spiralling in front of his eyes. He slumped in his seat.

"Can you stand?" it was a male voice, older.

Alfred tried to stand up. His legs felt like the reproduced goo that he ate most of his life. He collapsed back into his chair.

"Did...did you get me out?" Alfred stammered again.

"Yes, yes we did. We got you out. We have to escape. The Collective Zone ships are bombarding Europa!" the female voice again.

"Who? Who are you?" Alfred felt his face. He felt his eyes. They were still there. He squeezed them. There was nothing but colours.

"It's me, Draz, and Artisius is here too." The voice sounded hurt that it was not recognised. "Can you try to stand again?"

Alfred tried again, and failed. His body was failing him. He was caught mid way between a zet and reality.

"Is this normal?" asked Draz. "I mean, have we damaged you?"

"Maybe," whispered Alfred. "I hear it!" he started to claw at his implant again. "It's inside!"

Alfred felt some strong arms grab his arms and restrain him. "We need to get him to the *Green Dragon's* infirmary. We can treat him there," came Artisius' voice. "We'll have to carry him."

Alfred felt himself being lifted by his arms and some strong bodies positioned themselves under his arms. He had a limb around each person's shoulders, and he was trying to move his legs, but they were simply dragging him along.

"He's heavier than I thought!" came the female Draz's voice. "Alfred, we need your help...please!"

Alfred tried his hardest to make his legs work. They obeyed a little and he managed to stand and stagger along for a period of time.

"You need to walk now!"

"I...I can't!" said Alfred.

"What?" said the male Artisius' voice.

"If you ever want to zet again, walk! You idiot!"

"I...I must!" Alfred whispered and steeled himself. He managed to take one step, and then another, and he kept going one step at a time, which took the burden off his assistants.

"He's hearing voices again," said Draz.

"When we get him to the *Green Dragon* we can diagnose what's wrong," said Artisius, straining under Alfred's weight.

Alfred heard a large boom and a whooshing noise. "What's...?"

"Collective Zone. Shelling the planet. That's why we need to move, now!" gasped Draz.

After what seemed like an age, Alfred was allowed to sit down on a hover train. He heard the sound of many panicked people around him. They seemed to be escaping from the shelling. They were afraid as much as he was. He was scared. He was terrified. He had never been blind before. In front of his vision swam images of network pathways and zetting systems.

After a while that seemed like forever, he and his assistants exited the train and headed up a lift towards their docked ship.

"We're almost there!" strained Draz. She was obviously tired from lifting Alfred.

Alfred heard the activation of a number of airlocks and the rush of air from within their ship heralded their arrival.

Alfred was helped to the infirmary and ushered down onto one of the medical slabs. It felt cool to the touch. Alfred was so confused. He tried to ask what was going on, but no one answered. He heard Artisius and Draz talking to someone who seemed to be a doctor.

"Alfred, the doctor will take care of you now," Draz said as she squeezed his left hand. It was apparent to Alfred from her voice and action that she was concerned about him.

"Okay..." he said. But any further reassurance was gone, like her, as she and Artisius had exited the infirmary.

"Alfred? I'm Doctor Antonia. I met you earlier, do you remember? I'll take care of you. First, we have to scan your systems for damage. Is that all right? To see what new damage has been done." the voice was soft and female. It seemed kind. It was the voice of the doctor he had seen after the pirate base. He thought he recognised her smooth, soft tone.

Alfred, still blind, nodded.

Alfred felt the diagnostic needle slide into his implant on the side of his head. It was cold. He flinched a little. Why were all the doctors' tools always cold, he wondered?

"Sorry," said Dr Antonia. She had obviously seen him react to the needle. "This may take a little time, but it shouldn't hurt."

Alfred lay on the slab, motionless and blind. He saw shapes of circuits and pathways through networks spiral in front of his eyes.

"Will I see again?" he asked meekly. He was afraid.

"The blindness should be temporary, but that's what we're trying to find out. Just hold still." The last sentence was said with what sounded, to Alfred, like a smile.

Alfred heard the machine by the slab spitting out information onto synthetic paper reels. He wondered if he was going to be okay. As the process was taking place, the doctor spoke to him softly and reassuringly. He felt grateful to be cared for by a caring doctor.

"I...I know your voice," Alfred stammered.

"I treated you after the pirate base, as I said; don't you remember?" The voice had a concerned quality.

Alfred thought for a while and then answered. "Sort of...I remember the tone of your voice. But I cannot remember a face," he sounded sad.

"Almost done," said Doctor Antonia after a few minutes.

"What's the diagnosis? Am I damned?" Alfred said rather melodramatically.

"One question I have," said Dr Antonia as Alfred heard the rustle of paper, "are you still hearing voices? Last time I saw you, you said you were hearing voices."

"Do you want to tell her?"

Alfred flinched. The voice came back to him as if it were totally sentient and a different entity. He knew it was in his mind, but it sounded and seemed so real.

"I...I don't know?" Alfred's voice rose in an inflection.

"You don't know if you're hearing voices?" Dr Antonia sounded confused.

"Oh well done; now you've given it away. Don't you like me?"

Alfred shook his head and the lead cable jerked.

"Easy now!" said Dr Antonia. "I didn't mean to anger you."

"No, no, it's not that," said Alfred. "I do hear voices. It's like it's another person, inside my head, talking to me. I can't describe it any better. It's as if it has a mind of its own. It scares me. At first I thought I was imagining it, and then I thought I was mad, and now, I don't know..."

"When did it start," asked Dr Antonia.

"In my last zetting times aboard *Florida Station*. I thought it was the computer core talking to me. That's why I thought it was imaginary. Computers cannot talk to people." Alfred laughed uneasily.

"Well, actually," said Dr Antonia. Her tone scared Alfred, "computer cores have been known at times to talk to their zetters. It's extremely rare, but *Florida Station* was old enough for the computer core to perhaps have developed a personality..." she trailed off.

"So, then what's this in my head now?" Alfred said.

"Have you noticed a difference in the voices? I mean, did the computer core sound different from the voices now?" Dr Antonia continued her questions, calmly.

"I...guess," said Alfred. "The computer core talked about me joining it. These voices talk to me like a malicious person who wants to influence me."

"Exactly! I thought as much," said Dr Antonia. "The voices you hear now are a cause of the decay in your implant."

"And the older voices in the network?" Alfred asked. He was worried.

"They may have been the computer, or may have been early stages of decay. We can probably never be sure. It's more likely that they were the decay of your implant manifesting earlier as the computer's voice while you were zetting, as that was when your implant was under stress. I am sure now that the voices you are hearing are simply due to the decay in the implant." Dr Antonia paused to read some of the papers that came out of the machine plugged into Alfred.

Alfred, still blind, heard the rustle of papers.

"She might be right...but how do you know? She could just be lying..."

"There!" Alfred exclaimed. "There it was! The voice!"

"What did it say?" asked Dr Antonia.

"She might be right...but how do you know? She could just be lying..." Alfred repeated what he remembered.

"Interesting," Dr Antonia said. "Are all the voice's comments vicious or negative or attacking you in some way?"

Alfred thought for a moment. "Mostly...most of the time they are somehow against me, as if the voice is somehow trying to be on my side but is actually some kind of malicious being. Sometimes they give advice, but mostly it's just put downs."

Alfred heard Dr Antonia snap her fingers. "I've heard of this. It sounds like a kind of decay induced schizophrenia. It's rare, but it does happen to zetters when their implant decays to a point.

"Is it reversible?" Alfred asked. He sounded strangely relieved to himself. It was as if, just perhaps, he had a diagnosis, and the problem could be fixed.

"No!"

Alfred flinched.

"It said something then, didn't it?" asked Dr Antonia.

"It said 'no!'" Alfred repeated.

"Well, it's wrong. I'll run some further tests, but if I'm right, and I'm not saying I am, but if I'm right, then I will be able to prescribe you medication that could do something about the problem."

"Will my sight and memory come back?" Alfred asked. He was not sure if he wanted to know.

"Sight, yes, probably in a few hours. Memory, no. I'm sorry. That damage is permanent." Dr Antonia paused, and then continued when it looked like Alfred was about to ask another question. "You have to stop zetting. The more you zet, the more the memory loss worsens. And the voice will get worse too. At this point, things are manageable. But if you keep going, I cannot guarantee anything."

"You'll never be rid of me"

Alfred paused. "Is there any way of removing this?" He tapped at the implant in his head.

"Removal of the zetting implant?" Dr Antonia repeated. "It's possible. I've heard stories of people who have gone to Pluto's medical facility to have their implants removed. It's all pretty hazardous stuff though. You go to Pluto at your own risk."

"Pluto..." Alfred said. That was where the two corporations did not reach. It was beyond their jurisdictions. It was not like Mars, that was a buffer zone of criminals between the two empires; but it was its own government, and it had its own laws. There was a thriving colony out there. No one really paid it any attention as it was so far away. Alfred had heard all this while he had been on *Florida Station*. He did not know, however, that they could remove zetting implants out there. And that was all he could remember about it.

"I don't advise it," repeated Dr Antonia. "But if you had to get the implant removed, that's where you'd get it done."

Alfred relaxed onto the slab. He knew what he had to do. He had to get to Pluto and have the implant removed.

Over the doctor's communicator, Alfred heard that Artisius was calling for Dr Antonia to meet him in the boarding airlock. He had some refugees that he needed to take on board and they needed medical checks.

"Just wait here a few hours. Your vision should start returning shortly," she said as she touched him gently on the shoulder.

Alfred nodded. His sight was already partially returning. He could see the bright flare of the lights of the medical bay above him. The lights were interspersed with the pathways of the network that were still superimposed across his vision.

"Will the voice go away if the implant is gone?" he asked the departing doctor.

"That...I also do not know, but the medication should dampen it. I'll be back when your vision returns to guide you through the medication. Rest now," she said and then Alfred heard the hissing of the medical bay door slide aside and click shut. Doctor Antonia had left.

Alfred lay back on the slab and waited. He realised how exhausted he was. He had been zetting for so many of the past hours. His vision started to return slowly. And for the first time, in a long time, he felt more in control of his brain and his implant. He knew what he had to do. The voice stayed strangely silent.

Alfred drifted off to sleep. The slab was hard, but he was so very tired.

Chapter 18

Draz and Artisius were busy loading the families of the people fleeing Europa onto the *Green Dragon*. Artisius had promised ten families would be taken. However, there were many more people now crowding into the docking tube simply hoping to survive; to escape.

The shelling of Europa was still happening. Outside the entrance to the *Green Dragon* the people in the docking tube could hear the whooshing explosions as the Collective Zone ships around Europa conducted the orbital bombardment; and the tremors as parts of the ice sheet slid into the oceans below when the city above became unstable and disappeared into the depths.

Artisius was trying to guide the groups of refugees onboard, while Draz and some of the security crew were busy scanning their eyes and reading their forehead temperatures for any signs of illness. Artisius had insisted that the refugees be scanned in order to protect his crew and his ship. Their details would be logged, and it would be made sure that the refugees were healthy.

Even though the scans only took a few seconds for each person, Draz felt they were wasting time.

Draz looked over at Artisius. She wondered why he was wearing his brace of pistols when ushering in the refugees.

"But does it matter if they're unwell or not? They'll die if they stay on Europa anyway!" said Draz to Artisius as she scanned another family. Her voice did not inspire hope in the little girl of the family in front of her and she burst into tears. Her mother tried to comfort her while scowling at Draz. Draz looked sorry.

"I will not have my ship as a bringer of disease..." snapped Artisius, directing the family through the airlock.

"You never scanned Alfred or me!" Draz snapped back. She held the scanner in her right hand, and it was slack at her side.

"That was different!" Artisius said with a tone of annoyance.

"How?" said Draz. She knew she had won the argument.

"I just want to be sure these people are all right! Here I am, offering them a berth on my ship, and now I'm the bad guy!" Artisius threw up his hands. "Come on, Draz. We don't have all day!"

Draz knew she had won the argument, but she still felt like the loser. Artisius was right, he was helping these people, but sometimes his ways jarred with hers. She hurriedly scanned more people.

As she knelt down and scanned a small boy, he said to her. "Will we be safe?" The child would have been no more than five or six years old. Suddenly Draz had a flash back to her previous life; to her life as a Corporate Wing scavenger; to her fight against the Shipping Wing; to when she had boarded that hover train and the young child, who she could not quite remember, had asked her something similar. Draz could not quite remember the face of that young child, all those years ago, but she could remember the eyes, the fear in the eyes, they were the same. The child in front of her was clearly terrified and had seen things that no six-year-old should ever see.

Draz put her scanner down, and put her left hand on the child's head. "You'll be fine," she said. "We'll protect you. You'll be okay!" Draz said it as much to help herself as to help the child. "What's your name?"

The child smiled. "John."

"Well John, I'll make sure that you, and your parents, make it through this." Draz looked at the mother and father behind the child. They smiled with gratitude in their eyes. "Now come on, get yourself on board. It's time to go on an adventure!"

"Where are we going?" asked John. He sounded a little reassured.

"We're following the Solar Solutions fleet," said Artisius who had come over. He picked up Draz's scanner and gave it to her. "We don't have long," he whispered to Draz.

She nodded. She knew. But she had to help the child, John. Draz stood and waved John and family through to the *Green Dragon*.

Draz scanned family after family and waved them through. Dr Antonia had shown up after Artisius called her in order to give the families a more thorough check up.

Soon the quota of ten families was exhausted. But there were still more people crowding into the boarding corridor between the tower the *Green Dragon* was docked with and the *Green Dragon* itself. If the *Green Dragon* decoupled and undocked now, the people in the docking tube would be killed by the harsh Europa atmosphere. On the other hand, if they stayed behind, they would be killed by the orbital bombardment.

"That's enough!" said Artisius, walking over to Draz. "We need to go, now!" he said it with urgency. And it was plain why, the rocking and blasting from orbit was intensifying.

"But, the people!" Draz said.

"You may think me harsh, but I cannot save everyone," said Artisius. "Those I do save, I cherish, and those I cannot save, I mourn. But the thing is, you can never save everyone. Some people will always die. I learnt that a long time ago. It's served me well."

"I...haven't seen this side of you before. You always helped Alfred and me," said Draz.

"Perhaps that's for the best that you haven't seen this before. But war brings out the old soldier in me. And be realistic. Do you expect me to take the entire population of Europa onboard? I chose ten families. It was arbitrary. It could have been nine it could have been eleven, but what I say goes on my ship. In war you learn, you cannot save everyone." Artisius retreated inside the ship where Dr Antonia was.

Draz was left, holding the scanner, at the end of the docking tube with an increasingly panicked group of people. They had gathered that the ship would not take them and were beginning to surge towards the airlock.

Draz, realising she would be torn apart by the crazed and terrified mob, ran inside the airlock and Artisius closed it behind her with the aid of two security personnel.

Draz watched Artisius. He appeared to slump as the airlock closed and the thumps of fists and feet on the other side intensified. The airlock would not open again without his permission. But Draz saw the real man for a moment. He looked tired and run down. He was leaning against the ship corridor wall. He looked like the weight of the world was on his shoulders. His eyes were blank and empty, yet haunted by ghosts that would always chase him down, and always find him in his sleep.

In a second it was gone, and the boisterous Artisius was back. He smiled at Draz. Draz gave him a cold look. For all his talk, he was going to kill a number of people when the ship decoupled from the moorings. But Draz knew, he really was a good man. He did not have to take any families at all, but he had taken ten.

"Come on, Draz," Artisius said quietly. "We've got to get these people settled in. We'll put them in storage bay C. That's empty."

Draz helped Artisius and the security crews usher the families into the storage bay where they would spend most of the time. They pointed out the nearest bathrooms and the places where they could gain access to food and water.

It became very clear to Draz that even just ten families would put a large strain on the ship's supplies, and she was beginning to regret her attack on Artisius for only taking ten families.

After settling the people in Draz approached Artisius. "Now I realise the logistical problems. I'm...sorry..." she said

Artisius smiled. "That's okay. As the captain I have to wear these things. I know you meant well. Believe me I wanted to save more, but sometimes a few is the only thing possible. If we cannot do a lot of good in the world, we must at least try to do a little. But sometimes that little feels like doing worse than nothing." He smiled at her again.

Draz stayed silent for a while. "What about the people in the tube?" she said.

"If they don't go back to the tower, they'll die. If they do go back to the tower, they'll die. I'll have the security teams clear the docking tube," Artisius said. It was apparent he wanted to say the truth without sounding callous.

Draz nodded. It was a terrible truth.

"What will you do now?" Artisius asked her.

"What do you need me to do?" was Draz's reply.

"Nothing much at the moment. We'll make the final checks and take off soon. We have to make it fast as the planetary bombardment is strengthening. Any ideas on escaping?" Artisius said.

"I'm not the ship captain, that's your job to decide..." Draz stated.

"I see, well, I have an idea what to do." Artisius smiled. "We can break out with the refugee ships as they flee and use our cloaking device."

"How long before Europa is no more?" Draz asked, her brow furrowed with worry.

"Well, it's a large moon, and at the moment they've only put a few small cruisers onto the job of bombardment, so it may take a few more hours. If they bring the bigger ships into play though..." Artisius fell silent. He need not have said any more, Draz nodded her understanding.

"How long until we can leave?" Draz asked with worry in her voice.

"Less than half an hour, if that. The enemy ships haven't moved to our sector yet so we should be reasonably safe, for now. Anyway, I need to get back to the bridge. You're welcome to join me..." Artisius extended his hand.

"No, thanks, but I'm going to look in on Alfred. I'd probably just get in your way. It's your ship." Draz turned at headed towards the medical bays. She knew she should be helping with the escape, but she wanted to check on Alfred. After the refugees, she desperately wanted to see him smile. And she did not want to witness the docking tube.

Artisius nodded his understanding and headed to the bridge.

***

"Captain on the bridge!" came the well-worn cry from the First Officer as Artisius strode through the bridge doors.

Artisius paused before stepping onto the command dais. He waited for a moment. He knew what he had to do, and he knew that because of him, not only the frantic people in the docking tube would die.

He desperately wanted to be a good man, but everything that he did seemed to punish people and end in destruction.

"Sir?" said the First Officer, a note of trepidation in his voice. Artisius knew what it was about: he had never hesitated to take command before.

Swallowing hard, Artisius ran a hand through his greying hair. He was getting old. He was getting tired; tired of seeing people die.

"You have saved some, sir," said the First Officer. He was not oblivious to his captain's feelings.

"I know. I know." Artisius smiled at his second in command and friend. "I know, but it never feels like enough."

"That's how you know you're doing the right thing..." The First Officer smiled.

Artisius nodded and stepped into the light of the command dais. "Bring us up to full power. I want to be away from this rock as soon as possible. What is our estimated time to departure?"

The Energy Officer replied briskly. "Reactor will be a full power in ten minutes, sir!"

"And the cloaking device?" said Artisius.

The Energy and Shield Officers conferred for a moment and then the Shield Officer responded. "It's ready to be operational, sir. All that's required is the reactor at full power."

"Good." Artisius paused and looked up out of the observation dome at the few Collective Zone ships that were hovering above Europa and that were pummelling and blasting the once proud surface of the colony with bright beams of auto-turret lasers and plumes of missile fire.

From this vantage point, high above the surface on one of the towers reaching out into space, Artisius could see the numerous evacuation ships that were streaming from the spaceports dotted around the moon's surface. Some were making it to open space and trying to reach the retreating Solar Solutions fleet. Others were being vaporised by capital ship grade auto-turrets and falling back to the surface of the moon as burnt, charred husks.

Artisius' blood boiled. They were massacring innocent people, and he could do nothing about it. As he watched and willed each little ship to make it past the Collective Zone; and then he saw the ship shot down and crash into the surface of the moon, he fumed.

"How dare they!" he said and clenched his fists.

"That, sir, is why your saving ten families is a good thing," said the First Officer next to Artisius' shoulder. Artisius had not noticed him approach. He nodded silently.

Artisius wondered why the Collective Zone had not simply targeted him with its artillery. He wondered why the tower he was on was still standing. Perhaps they had not recognised his ship docked to the tower. It was possible. It had been powered down and the Europa Moon Colony was vast. They had to start their bombardment somewhere and had not started where he was docked. Nevertheless, it puzzled him.

"Reactor fully powered, sir!" shouted the Energy Officer.

"Prepare to undock and deploy cloaking. I want us gone." Artisius ordered.

"Sir, there are still families in the docking tube?" said the head of security, Sergeant Ithia.

"What? I thought I ordered you to clear them!" snapped Artisius, rushing to her holo-screen station.

"I tried, sir, but they refused. I couldn't exactly force them to leave," Sergeant Ithia said, she turned to meet Artisius as he rushed to her terminal.

"Show me!" Artisius said.

Sergeant Ithia pulled up a camera vision of the docking tube from the camera mounted above the airlock door to the ship. There were still families packed into the tube with children. They were banging on the door. The camera had no microphone so there was no sound, but the horrid spectacle shot through Artisius to his core.

"What do we do, sir?" asked Sergeant Ithia quietly.

"What we have to do," said Artisius. He hated being put in this situation. "Detach from the tower. I want us out of here!"

Suddenly a bright flash streaked across the observation dome. One of the Collective Zone capital ships had begun to bombard the tower where they were.

"They've detected our reactor signature. If we don't move now, we're dead!" Artisius bellowed to the bridge. "Retract the docking tube!" He was still standing at Sergeant Ithia's terminal.

"I'll turn this off then," Ithia said. She went to turn off the camera.

"No!" said Artisius. "I want to watch my failure. I owe them that. They need to be remembered. I failed them. I killed them. I will watch their last moments."

"As you wish." Ithia grimaced.

Artisius watched through the camera as the atmospheric seal around the docking tube broke, and the breathable atmosphere fled, and the Europa atmosphere invaded. The people panicked. They ran to the ship's airlock. They pounded on the door. Their faces contorted in agonised screams. As their breath ran out, they fell to the floor of the tube, gasping, screaming, clutching at their throats and faces and eyes as the pressure equalised with the outside. They began to bleed from their open orifices. It all took a matter of seconds. Artisius watched it all, unblinking. The tube retracted into the hull of the *Green Dragon* and the bodies, now still, that lay in it, fell away out of sight of the camera; past the supports for the landing pad, down, down onto the surface of Europa many hundreds of metres below.

"Turn it off," Artisius said. His face was ashen.

"Sir!" snapped Sergeant Ithia. She turned off the camera outside the airlock.

"I will carry them with me until my dying day," Artisius whispered to himself. "I will remember them." He was thankful Draz did not have to see what had just happened.

Artisius moved stiffly back to the command dais. "Take us out of here. I want to get to the Solar Solutions fleet as soon as possible. I have some words for their...CEO," Artisius spat the last words as if they were disgusting.

"Sir!" shouted the First Officer and the *Green Dragon* began to climb away from the wreckage of Europa.

"Engage cloaking device!" ordered Artisius.

"Sir!" shouted the Shield Officer. After a few switches were flicked, the bridge descended into the dull red glow of the cloaking low power mode. "Full cloak activated, sir!" finished the Shield Officer.

The *Green Dragon* slipped past the blockading ships with ease and headed out into more open space. They avoided the path taken by many of the evacuation ships from Europa that had gotten past the Collective Zone ships. They did not want to collide inadvertently with any escaping ships.

After about half an hour of space travel, a blip appeared on the scanner of the Scanning Officer.

"Sir, I have something, something small, but with an energy source..." the Scanning Officer reported.

"What is it?" asked Artisius, he moved to the scanning terminal and looked over the shoulder of the Scanning Officer.

"I'm...not sure. A pod maybe? Should we pick it up?" said the Officer.

"Yes, do. It might be a refugee shuttle that's become stranded. It's a bit off course though..." Artisius pondered the situation before straightening up and barking an order. "We're picking up a shuttle, jump to it!"

After another half an hour the shuttle was brought on board into the small, but big enough, docking bay for shuttles on the *Green Dragon*.

"Sir, it'll be hours before we reach the Solar Solutions fleet," said the First Officer. "We've picked up the pod. You can look at it if you like? It's been scanned for radiation and it's safe."

"Good, yes, I will. Sergeant Ithia, send a security team down to the shuttle bay and I will meet it there," said Artisius as he left the bridge.

"Do you want me to lead the team?" asked Ithia.

"No, you stay here, send someone else, it's guard duty after all," replied Artisius as he headed down to the shuttle bay.

Chapter 19

The Europa Colony was broken. It was burning. Its glass passageways and vaulted halls were smashed and exposed to the harsh Europan atmosphere. Its Churches were devastated and rendered into molten slag. Many parts of the ice sheet that covered the moon were melted and the city built on top of them was cast down into the oceans below. The oceans were no longer quiet and sedate, they boiled and thrashed as the lasers and missiles stirred them up and burned the ice covering.

Colony Commander Anya had been walking. She had walked through the throngs of panicked people as they rushed for the last transports. She had listened to their shrieks of desperation as their world came apart around them. They had ignored her. She had nothing to say to them. She just watched their mad scramble for their lives with a certain shame. She had walked.

She had walked through destroyed Churches. She had seen their boards of prayer no longer showing the green or red of the Bull and Bear Gods. They were smashed and cast down into the jagged craters. The priests and Traders were gone. There were some people left in the Churches. They huddled and crawled around seeking shelter as the world was torn apart around them. She had walked.

She had walked back, through the still habitable areas of the colony near the command centre. There was still breathable atmosphere in the passageways and corridors. She had walked.

Anya was now back in the command centre. It was abandoned. It was smashed. It had taken a direct hit by a missile a little earlier. The emergency shielding on the dome was just about holding as the main observation dome had cracked and had let some of the atmosphere inside leak out before the emergency safeguard took hold. Even so, the atmosphere was slowly leaking through the damage, and this caused a slight gust of air, which fuelled the fires that had sprung up around the computer terminals and electrical wires that filled the command centre.

The main paths up, around and across the chamber were damaged beyond a useable level. Anya picked her way along the main path through the centre of the command centre. She ducked and dodged the mangled and twisted walkways that had collapsed down onto it.

Anya looked around. The room was smoky from the fires. It stung her eyes. They watered a little, not just from the smoke. There was no one left to see, yet Anya wiped her eyes dry from pride.

At some of the terminals, there were the corpses of the now dead operators of those computers. Many had been able to escape the command centre, but some had not, before the missile struck. Their mangled and charred bodies with contorted and disfigured faces cried out to Anya in her mind.

She had not saved them. She had not saved anyone. She had hoped that Gunter and the Solar Solutions fleet would save them all. They had not. What else was there to say on the matter? Anya had accepted her fate. She had remained behind, like so many of her people. She would die with them. That would be her punishment for her arrogance. She would go down with the ship. She would not shrink from that task, at least. She knew, she should have listened.

Anya looked down. She had trodden on the charred remains of a body. She did not know who it was, it was impossible to tell now. She lifted her foot, and shivered. She was scared.

Anya's black and green uniform was smeared with blood; hers and other people's, she knew not where one ended and the other began. She had been cut by falling debris during her mournful walk, but she did not feel the pain. The ache in her heart was far stronger. Her own arrogance had meant the downfall of the whole colony. If she had only signalled the evacuation earlier. If only she had listened to Artisius. But now he was gone, and so was all hope.

Anya picked her way to the centre of the main walkway in the middle of the failing observation dome. Sparks were falling from cut overhead power cables. She ducked out of the way of one as a particularly violent electrical spark arched to one of the walkways.

Standing in the centre of the central walkway, Anya looked up. Above her were the floors and tiers of the command centre that were now smashed and battered. Higher than that was the cracked dome, venting its atmosphere into the void, just kept intact by the emergency energy shield. Above that was the looming form of a Collective Zone cruiser that had taken up the effort of bombarding this part of the Moon.

Large bursts of energy and missiles rained down on this sector of the moon. Anya looked out of the dome across the expanse of the colony; her colony. Large portions had disappeared, and many more parts were burning.

One day, one day sometime in the future, Anya hoped that the story of this crime would be told, and the Collective Zone would pay for it. However, with the defeat and retreat of the Solar Solutions forces, and the inevitable victory of the Collective Zone, Anya knew that such a thing would probably never happen. History was written by the victor, after all.

The Europa Colony had some defences. But nowhere near enough to stand up to the Collective Zone fleet. The colony had put up a bit of a fight, but the Collective Zone's guns had silenced the defences in short order.

Anya ran a hand through her brown hair. It too was smeared with blood and her fingers caught in the mats and knots. It would not matter soon. She had placed all her faith in someone, and he had let her down; he had let the entire Solar Solutions Corporation down.

Anya looked up. She saw the missile pods and auto turrets aiming down at her command centre from the cruiser. She knew this was it. She was ready. All she regretted was trusting someone who had let her down, and in turn, she had let her colony down.

"Come on!" she shouted up to the orbiting ship. "Come on!" she repeated.

The missile pod flashed, and a volley of missiles streaked down from the ship. Anya raised her arms perpendicular to her sides. She was still looking up. The missiles got closer. She closed her eyes. She heard the shattering of what was left of the glass dome and the dissipation of the emergency energy shield. She felt her breath stolen from her as the atmosphere fled in an instant. And then there was a terrific roar as the missiles struck home.

"Damn you all," she said as she died.

***

And so, humans, the only being in the solar system to tame fire, brought fire to the surface of Europa and expunged the colony from existence.

Chapter 20

Artisius exited the lift into the shuttle bay. The shuttle bay was small, almost claustrophobic. It only held a few shuttles and was not that frequently used as the *Green Dragon* was small enough usually to dock with the other ship, planet or space station. The need for the shuttles was limited, but they were there just in case the *Green Dragon* was required to remain in orbit and a small group was needed to investigate something or the crew of the *Green Dragon* had to meet with another ship that had no docking capability.

The walls, like most of the *Green Dragon*, were white. The floor was a dark grey, and fluorescent strip lights lit up the whole chamber with an eerie, unnatural light.

In the far wall there were three launch tubes for the *Green Dragon's* shuttles. They were empty as the *Green Dragon's* shuttles were in storage as they were not needed at the moment. The shuttles were stored in recesses in the floor covered over with large movable doors that slid aside to reveal the shuttles, which rose up and slid into the launch tubes.

In the middle of the chamber there was the shuttle that they had picked up. It was sitting on top of one of the storage doors. It was squat and lozenge shaped. It had one view port that stretched across the tapered front and at the back it had a couple of small engines. In the side, there was the outline of a door. The shuttle sat on four small landing skids.

The shuttle sat in place. It seemed rather beaten up with paint scratches and it was a rather old model. It bore the markings of the Europa Colony on its sides, and it seemed rather sad in its squat way of sitting there.

Artisius had an apprehensive feeling as he approached. The security team of six guards was standing around it, weapons drawn.

"Sir!" They all saluted as Artisius approached.

"We have secured the vessel and scanned it. It seems safe. We read one life form aboard," said the male sergeant.

"Only one?" said Artisius. "I thought this was meant to be a refugee boat?"

"I, I don't know, sir. Maybe there are some dead on board? All I know is that there's one life form aboard and that's all," replied the sergeant.

"Well done." Artisius tapped the man on the shoulder. "Open it up!"

"Sir!" snapped the sergeant and indicated to his soldiers that they were to trigger the mechanism to open the shuttle's door.

Two of the soldiers stood either side of the door in the side of the shuttle while a third pressed the door release catch and with a hiss, and a venting of pressurised atmosphere, the door swung open, and a small ladder descended. The inside of the shuttle was not lit and there were no sounds of refugees aboard.

Artisius was about to climb the ladder into the dark interior, when the sergeant held out an arm and indicated that he should go first. "Me first, sir." Artisius nodded and let the sergeant climb up the ladder and entered the shuttle.

After a short time, the sergeant called out. "All clear, sir. You can come up now."

Artisius mounted the small ladder and climbed into the dark interior. His eyes took a second to adjust and what he saw surprised him. When his eyes had become accustomed to the dark, he saw the small interior of the pod had no refugees in it, alive or dead. The majority of the interior was taken up by a cryo-pod.

Looking in through the porthole of the cryo-pod, Artisius saw that it had a man in it. An older man. An older man in Head Trader clothes. The man's face seemed strained and pained as if he was in some sort of discomfort and that something was haunting him.

"It can't be..." said Artisius.

"Do you know him, sir?" asked the sergeant.

"No, no I don't know him, but I think this is Head Trader Virtus. We were searching for him. He's the one who blew up *Florida Station*." Artisius paused.

"Sounds dangerous. What do you want to do with him, sir?" said the sergeant.

Artisius replied, "I think we have someone on board who can make that decision. I want to see what he wants to do with this...man," the distain was obvious in his voice.

Artisius checked the vital signs on the pod. His finger hovered over the emergency shutdown button. It would be so easy. It would be so simple. He could say that the man was found dead and that his cryo-pod had malfunctioned. He scrunched up his hand into a fist.

"Sir? What are you doing?" said the sergeant, seeing what his captain was doing.

"Oh, pay me no mind. This man is dangerous, and I just thought, that it would be so easy..." Artisius trailed off.

"You said he destroyed *Florida Station*?" said the sergeant.

"Yes," responded Artisius, wondering where the sergeant was going.

"Well, sir, I see it like this: if you kill him now, and don't let the man give an account of himself, then you're no better than he was killing all those on *Florida Station*." The sergeant paused and let Artisius ponder the moment.

"Yes...but...he's only one life, and it would be his life against thousands...he deserves it." Artisius was clearly conflicted.

"Ah but," said the sergeant sagely, "how can we be good if we let ourselves slip? Who are you to judge if he deserves it? He may be only one life, but he needs to be heard. Don't kill him now. We have him here as a prisoner, let him speak his mind. We can always kill him later, if he deserves it. Who was it that would be interested in this acquisition?" the sergeant changed topic.

"Alfred, he was from *Florida Station*; and you are wise..." Artisius looked into the pained face of the man in the cryo-pod.

"Ah, Alfred, one of our...guests," said the sergeant with a grimace.

"You disapprove of him?" asked Artisius looking at the sergeant. He raised his eyebrows.

"I don't like zetters, sir, never have," said the sergeant. "Unnatural."

Artisius said nothing, and looked back at the cryo-pod. He was conflicted. He wanted simply to end this man's life, if you could call him a man, concocting a sect and being a fanatic that killed many thousands if not tens of thousands of people. However, there was a reason that he was here in this pod. He had fled Europa and left himself adrift in this pod. Artisius was curious as to why. Why had this man done this?

Artisius put his hand on the porthole in the cryo-pod, fingers outstretched. "Why are you here?" he whispered. "Okay, sergeant, you win." Artisius turned to the sergeant. "We'll keep him alive, for now, to interrogate him when Alfred is ready. I want to see what he does with this...man.

Set up a guard on the shuttle. No one is allowed near it without my express permission. Except for Alfred. He has a clearance to access this without my permission." Artisius waved his hands around indicating the shuttle.

"Sir!" snapped the sergeant as he came to attention. It was evident he was more comfortable taking orders than offering moral advice.

The pair exited the shuttle and as the sergeant barked orders to the security detail in the method of guarding the shuttle, Artisius headed back towards the bridge. He had to choose the right moment to tell Alfred.

Chapter 21

Alfred stirred. He felt as if he were floating. He felt the hard slab that he was lying on. He felt light headed. He did not know how long he had slept for. All that he knew is that he did not feel tired anymore. It had been a long time since he had had a restful sleep.

Alfred tried to open his eyes. They resisted. He thought that he could sleep here forever. Even though the slab he was lying on was uncomfortable.

He tried again to open his eyes. They obeyed this time. He could see! The bright light on the roof of the room temporarily blinded him. He blinked. He wondered where he was. He was not sure.

In a flash, it came back to him as his eyes adjusted to the light and he saw a bit more of the room. He was in the medical bay of the *Green Dragon*. He did not care. He felt rested.

Alfred heard breathing nearby. It was rhythmic. It was the breathing of someone who was asleep. Alfred turned his head and looked in the direction of the sound. He grimaced, as his neck was stiff from lying on the hard slab for a while. He did not know how long he had been asleep. He did not care about that either.

As he turned his head slowly, Alfred saw Draz with her head against the slab he was lying on. She had her arms folded and her head on her arms. She was sitting on a chair. Her brown hair was draped over her face. She was asleep. It looked, to Alfred, an awkward position to fall asleep in, but it was plain that she, too, had been exhausted from the activities on Europa. He did not want to wake her.

Alfred watched her sleeping. She breathed rhythmically and her hair moved as she inhaled and exhaled. She was still wearing the uniform that Artisius had given her, though it was a bit more worn now. Alfred looked down at his own uniform that he had been given; it had seen better days.

Turning his head back to watch Draz again, Alfred thought it looked uncomfortable for Draz to breathe through her hair, so he reached out with a stiff jointed arm and gently moved the hair from her face. He tried not to disturb her.

With Draz's face exposed, Alfred noticed how serene she looked. She was deeply asleep.

Alfred moved his body in an effort to sit up. He accidentally bumped Draz's arms folded on the slab. Draz stirred. Alfred cursed himself silently. Draz opened her eyes and began to move. She blinked a few times.

"Sorry," Alfred said. "I tried to move and knocked you..."

"No, no, that's all right," Draz said. "I shouldn't have been asleep anyway. I came to check on you and, well...I was exhausted."

"Hah I know that feeling." Alfred laughed. "How long have I been asleep?"

"You just woke up?" Draz asked.

Alfred nodded. "It was a good sleep."

Draz checked her communicator for the time. "About four hours. Which means I've been asleep about two hours, but it feels more..." Draz stretched. "How did you sleep? I mean, you said before that your dreams were full of nightmares. Did they return?"

Alfred paused for a minute to think. "I can see now, that's something. You know, I can't...I can't remember how I slept. I don't know if I had nightmares or not."

"Well, that's something," said Draz.

"But it means my memory is getting worse!" said Alfred, looking despondent.

"You don't know that; most people cannot remember if they dreamed or not. Maybe you didn't have nightmares, maybe you did; it doesn't mean your memory failed." Draz stood up.

"You were looking in on me for two hours?" said Alfred quietly. The meaning of the time telling hit home.

"Well." Draz looked at the floor. "Really I was sleeping for two hours, but the intention was there," she said, smiling.

Alfred smiled. "Thanks, I mean it. I need all the support I can get at this time." He tapped the side of his head.

"I know..." said Draz. "How do you feel?"

"Rested, but my head feels...unsettled. The implant feels decayed and damaged. Now that I'm starting to feel it outside of the zet I know that my time is limited," Alfred said.

"Don't say that! Surely there's something that can be done?" Draz asked.

"Well, I can have the implant removed; on Pluto. The doctor said. But I don't know if that would help stop the damage now..." Alfred trailed off.

"Pluto...I see..." said Draz, by her tone of voice it was clear she was thinking. She ran a hand through her hair. "Well, that's something. We're headed in the right direction anyway, outwards from the Sun. Hold onto that hope, Alfred. Hold onto it!" She looked him in the eyes and took him by the hand.

Alfred looked into Draz's eyes, and saw concern combined with caring. "Thanks," is all he said. He felt awkward. He was unused to such situations. It was clear, even to him, that Draz liked him. However, he was unsure

165

whether he could reciprocate that like in the situation he was in. He could not control his own mind, how was he supposed to deal with someone else's too? So, all he said was "thanks" and left it at that.

Draz withdrew her hand and seemed rather embarrassed. She looked at the ground. Alfred felt bad, but the moment passed, and he could not bring it back.

"How's your mind treating you?" Alfred asked, to change the subject. "You holding up okay?"

Draz rallied and looked back at him, a resolute expression in her face. "I'm okay. It's hard, but I'm okay. The cravings are still there. But the temptations have been removed, so that's easier. But I just have to live with it. There's no simple surgery to have and then the problem goes away...Sorry" Draz realised what she said was harsh and that Alfred did not deserve what she said just then. It was portrayed on her face when she saw his face change.

"No, that's all right. I guess we all have our demons to deal with." Alfred smiled. He knew he had to say something about the moment before. "Look, I can appreciate the way you feel towards me. It's rather obvious, but at the moment, I cannot control my own head. It gets difficult having to deal with someone else when I cannot even deal with me. I appreciate your affection, I really do, but I can't do anything like that right now. Please, ask me later, when I've sorted my issues..." he trailed off seeing Draz's reaction.

Draz was looking down at the ground. She looked downcast. "I see..." is all she said for a while. "I...appreciate your candour and I respect that. But that doesn't make it easy for me..."

"I know, but understand my position. Wait for me," Alfred said softly.

"I will wait. I will hold you to that!" Draz smiled.

Alfred laughed.

"But don't delay too long," Draz said. "I've been exposed to a lot of radiation back on Earth in my scavenging days...I don't know how long this body will hold out..."

"How's Artisius doing?" asked Alfred, changing the subject rather obviously. He did not want to talk of any more of his or Draz's problems.

"Well last I saw him he was screening the refugees on the way into the ship and then he went to the bridge to make good our escape," Draz said, she seemed welcome to the change of topic.

"I see, and how did that go?" Alfred asked. He swung his legs over the edge of the slab.

Draz shook her head as an indication of not well. "There were issues about how many to take, and such..." Draz trailed off.

"Nasty. Damn those Collective Zone! Sorry..." Alfred retracted when he part remembered that Draz was originally Collective Zone.

"Relax, I don't approve of what my former Collective is doing." Draz waved her hand. "Curse them all you like. I consider myself neither Collective Zone nor Solar Solutions. If that's possible. It's rather weird. I sort of get why Artisius chose the life he chose now."

"Although he would seem to consider himself in the Solar Solutions camp now. He burned his bridges with the Collective Zone," said Alfred, standing up. His legs felt weak, and he steadied himself on the edge of the slab.

At that moment, the doctor returned through the sliding doors of the medical bay.

"Ah, Alfred, you're awake. Can you see?" asked Dr Antonia.

"Yes, yes I can. It's a relief I can tell you!" Alfred said.

167

"So, the medication...I've confirmed your condition..." Dr Antonia began.

Draz nodded to Alfred and the doctor and began to head out the door.

"Don't go..." said Alfred.

"You sure?" said Draz. "Don't you want privacy?"

"Moral support more..." said Alfred with a tremor in his voice.

Draz nodded and stayed at a respectful distance.

Dr Antonia produced a vial of medication, some clean syringes, and a tourniquet. Alfred baulked. "Needles?" he gasped.

"Really?" Dr Antonia said pointing to his implant. "You're afraid of needles and you stick one in your head all the time?"

Alfred blushed. He realised the silliness of his reservations. "Okay, okay, point made. But I mean, the last things I had back on *Florida Station* were pills, and I've never really liked drugs..."

"Things are worse for you now. You need to have more drastic treatment. One injection, into the arm vein, every day. It's your choice when, but you need to do it every day. I can supply you with clean needles," the doctor concluded the demonstration. "Now you."

Alfred took up the vial and loaded it with serum. He put on the tourniquet. He found the vein with the needle and delivered the injection. He winced at the feeling of the chemical rushing through his system. It felt different. The fizzing in his head and implant seemed to recede a little.

"Masterfully done!" said Dr Antonia, clapping her hands together. "How does it feel?"

"Odd," said Alfred, cocking his head on the side. "Somehow...better...but odd..."

"Remember: every day. Now if you'll excuse me, I have more work I have to do on the refugees. Some need medical treatment due to wounds sustained in the bombardment," with that, Dr Antonia left Draz and Alfred alone again.

Draz looked at Alfred and asked, "Does it really feel better?"

"Yeah, a bit. I still need to go to Pluto, but if this arrests the decay a little, I might survive until then!" Alfred said happily. "I don't like the needles though!"

Draz laughed. "I prefer mine up the nose!" She laughed again at the dark joke.

Alfred laughed too.

"Come on, let's find Artisius," she said, and they left the medical bay. "Artisius where are you?" Draz spoke into her communicator.

"On the bridge, where are you?" came Artisius' voice over the communicator.

"Just exiting the medical bay," replied Draz.

"Is Alfred with you?" crackled Artisius' voice.

"Yeah I'm here," said Alfred.

"Ah, well meet me in the shuttle bay, both of you. I have something that might interest Alfred there. And Draz, I want you there too," the voice cut off.

"I wonder what he means?" pondered Alfred as they headed towards the shuttle bay.

***

The pair emerged from the lift down into the shuttle bay to see the shuttle that Artisius had brought on board being guarded by a number of soldiers.

"I guess we wait here for Artisius," said Alfred.

The lift hissed behind them and Artisius stepped out onto the landing pad.

"Ah, good," he said. "Alfred, now, I want you to come and see this. And Draz I want you to be here too." He turned to Alfred. "Alfred, I want you to remain calm, whatever goes on in there."

"Uh, okay?" is all Alfred could manage through the confusion. "What, exactly, will rile me up?"

"I'll leave that for you to see..." Artisius beckoned for them both to follow him and board the shuttle. The soldiers saluted as Artisius went past.

The trio made their way inside the shuttle and Alfred's eyes took a little time to adjust to the gloom. But when they did he saw a large cryo-pod.

"And?" Alfred said, looking at Artisius.

Artisius indicated that Alfred should look through the vision porthole on the pod.

Alfred walked over and looked through the porthole. He stopped. His blood ran cold at the sight he saw, frozen, beyond the glass.

"It's him...IT'S HIM!" Alfred babbled. He turned in a flash towards Artisius. "How?"

"We picked him up thinking his shuttle was a refugee craft gone off course," Artisius said.

"Who is it?" asked Draz.

"Virtus..." said Alfred.

"Virtus!?" exclaimed Draz. "Holy shit!" She rushed over to have a look. "He's...older than I imagined."

"What do we do with him?" panted Alfred in a rage. His fists were clenched. His fury boiled inside him.

"That, I think, is up to you..." Artisius said quietly.

"Let's turn him off and vent him into space!" whispered Alfred.

"Don't you want to question him?" said Draz.

"Do I need to? He destroyed my life!" Alfred raised his voice a little. He was still transfixed by the face beyond the glass in the pod.

"He can't escape here, Alfred. We should talk to him," said Artisius agreeing with Draz.

"All right, but I'm not waiting around. Do a fast thaw, and if he dies in the process, good!" Alfred stepped back as Artisius pressed a few buttons on the side of the pod and an emergency fast thaw was engaged.

About twenty minutes later the pod hissed and began to open. The life signs for the occupant were faint but he was alive. Alfred cursed that he had not died in the process.

Virtus, frail and ragged, stumbled out of the pod. "I...I'm alive? Who..." He turned to see the three of them facing him in the pod. "Where am I?"

"On the *Green Dragon*, still near Jupiter. We picked you up. Now, I believe you owe some explanations to this man," said Artisius. He pointed to Alfred.

"Who...?" Virtus stammered. It was evident he was semi delusional.

"I'm Alfred, or perhaps you know me as Theta 7B. From *Florida Station*..." Alfred was clearly livid.

"Oh...oh Alfred! Yes...uh...*Florida Station*..." A haunted look crossed Virtus' gaunt features.

"Yes, the station you blew up. And framed me. Why? Why did you do that?" Alfred was trying to control himself.

"The Computer...The Sect!" Virtus collapsed onto his knees in front of Alfred. He reached up with ragged arms, his priest robes crumpling on the floor around him.

"Damn your fucking Sect and Computer god. It's all a sham. It's just your implant malfunctioning. Don't you dare talk to me about your little cult!" Alfred spat the words. He had seen the telltale signs of the zetting implant in the side of Virtus' head.

"But...but...my implant?" stammered Virtus, still on the floor. He clawed at his zetting implant in the side of his head. "It's the Computer...Uxus said he didn't believe it, but it was the Computer!"

"Uxus?" asked Alfred. "What about him?"

"Uxus...he said he wanted me to clear the way for him. He didn't believe in the Computer either. But I do...I still do!" Virtus began babbling incoherently and crumpled even more on the floor of the shuttle. He looked into his hands and began to sob. "I am a broken man, Alfred," he said rather coherently. "Do as you wish..."

Alfred spun around and grabbed one of Artisius' pistols from its holster and aimed the muzzle at Virtus' head. "I have a good idea what to do," he said with white-hot rage.

"Alfred!" gasped Draz.

"What? You're going to tell me I can't? Like with you and Crathka?" Alfred glared at Draz. "Yes, I remember that. There's something about brain splatter that makes you remember."

Artisius stayed silent. He simply reached out and held his hand open to receive the pistol.

Alfred glared at him too. "And you're not such a good man as to talk me down either!" It was clear this wounded Artisius with his facial expression change, but Artisius still said nothing.

Alfred turned back to Virtus who was mewling and whimpering on the floor.

"Look at him; he's a broken man, Alfred. Killing him would be a mercy," said Draz. "Put the gun down. Be better than him. Be better than me..."

Alfred was torn. All he wanted to do was kill the man in front of him for ruining his life. But he knew that it would bring him no peace. He knew that it would bring him no clarity. He knew it would bring him no resolution; just like killing Grekthax had brought no peace, just more fitful dreams.

His hand trembled. He tried to force it to stay still which made the tremor worse. He placed the muzzle of the gun on Virtus' head.

"Do it!"

"Yes! Yes! Kill me..." said Virtus.

Suddenly it became apparent to Alfred that his friends were right. The man in front of him was broken. He was in his own Hell. Killing him would have been a mercy. Alfred lowered the gun.

"No...NO! Kill me!" cried Virtus.

"Kill him, Alfred!"

"I know what to do with you," Alfred said handing the gun back to Artisius. "We're heading to Solar Solutions space aren't we?" He turned to Artisius.

"Yes, we'll dock with the *Silver Ark*, their flagship," Artisius said.

"Then we'll hand this...man...over to them," Alfred spat the words. "They can determine his fate, as a traitor!"

Draz smiled.

Artisius smile too. "Good," he said.

They escorted Alfred out of the shuttle. "Where are you going to keep him," Draz asked.

"Put him in the cell I was in. In the cargo bay. Where I saw my life change forever when the Station blew up," said Alfred looking at Artisius.

"The cell is still there...and I think that would be appropriate, Alfred, yes..." Artisius trailed off in thought before speaking to one of the guards and ordering that Virtus be imprisoned in the cargo bay cell.

The trio left the shuttle bay and headed back to the bridge.

Alfred looked distracted as he walked slightly behind Draz and Artisius on the way back to the bridge. After a few minutes, he stopped entirely.

Draz noticed that Alfred was no longer with them and turned. "What's wrong?" she asked.

"I...I have to talk to him," Alfred stammered, looking at the ground.

Draz and Artisius looked at each other in an anxious fashion.

"Are you sure that's wise?" asked Artisius.

"What about the refugees?" said Draz.

"There are no refugees in that cargo bay," said Artisius. "That cargo bay is purely for storage."

Alfred paid the two of them no heed and turned and headed back to the cargo bay that he had been imprisoned in all those years ago.

***

Alfred paused on entrance to the cargo bay. He looked around at his surroundings and, despite his memory problems; he seemed to remember the place. He walked slowly between the remaining slave cryo-pods and robots that tended to them.

Alfred approached where he remembered the cell to be and heard the talk of the guards. He did not bother to listen to them to make sense of what they were talking about; he was absorbed with his own thoughts.

He was wondering why he had come here; why he wanted to speak to Virtus; why it mattered to him at all what happened to the broken man. Alfred did not know, but all he knew was that he had to face him and talk to him. All he had to do was talk. Alfred felt that stronger than any emotion he had felt in a long time.

Upon rounding a corner in the cargo crates, Alfred stepped out into a small opening in front of the cell bars. The guards had not heard him approach and spun to meet him, weapons raised.

"It's all right, it's just me..." Alfred nodded.

The guards lowered their weapons. They then gave a silent look to each other that Alfred could only interpret as: they were worried about what he would do.

"Leave me with him," Alfred said, more forcefully than he intended. It had the desired effect though: with another silent glance, the two guards left the prison cell and walked a distance away into the cargo bay. They were not quite out of earshot, but they were far enough away for Alfred.

Alfred approached the bars. He wrapped his hands around the bars. They were cold. He looked in through the bars to see the crumpled form of Virtus sitting and leaning up against the far wall with his legs stretched out into the space in front of him. He seemed to have shrunk as a man. His white priest robes engulfed him in their voluminous expanse. It was evident the man was broken.

"What...do you want?" Virtus rasped. The voice seemed to come from somewhere within the robes.

Alfred sat down outside the bars. He slid his hands down the bars as he did so. He came to rest, slowly and gently and sat cross-legged in freedom, while his tormentor sat in captivity.

"I have come to ask, why?" Alfred said quietly. "And what it feels like, to be in there?"

"You have come to gloat?" asked Virtus. He looked out at Alfred with a hollow expression.

"No, not gloat; just wonder." Alfred paused.

Virtus looked confused.

"I wonder," Alfred continued, "I wonder what it feels like, to you, to be stuck; to be trapped; to be in there." Alfred pointed at the bars. "What does it feel like to you?"

"Like death..." Virtus said.

"Indeed. And how do you think I felt, all those years ago, when you framed me; and I was there, in here? How do you think that felt?" Alfred paused, he felt rage building up inside him, but he tried to repress it. Getting angry and shouting would ruin his point.

"Like crushing claustrophobia?" said Virtus.

"Right!" snapped Alfred. "And then, when I thought it could get no worse, you blew up my home. You destroyed everything I knew." Alfred was losing control of his anger and beginning to sound enraged. He tried to calm himself. He breathed and paused for a short time.

Virtus stayed silent.

Alfred continued, "You...you destroyed my home...And then I was imprisoned, and my life turned upside down because of your damn beliefs. How does it feel to be in a cage, like vermin? I felt that, because of you. I was hunted and imprisoned and my life was ruined, because of you!"

"I'm a ruined man, Alfred..." Virtus said. "I have lost everything I knew, and loved. I have destroyed all the peace I had in the world. I will be sentenced to death, most probably, I am damned." He paused for a time. "Our situations are not so different, I think. I understand, now, what you went through. And I am sorry."

Alfred was a little shocked. He had not expected an apology. It caught him off guard. "Just tell me why?"

"I already told you in the shuttle. It was the belief in the Sect. I believed that the Computer was talking to me and that it wanted me to release it from its prison. I believed that I could by blowing up the station. I believed that CEO

Uxus wanted me to spread the religion and open up a new era of worship of Computers." Virtus paused.

Alfred did not interrupt. He simply sat and let the man talk.

Virtus continued. "But it was all fake. Uxus just wanted the colonies destroyed so he would have less military opposition. He played me, Alfred. He played me." Virtus looked pleadingly out of the cell at Alfred.

Alfred felt a twinge of remorse.

"Did you hear the voice of the Computer?" Alfred asked calmly.

"Yes! Yes! At least I thought it was..." gasped Virtus.

"So, did I. And it may have been the computer. My old doctor on *Florida Station* believed it was the computer talking to its servants. But I've come to believe that it might just be a malfunction in the implant. That it is the implant decaying that causes the brain to hear voices and fail." Alfred stopped at the look on the priest's face.

"Really? Well...I find that hard to believe. It was so real!" Virtus said.

"As I said, it still could be computers talking to us. But it's more likely all in our heads. Here's a question," Alfred paused to think, "have you ever heard of someone hearing the Computer's voice early on in their zetting life? Or was it always later in their lives when they had been zetting for years?"

"Always later..." Virtus said.

"Indeed. That would fit in with the theory of the implant failing. People only hear the "Computer" when they're experienced, and the implant is already decaying..." Alfred paused.

"So, my whole existence was a lie?" said Virtus.

"I'll leave that for you to decide..." Alfred said.

Alfred sat where he was for some time. He simply watched the man in the cell. He remembered his own time in there and the terror he had felt when he saw his home destroyed. However, he felt strangely calm, as if the sight of someone else, in a similar situation to him, made him feel at peace; somehow at ease. It left him feeling whole and complete.

It was plain to see that Virtus was now a broken man. His beliefs and position had been soundly shaken and destroyed. He had lost everything he cared about; and he was on his way to some form of trial and imprisonment and even execution if that was decided.

"So, you're just going to sit there and watch me?" said Virtus.

"I will do what I like, because I can. I will watch you. I will see you tried. I will see you sentenced," Alfred said.

"So, you are gloating," snapped Virtus. "I'm not some animal to be forced to dance upon instruction!"

"That's an insult to animals..." Alfred snapped in return.

"Pah!" exclaimed Virtus, with a wave of his hand.

Alfred felt his anger rising again, and then realised that Virtus was playing him again, as he always had. "I will not lose my temper for you..." he snapped and tried to calm down.

Alfred sat and watched. The guards came to check a number of times if everything was okay, but Alfred sent them away again every time. All he wanted to do was watch. He felt at peace.

After a while, Alfred got up and left. He had other things to do.

The guards returned to their positions as Alfred walked past them silently and went for a walk around the ship.

"Your response to that situation was...interesting."

The voice came again as he walked. Alfred shook his head to clear it.

Chapter 22

OE15 banked his fighter around over the retreating Solar Solutions fleet. He was low on fuel, but he did not want to let any of the pursuing enemy fighters exploit any advantage. There were only three fighters left in their squadron that were still functional. AA3 was in the lead; OE15 was off his left wing and another pilot, who OE15 did not know, off his right.

"How's everyone's fuel?" crackled the question over the radio from AA3.

"Low, sir," responded OE15 and the other pilot.

"Same," replied AA3. "We'd better land. There's not much we can do here. Just make one more pass over the *Silver Ark* and we'll call it an end."

OE15 felt like saluting, but that would have been silly in the cockpit. The commander could not see him; but OE15 had felt like he had formed a lot of respect for the commander of the fighter wing.

As they screamed low over the *Silver Ark*, OE15 could see the expanse of the Solar Solutions fleet in full retreat. They had lost almost a dozen ships and a number of those still with them were severely damaged. OE15 did not have time or the ability to do a full count, he was concentrating on flying, but he knew that the losses had been harsh.

Off in the distance OE15 could see the Collective Zone fleet. It seemed undecided in what to do. Part of the fleet seemed to want to pursue the Solar Solutions ships, and yet another part was holding its position around Jupiter and Europa in particular.

OE15 could see the bright flashes and sparks as auto-turret and missile fire pounded the surface of Europa. It was at an extreme distance, yet he could see the tell-tale explosions. Europa was burning.

OE15 gritted his teeth and turned his head to scan the space around him. The enemy fighters had mostly retreated due to their own fuel requirements and the larger distances that were now developing between the two fleets.

He looked at his instruments. "AA3," he said, "I have to land; I'm almost out of fuel..."

"Copy that, OE15. We'll all land. We've done our job. You've been a good pilot! If you ever want to switch from bomber detail to fighters, give me a shout!" crackled the response from AA3.

If the weight of the loss were not sitting so heavily on OE15's shoulders, he would have felt proud of what was just said. He had performed well. It felt good to be able to dogfight. He might take AA3 up on his word sometime in the future; if there was a future for the Solar Solutions Corporation.

The flight flew underneath the *Silver Ark* and slowly into the cavernous interior of the landing bay. OE15 struggled with his sluggish controls. When they entered and had landed, the vacuum protected tech-slaves clomped out to the three remaining fighters.

The landing bay was still depressurised. At least there was gravity again, OE15 thought, just like when the bombers returned.

OE15 extricated himself from the cockpit and climbed down the ladder that a tech-slave had placed on the side of the craft.

When he reached the floor of the landing bay, OE15 looked around and saw AA3 and the other pilot making their way to the airlock on the side of the landing bay. He took his time and looked around at the other fighters in the landing bay. There were six. Six were left out of a flight of twelve. That meant that six brave pilots had not made it home. OE15 swallowed hard. The other ships that had landed earlier were either low on fuel or damaged and had had to land before their flight leader.

"Only six..." said OE15.

He made his way through the airlock and stripped off his helmet. He breathed fresher air again. He deposited his air canister and vacuum suit in their lockers. After that he caught up with AA3 who was heading towards the debriefing room.

As he ran up to AA3, AA3 said, "OE15 is it?"

"Yes, sir," replied the pilot.

"I meant what I said," said AA3. "If you ever want to join my squadron, you can. You're a good pilot!"

"Thank you, sir!" said OE15. Still a little overcome with the honour.

"It's rare for a bomber pilot to succeed as a fighter pilot. Why'd you choose bombers?" AA3 asked before the door of the debriefing room.

OE15 thought for a bit and then said, "I guess I just wanted to be in a team rather than a lone hunter. And it was more like I was chosen for bomber detail rather than a choice of mine, sir."

"And you think a squadron of fighters has room for lone hunters? Hah, we're a 12 person team. But I see your point. Also, it must be satisfying putting a nuclear torpedo on target?" AA3 said.

OE15 nodded.

They entered the debriefing room.

In the debriefing they learned that the Solar Solutions fleet had been soundly trapped and defeated and was now retreating towards Neptune. Which, due to the rotation of the planets, was the closest planet to Jupiter by some horrid chance. There would be no more delaying actions around buffer planets. The next fight would decide the fate of the Solar Solutions Corporation around its home planet.

OE15 left the debriefing feeling queasy. The fighter and bomber details would stay on duty for another few weeks while the Solar Solutions fleet distanced itself from the Collective Zone. Then they would go into cryo-sleep for the long trip to Neptune.

***

Gunter sat on the edge of his bed in his private quarters of the *Silver Ark*. They looked a lot like his quarters back on Neptune. They were opulently decorated and had ancient wooden furniture and rich furnishings.

He sloshed the glass of brandy in his hand and drank it all in one go. He poured another. This was his fifth. He felt drunk. He was drunk.

Gunter held his head in his left hand. He moaned quietly to himself. He felt dreadful. His communicator sounded for the tenth time.

"Yesh, yesh, yesh," he mumbled before turning it off.

He finished his brandy and poured himself another. Was it his sixth? He had lost count. All he knew was that the decanter was almost empty.

He collapsed backwards onto his bed. His head was spinning. He had failed. Thousands, no, millions had died because of his hubris and overconfidence. Europa was destroyed and his fleet had been caught in a trap and defeated, all because of him.

Gunter sat up again. His head swam. He felt ill. "If I had told them that...If I had told them," he slurred. He knew that if he had told them that he wanted someone else to lead the fleet, then things may have been okay. But he had not shirked from his duty. He had followed in the line of all the other CEOs who had had to fight. But he had failed due to his ineptitude and incompetence. The blame lay with him.

"If they had jusht lishened..." he cursed himself again. "Damn Cranmere and his fawning! Forshing me into the command role..." Gunter went to throw the glass across the room, but caught himself before he did. He finished the brandy in it first, and then threw it across the room. It smashed against some table and skidded to rest in some unknown corner, glass shattering everywhere.

A faint tap came from outside the room on the door. "Sir, are you there?"

"No!" said Gunter. He smiled to himself.

"Sir, I can hear you," said the voice. It was the First Officer. "We need you on the bridge, sir, to give orders..."

"I...I can't!" slurred Gunter. There was a pause.

"Sir...are you drunk?" The voice was more accusatory now.

"Sho what if I am?!" Gunter had grabbed another glass and poured the rest of the decanter into it.

"Sir...we need you!" The First Officer sounded worried.

"Well, you can't have me!" Gunter sighed and began to cry a little.

"CEO Sir!" The voice was now quite angry. "You're abandoning your fleet!"

"Sho what? We're losht anyway..." Gunter stood up, and regretted it. His mechanical leg protested, and he fell back onto the bed.

"There are refugee ships, sir. We need your orders to pick them up!" snapped the First Officer.

"Well, pick them up then!" ordered Gunter. "But shtop bothering me...I'm bushy..."

"In that case *sir*," the 'sir' was laboured, "I will have to take command. Do you object?"

There was a lengthy pause. Then Gunter responded with an almost sober voice. "No, I don't object..." He was crushed. His crew had mutinied against him. But who would have objected to that? In his situation he was in no way fit to lead, and he had lost the trust of his soldiers.

Gunter predicted in his drunken state that when they got back to Neptune he would be voted out of the CEO position. That was pretty certain. The question was, who would replace him? Cranmere? Cranmere was as bad as him. There was no one. The Solar Solutions Corporation was doomed. It would be absorbed into the Collective Zone in time.

Gunter staggered to the door to see if the First Officer was still there. He opened one of the double doors and looked out at the landing. He saw the First Officer about to descend in the lift.

"We will all die!" he yelled. He staggered against the doorframe.

The First Officer turned to face his CEO. He shook his head, and the doors of the lift closed.

"You! You can't judge me!" slurred Gunter. He staggered back into his room and the door closed.

Gunter turned his spinning vision to the brandy decanter. It was empty. He did not remember drinking the last bit. He got out another glass and put it down on the counter with a bang. He rummaged carelessly below the counter and pulled out another bottle. There were plenty more where that came from stashed in his room, he smiled. He opened it roughly and tried to pour a glass. He spilled some on the counter.

"Whoopsh..." He staggered. Eventually he managed to pour some in the glass. This bottle would carry him through, he thought.

Chapter 23

Fleet Commander Boltha stood on the bridge of the *Iron Bastion*. She stood near the glass window section of the bridge so that she could see what her fleet was doing to Europa.

"Damn it," she whispered to herself. "This is not what I meant by wanting to wage war..." She watched as missile after missile and auto-turret laser after laser slammed into the surface of the Europa Colony and reduced it to molten slag and boiling ocean.

What particularly galled Boltha was that when a little ship tried to run the gauntlet and escape from the destruction, it was mercilessly targeted and blasted apart before it could get out of range of the guns of the Collective Zone fleet. Some refugee ships had escaped, earlier. Now, with the majority of the Collective Zone fleet engaged in bombarding the hapless moon, nothing was getting away.

"Ma'am?" A voice came to her side. It was her First Officer. He waited for her instruction.

"We could have pursued the damn Solar Solutions fleet when it was caught in my trap! It would be over by now! But damn Uxus..." Boltha stopped herself. She did not want to commit treason.

"Yes, ma'am..." the First Officer nodded agreement. He was not just agreeing with her for the sake of it, he was experienced enough to know that she was right. They could have ended the war right there, but Uxus had pulled the ships to destroy Europa.

Boltha watched the fires rage on the surface below her. They were so numerous and fierce that they illuminated the *Iron Bastion* and the other ships above the moon. The glow of the flames flickered on her face as she gazed through the glass windows on the bridge.

"Get me Uxus..." she snarled.

"Ma'am!" saluted the First Officer and rushed off to organise a direct radio link between the two ships. After a short time, he returned and gave Boltha the signal that the channels were open to talk.

"CEO Uxus!" demanded Boltha. It was not a question.

"Yes, Boltha? What is it?" replied Uxus. He sounded distracted. "I'm busy here, what do you have to say. Make it quick!"

Boltha was incensed. "You dare talk to me like that?" she growled.

"Careful, Boltha. I can remove you from command..." The voice was threatening and also delighted, as if Uxus was daring Boltha to try him. "Don't try my patience..."

Boltha swallowed her rage. "CEO Sir, we had the Solar Solutions fleet in a trap; my trap. Then...then this happened." She gestured to the burning, boiling moon in front of her. She knew that Uxus could not see her action, but she had to add emphasis somehow. "You usurped my command. I had full command of the fleet and sprung that trap!"

"And? I'm simply adding to your glory!" Uxus replied. He sounded hurt. "Don't you want glory?"

"With all due respect, CEO Sir. I don't view killing innocent people as glorious." She paused. There was silence on the end of the line.

After a short time Uxus replied. This time his voice was cold, and harsh. "I don't view these people as innocent. They participated in hiding our prey, which, by now, I assume, has left. I consider that your fault, Boltha!" The last word was spat with some vitriol.

"CEO Sir! If you had let me continue my battle plan, there would be nowhere for the *Green Dragon* to go! I would have caught the Solar Solutions fleet and destroyed it! Then you--" Boltha was interrupted.

"Then I what?" snapped Uxus. "Look Boltha, I assigned you as commander, yes. However, I am the Supreme Commander. I made a tactical decision. I believe it was and is necessary to punish those who harbour our foe. I believe that it is necessary to teach the Solar Solutions scum a lesson. So, Mars had to pay, as did Europa." There was a pause as Uxus sounded like he was giving orders to his bridge and then he continued. "I believe that this was necessary to send a message. I know about politics. You might not agree with me, but I am your superior and so you have to obey."

"Yes, yes I do," Boltha sighed. She physically slumped. She knew it was not the total truth. She could rebel, but the consequences of that were horrendous. And she, a career officer in the Collective Zone, would never think of doing such a thing. She was behind her leader to the last. It was her duty and her curse.

"Good. Now, target quadrant 2B for me please with your ship's guns. There seem to be a large huddle of life forms there on the surface," Uxus paused.

Boltha started scans of the target and let the reports come back as to what was there.

"CEO Sir, those are people. They're in a bunker. You don't expect me to--" she was cut off.

"I expect you to follow my orders! Remember Mars!" Uxus said.

"But you put me in command of this operation! And Mars was different. They fought back for one thing. They

188

were criminals...And I believe I stopped you from obliterating that planet," Boltha protested.

"We've been through this, Boltha. You are in command of the fleet action. I can intervene when I believe it right to do so. Target. That. Bunker." Uxus' voice was calm and full of ice.

Boltha sighed. She called her First Officer over. "Target quadrant 2B. Reduce it to rubble."

"Ma'am," replied the First Officer. He gave her a sympathetic look.

Soon auto-turret lasers and missiles were landing where Uxus had ordered. Boltha could only imagine the terror and destruction that they wrought on the defenceless people below.

"Good. Now, Please continue this operation, Boltha, I will tell you when we can pursue the Solar Solutions fleet." Uxus sounded smug. The line went dead.

Boltha leaned against one of the supports for the window in front of her. She had not joined the Collective Zone Navy for this, not to target innocent civilians!

"If we win this war, we're damned. If we lose, we're war criminals," she said quietly to the First Officer.

"We must all do our duty and follow orders," said the First Officer.

"I know, I know," said Boltha. She looked out of the bridge window at the boiling surface of the moon. "But what is the price?"

"Well, to take your mind off it, Lieutenant Vauz is ready to report on the boarding action on board the *Silver Ark*." The First Officer offered a way out.

"Ah, yes, good. Send him in." Boltha composed herself and watched as Lieutenant Vauz was ushered onto the bridge and stood in front of her and saluted. His mechanical eye piercing the darkness with a red glow.

"Ma'am, I have your report ready," he said.

"Go ahead." Boltha gestured for him to continue. She respected Vauz, he was a good soldier, like her, once.

"Well, ma'am, they had bulkheads there that slowed us to a crawl, and our drill was damaged, so we had to abandon the action. Their resistance was fierce; stronger than I had anticipated. I must apologise for my failure." He bowed.

"Yes, it was unfortunate that those bulkheads were more prevalent that I had imagined," Boltha said. She paused, thinking.

"Ma'am, I will accept any punishment for my failure!" Vauz saluted again.

"Hah, there's no need for that, Lieutenant. You may have failed, but you are not the reason the Solar Solutions fleet got away." She looked out the bridge window towards the *Old Monarch*.

Vauz looked confused. "Ma'am?" he said.

"Never mind." Boltha waved a hand. "Don't think badly of yourself, Vauz. Things ended up not quite going as any of us had hoped. But you tested their defences, and your soldiers did well. How many did you lose?"

"23, ma'am. Out of 40." He grimaced. It was apparent he took the loss personally.

"It was a hard fought action then. Did you get close to the bridge?" Boltha beckoned for him to walk with her, and they paced the bridge walkway.

"We got within a few floors, ma'am. But their resistance was tough and as I said, we lost the use of the drill. It was damaged. If we still had that, then we could have done it. But the bulkheads needed to be breached by that drill, you see? If we had landed closer to the bridge..." Vauz fell silent.

"Yes, I see." Boltha paused and Vauz stopped beside her. "Well, good work with what you did, Lieutenant. I can't fault your actions. If you had retreated before the drill broke, then I would have cause to issue a platoon wide punishment. But I believe what you say. Next time we board the *Silver Ark*, we take more drill bits and more soldiers."

"Excuse me, ma'am. How will we get more soldiers? I mean, we're outside our space." Vauz looked confused.

"By combining platoons. Your 3rd Platoon will join with 5th Platoon. Together you make almost fifty soldiers. We still have quite a number of platoons left. It's not actually getting more soldiers, but focusing what we've got." Boltha looked at Vauz carefully.

"I...see..." Vauz said. "And who will be in command?"

This was the question Boltha was looking for. "You will be, Lieutenant. The leader of 5th Platoon was killed in his boarding action," Boltha replied.

"Right, that's a pity," Vauz said a little sadly.

"A pity?" Boltha asked, her eyebrows raised.

"Yes, we were friends, and he was a mean chess player..." Vauz trailed off, looking into the distance.

"You like chess?" Boltha asked.

"I do. It focuses the mind on what is truly necessary. There are no distractions. You have to plan ahead and it's all purely tactical. There's nothing...messy." Vauz paused and looked out the bridge window and then at Boltha. "But you've heard enough of my ramblings..."

"No, your opinions are interesting." Boltha smiled. "But you are dismissed, Lieutenant."

"Ma'am." Vauz saluted again and left the bridge.

"Chess...huh..." Boltha whispered. She turned to see the destroyed moon out the windows of the bridge. "What's truly necessary..." She paused for a while and then uttered.

191

"Now I must wait for my superior to unchain me again...Damn it. I don't want to be a war criminal. That's not why I joined all those years ago...And I think Vauz feels the same way..."

***

Trooper Althar sat on the edge of his bed, below his locker. He had been tidying up his effects after the engagement earlier on the *Silver Ark*. It was the Platoon's assigned down time after the combat, and they were allowed to do whatever they wished for a few days while the fleet rearranged and then presumably pursued the Solar Solutions fleet.

Althar had wondered why the fleet had not pursued the Solar Solutions fleet when they had been caught in the trap. He thought it was a waste that the fleet had not pressed home its advantage and it seemed a waste of all the lives of those lost in the boarding actions, but he was a simple soldier and he dared not question his superiors. They knew best, of course.

With a sigh, Althar looked across the gap between beds and looked at the empty space that should have been filled with his friend, Grox. He got up and moved to the locker that was above the bed. He put his hand on the cold, hard latch that secured the door of the locker and the contents inside.

Althar paused, it was left to other soldiers to clean out the lockers of those who did not make it back, and as Grox's closest friend, it was up to him to empty the locker. The contents of which would be sent to storage for a while, as Grox was not officially dead, just missing in action, and then after a time jettisoned into space.

Grox had been Althar's closest friend aboard the *Iron Bastion*. They had been friends from the start. Althar remembered Grox's foolish and comical mannerisms and actions. He had been a bit of a joker. He had been rather irreverent as a soldier. He had been a good soldier. He had been a good friend. And now he was gone.

Althar did not know if he was dead or somewhere captured aboard the *Silver Ark*, all he knew was that his friend was no longer here, and he wanted to make the Solar Solutions forces pay for what they had done. He would make them, personally, pay for the loss of his friend.

"I will avenge you," he said as he lightly banged his now balled fist against Grox's locker.

After a second, he opened the locker, and out of it fell a book. It landed first on his head, and then it hit the floor and flipped open.

"Damn it, Grox," Althar rubbed his head. "You arse..." He reached down and picked up the book. It was the copy of *The Collected Works of William Shakespeare*. It had landed open on a page. At first Althar wanted just to slam the book shut and throw it across the room, but he resisted the urge. He read the page.

"Alive, in triumph! And Mercutio slain! / Away to heaven, respective lenity / And fire-eyed fury be my conduct now! / Now, Tybalt, take the villain back again, / That late thou gavest me; for Mercutio's soul / Is a little way above our heads, / Staying for thine to keep him company: / Either thou, or I, must go with him."

It was from something called *Romeo and Juliet*. He read it slowly. It was written in a way that was difficult for him to make sense of. But he understood it. He understood what was said all too well. His friend was gone and that made him sad, and full of rage. He would have given anything to see or hear that fool of a friend again. But this was war, and in war, people died. Grox may as well have been dead. Even if he was captured, Althar was very unlikely ever to see his face again in this lifetime.

"Damn you, Grox," Althar whispered.

He closed the book and went to put it in the pile he was about to start to throw out his friend's possessions, but he stopped. He turned the book over a few times in his hands, and then opened his own locker, and placed the book in there. He did not know why he did this. He was not really a reading person. But as a memory of his old friend, he could not throw it out. There was something about the book that yearned to be kept. The plays and poems in it had survived for a thousand years, and who was he to throw them away?

Althar sorted through the rest of the locker. There were more books, which he kept, and various other bits and pieces.

Althar came across a photo. It was of a woman. She was young and pretty. It must have been Grox's girlfriend. He had strangely never talked about her. This was understandable as the length of time people spent in cryo-pods and travelling between planets meant that anyone left behind was many years older physically than them when they got home. Many soldiers simply avoided long term relationships or had relationships with other soldiers in order to avoid the pain of coming home and seeing someone grown old. He placed the photo in his own locker. She would need to be told of his fate one day. Perhaps she had already given him up for dead as they had been travelling already for years. Althar did not know.

He was able to put most of the contents of the locker into the storage pile, but the books and the photo he saved. He had to, for his old, lost, friend.

He called for a tech-slave and soon one arrived. It picked up the pile to go into storage for a time and stumbled away. Grox's bed and locker lay empty.

Althar sat down and then lay back on his own bed. He was so tired. He knew he had a while before he had to report for duty again. He fell asleep in his uniform on top of the covers. He dreamed fitful dreams of his lost friend and the battle just fought.

***

Grox woke up with a scream. He was strapped into a chair. He had no idea where he was. He tasted blood in his mouth. He looked around at what he could; his head was locked in position by a vice either side of his head. He realised he was in pain. There was a light shining in his face. He could not see much outside of that. Everything else was in silhouette. His arm and leg hurt a lot.

"Ah. Awake." fizzed a tech-slave. He could tell it was a tech-slave due to its jerky movements and the way it spoke.

Grox felt a sharp pain as the tech-slave administered an injection to him.

"Where...am I?" he asked.

"Not. Asked. Question. Don't. Answer." snapped the tech-slave and administered an electric shock.

Grox screamed.

"What's going on?" Grox said through clenched teeth.

"Again. Not. Asked. Question." Another electric shock.

Grox realised he was in a torture cell and the tech-slave was programmed to ask him questions, and only then could he speak. His head swam with the chemical that was injected. He stayed silent.

"Name?" fizzed the tech-slave.

"Grox..." he replied.

"Function?" Again fizzing.

Grox did not quite understand, and he delayed. There was another electric shock and he screamed.

"Function?" demanded the tech-slave.

"Sol-soldier," gasped Grox through the pain.

"What were you doing?" came the question from the tech-slave beyond the light.

Grox wanted to resist, but the pain was so intense from each shock that he could not fight it. He tried multiple times to lie or resist, but the tech-slave torturer knew when he was not truthful and administered electric shocks and more serum.

The torture went on for what seemed like hours, although it was probably less than an hour, reasoned Grox through the haze of pain and serum.

"How dare you!" he snapped through another electric shock. "You barbaric Solar Solutions bastards! This is why we're invading your space! To show you civilisation. Our soldiers will win and," he screamed with another shock, "...will win and hold you responsible for this outrage! How many of us have you tortured!?" Another shock followed.

"Perhaps. Would. Like. To. Know. I. Programmed. With. Collective. Zone. Torture. Protocol." fizzed the tech-slave while administering more serum.

Grox's head swam. He felt very ill. He began to lose consciousness and the last thing he felt was the sting of another shock, but he was too drugged up to notice. He faded into blackness.

Chapter 24

Alfred sat in his quarters and reached for the tourniquet; he prepared to give himself another injection. He felt the sting of the needle and the rush of the medication as it coursed through his veins and through his head. He felt a little light headed, but that was better than the alternative.

His desire to zet was diminished a little, but he still felt the craving. Now it was not the only thing he wanted to do, but it was still weighing heavily on his mind. He still craved the sensation.

"So, what do we do now?"

"You can piss off!" Alfred whispered to himself.

"Don't talk to me like that. You know I'm right. You know you have to zet..."

Alfred shook his head. He had been having more and more conversations with the voice lately. It seemed less chaotic and random and instead it appeared to be more reasoned now that he was on the medication. But it was still there. It was always there now, commenting, judging, waiting...

"Alfred, you there?" chimed his communicator. It was Draz.

"Yeah, Draz. I'm here. What is it?" He liked to hear her voice; it broke the contact with the voice in his head.

"Come to the bridge. We're going to dock with the *Silver Ark*." The communicator cut off.

"Right," Alfred whispered to himself. "Maybe a chance to zet?"

He put the syringe and tourniquet down and left his room.

Alfred made his way through the *Green Dragon* from his quarters to the bridge. As he stepped through the doors onto the bridge he saw Artisius on the command dais in his full ceremonial regalia and Draz standing to one side. The bridge was back to normal light indicating that the cloaking device had been shut down a while ago. They were obviously out of danger for the moment. The First Officer was rushing around making sure that the orders from Artisius were carried out.

Draz saw Alfred enter the bridge and walked over to him. "You all right?" she asked.

"Yeah, I'm fine. New meds are working...sort of." He looked into the middle distance.

"Oh, are they?"

Alfred shook his head a little.

"You sure?" asked Draz. "You look a little...off colour..."

"No, no," Alfred reassured her. "Things are okay. Why was I required?"

"To observe the wonders of the Solar Solutions flagship, the *Silver Ark*!" boomed Artisius. He stepped down from the command dais and slapped Alfred on the back in a friendly way.

Alfred nearly fell over.

Draz chuckled.

"So...I don't get to zet?" asked Alfred.

"No, son, no. We don't need anything like that," replied Artisius. "I just thought you'd like to see that!" He spun around and pointed out the observation dome at the massive shape of the *Silver Ark*. Alfred had not noticed it on his way in as he had been paying attention to his head and Draz.

"That's huge!" said Alfred. He was rather dumbstruck. He had seen and lived on colonies and space stations that were bigger, but the *Silver Ark* was a massive ship. It glittered in the starlight. "Is that bigger than the Collective Zone flagship?"

"They're about the same size, actually. But this one is closer," Artisius said, smiling.

"And we're going to dock? Then what?" asked Draz.

"Well, we see what they need from us. Any assistance we can give I'm sure would be welcome. We just lost a battle. And I have some...cargo I'd like to unload..." Artisius said. "CEO Gunter is supposed to be on there. And in his...brilliance...he made us just lose that battle by falling into a trap." Artisius grimaced. "Now if you'll excuse me, I have orders to give!" He remounted the command dais and began barking orders for docking procedure.

"So, my CEO is on there," Alfred said. "I wonder if I can meet him..." Alfred said almost silently.

"Do you care about him?" asked Draz by his side.

"Well, not really...I mean, I don't worship him like some, but just to meet him would be special. Like some kind of holo-vid star, you see?" Alfred was staring out the observation dome as the massive bulk of the *Silver Ark* got closer.

"You want his autograph?" Draz said, laughing.

"Well...not like that...but..." Alfred blushed.

"Should I take your photo with him?" Draz stuck her tongue out at her friend.

"Stop it!" Alfred pushed her away in a friendly way.

They both laughed. And then they both paused. Alfred wondered how long it had been since they laughed; how long it had been since either of them had found the time to have fun. Draz stopped too. It was clear she was thinking the same. The war was not yet over, and no-one's life was secure at a time like this.

"It's good to laugh," Draz said, giving voice to both their thoughts.

"Indeed," Alfred said with a smile.

"Bring us alongside, Helmsman," boomed Artisius. A suitably emphatic response followed from the Helmsman. "Open a channel," Artisius continued. After a short time, it was indicated he had a communication connection to the bridge of the *Silver Ark*.

"This is the First Officer of the *Silver Ark*, what do you want?" came the curt challenge.

"This is Captain Artisius of the *Green Dragon* requesting permission to dock," demanded Artisius.

"Ah, Captain Artisius, good to hear from you; permission granted. Please dock at station four. It will be good to see you again," came the reply from the *Silver Ark*.

"One request," Artisius paused and ran a hand through his hair. It was evident he had trouble voicing the next sentence. "I may have...words...for your superior."

"Don't we all? He's a little...under the weather right now. But I'll try and get you an audience," said the First Officer of the *Silver Ark* sympathetically.

"Thank you, Artisius out," and the communication went dead. "You heard the man, Helmsman; docking station four!"

"Sir!" snapped the Helmsman and guided the *Green Dragon* to its docking port. After a short time, the docking tube extended, and the ship reverberated with the clang as the secure lock was obtained between the two ships. After a few more seconds the Helmsman replied, "Secure docking obtained, sir. We have atmospheric unity."

"Good," said Artisius. He checked his gold braid and red epaulettes. Then he smiled at Draz and Alfred. "Ready to go aboard?" he said with a grin.

***

As the trio left the bridge and made their way to the docking tube, Draz asked a question. "I thought you were furious with CEO Gunter, Artisius? Why are you so cheerful?"

"Because," Artisius paused, "I don't always get to go aboard such a magnificent ship. But yes, I am furious at Gunter. But I don't know the full story, yet. He may have been bluffed into falling into the trap. It may have been a genuine mistake. Shit happens in war, you know..." he paused again. This time coming to a stop in the corridor. "But I will have stern words with him, but there's no point in losing one's temper for no reason! So, in the mean time, I stay positive. Because in war, you really have to stay positive, or you're lost..." Artisius paused for another minute and then the trio headed towards the docking tube.

Alfred remained silent. He was dealing with the voice in his head.

"Do you really believe what he's saying?"

The trio made their way through the airlocks and into the *Silver Ark*. They were met by an honour guard of Solar Solutions soldiers who were arrayed around the end of the docking airlock on the *Silver Ark* end.

"Impressive," whispered Alfred to Draz.

At the head of the guards there was a man in full naval military uniform. Artisius greeted him like an old friend and the man responded in kind.

"First Officer of the *Silver Ark*! Edward! My friend." Artisius beamed as he embraced the man.

"Artisius, it's been too long!" said the First Officer with a laugh.

Draz and Alfred looked at each other.

"And who is this?" asked Edward heading towards Draz and Alfred.

"These are good friends, Edward. This is Alfred," Artisius indicated, and Edward shook Alfred's hand warmly. "And this is Draz." Artisius pointed.

"Delighted, I'm delighted to meet you. Any friends of Artisius are friends of mine." Edward shook Draz's hand warmly too. He turned back to Artisius. "I would offer you a tour in calmer times, but I have work to do on the bridge. What do you need?"

"I need to talk to the man in charge. I have some refugees to unload and also some...other things to deal with..." Artisius said.

"Ah...well...I'm in charge..." said Edward, rather annoyed.

"What? What about the CEO?" asked Artisius.

"He's...indisposed as I said before; when you were docking..." said Edward sheepishly.

Artisius growled. "Take me to him. But first, I would like some of your guards to assist my First Officer in unloading an unwanted prisoner from my ship. He needs to be tried and sentenced. His name is Virtus."

"What was his crime?" asked Edward, his brow furrowing.

"Mass murder. The destruction of *Florida Station*. And the incitement of violence and terrorism on Europa," Artisius said.

"*Florida Station*!" whispered Edward. "He did that? I remember that years ago...I thought a culprit was found already? I heard it on the official reports..."

"That was...a mistake. It was Virtus after all," said Artisius, giving Alfred an apologetic look.

Alfred nodded and said, "It's true! It was him." He felt afraid that his word would be doubted.

"Then we will arrest him right away and put him on trial when we can, war permitting, we may have to keep him in cryo-storage until things get better." replied Edward. "Anything else?"

"We have some refugee families that would do better on this ship, if you could take them I would be most grateful," said Artisius.

"We will do that! Thank you for rescuing who you could from Europa." With that Artisius indicated that that was all, and Edward indicated for some guards to go aboard the *Green Dragon* and take Virtus into custody and help the refugees.

Edward indicated for Artisius, Alfred and Draz to follow him and they headed towards what Edward said was the private quarters of the CEO.

After a few steps, Edward suddenly stopped and held up his hand. "I'm sorry but due to security concerns I'll have to ask for identification from the two others..." He pointed to Draz and Alfred.

"Uh..." began Alfred. His mind raced as he feared that he was going to be locked up again.

Artisius held up his hand and stopped Alfred mid sentence. "If I'm allowed, they are. They have my express trust and I would vouch for them anywhere," Edward gave Artisius a sidelong glance and was about to continue when Artisius interrupted. "Look, Edward, you know me, and I know you. They're trustworthy, I swear. We've been through a lot together these two and I."

After a minute thinking, First Officer Edward nodded and smiled. "I suppose we can make an exception for you."

Alfred and Draz breathed a collective sigh of relief, as they had no documentation. They glanced at each other in a thankful way and followed Artisius and Edward along the corridors and through the lifts of the *Silver Ark*.

Alfred was dumbstruck. The ship was so modern; so sleek; so advanced. He had been impressed with the *Green*

Dragon, but this was something else. This ship was massive and the peak of design.

"How old is this ship?" Alfred said in awe.

"About four decades old," replied Edward over his shoulder. "But we keep updating it and it really is our finest ship."

They walked for what seemed like ages through white corridors and lifts until they came to a lift with guards. Alfred assumed he, Artisius, and Draz were being led to the CEO's quarters in the upper areas of the ship.

The guards saluted as Edward approached. He saluted back. Then he produced a special key card and scanned it in a security scanner at the side of the lift.

Alfred suddenly had a faint memory of the airlock controls on *Florida Station*; it worked its way into his mind. He smiled. This technology was a long way from the crude button codes of that place.

The lift door slid aside with a quiet hiss and the four of them stepped inside. After a short travel, also upwards, the door slid open again and they all stepped out onto a landing that had a large double door in front of it. It was obvious to Alfred that this was their destination.

Edward held up his hand again and indicated that the trio had to wait a minute. Edward moved to the double door and tapped on it lightly.

"CEO Sir, are you there?" he said in a soft voice. There was no reply. "CEO Sir?" he said with a stronger voice.

"Go away!" shouted a voice from within the chamber.

Alfred's heart leapt. Was that Gunter? Was that his CEO?

"CEO Sir, I have some people to see you. I think it's important," continued Edward.

Alfred was surprised at the meekness of the man's voice in this situation. He had assumed Edward was more confident, but then again, he was talking to their CEO.

"Damn it, go away! I don't care who it ish..." shouted the voice. There was a crash from behind the doors.

Alfred was marvelling at the fact that he might get to meet his CEO, when Artisius, his face a pure beacon of rage, shouldered past Edward and banged on the door.

"Open the door, Gunter! We don't have time for this shit! I need to talk to you!" yelled Artisius slamming his fist onto the ornate doors.

Alfred was shocked at the way Artisius spoke, especially after Artisius said earlier that he would not lose his temper for no reason. But it was clear something was not right inside the chamber.

Edward tried to pull Artisius from the door, but that only seemed to make him angrier and pound even harder on the door.

Alfred and Draz looked at each other. Their look exchanged a thousand words. They knew something unpleasant was going to happen. This could not end well.

After a few minutes of banging on the door. Artisius stopped and rubbed his fist. "Gunter! Come out here! This is no time for self pity!"

There was a shuffling noise on the other side of the door, and then there was a click as the lock was disengaged and one of the doors opened. And there he was. The CEO of the Solar Solutions Corporation.

Alfred was dumbstruck. He had never expected in his life to see the man in person. Alfred was not the sort for celebrity worship, but this was different. This was his Supreme Commander. He felt that he was allowed some sort of knee weakening adoration. He felt Draz's hand on his shoulder. He did not look at her, but she steadied him.

But something was wrong. The CEO was swaying. He looked dreadful. In a moment Alfred realised, he was drunk!

"Now, Gunter..." Artisius began, and was interrupted by a tirade of insults from the staggering man in the dishevelled business suit.

Gunter, whose tie was crooked and shirt messy and was generally a sight of unkemptness, insulted Artisius. Insult after insult flew from his spittle speckled mouth.

Artisius took it all stoically. After about a minute Gunter stopped and swayed a bit. He leant against the door half that was closed. He seemed pleased with himself at putting Artisius in his place.

Alfred felt dreadful. Here was his CEO and he was a common drunk. He did not know if he was going to cry from shame at adoring this man.

It was obvious that Artisius was furious. He had clenched his fists and had turned a rather bright shade of red. Alfred tried to move forward to pull him away, before he did anything stupid. Artisius shook Alfred's hand off his shoulder.

"Now listen here! I am Captain Artisius of the *Green Dragon*. And you know me," Artisius boomed in his most threatening and authoritarian voice.

Alfred and Draz were taken aback, and it was clear that Edward and particularly Gunter were also shocked.

"I will not be talked to like that, by some common drunk!" Artisius said. "Before you protest, it is obvious that you are drunk and totally ignorant of your condition. You reek of alcohol!" Artisius paused. Gunter was about to jump in again, but Artisius cut him off. "I am not finished! Your incompetence has killed millions in the Battle of Jupiter. You gave everyone hope and then you threw it away! If you had not fallen into that obvious trap you would have won the battle, and the war! But no, you had to be the proud and great CEO and not pay heed to your tactical briefings. Now, when your people need you most, you have abandoned them and turned to drink! You disgust me! You are no CEO, you are no man, you are worse than a tech-slave. At least they know how to complete their duties! What do you have to say for yourself? And make it good!" Artisius paused again, obviously somewhat pleased with his counter tirade.

Gunter froze. It was evident that he had never been talked to like this before. He seemed not to know how to respond. He gagged on his words.

"Well?" snapped Artisius again, his keen eyes boring deeply into the puffy drunken features of his target.

Alfred and Draz had completely frozen on the spot. And as Alfred looked at Edward, it was evident he had no idea what was going to happen either. They all stood, dumbstruck. Only Artisius seemed in control of himself.

"I...I...didn't want to fight..." whimpered Gunter. He was totally deflated. "What do I do? Captain Arshteshius?" Gunter grinned at the mispronounced name.

Artisius ignored the insult and pushed Gunter back into the room. He kept pushing him until the CEO fell back onto his bed.

Edward, Alfred and Draz followed the pair inside the room. Alfred marvelled at the rich and opulent decorations and furnishings of the room. Then his vision snapped back to the confrontation between Artisius and Gunter.

Artisius was going around the room smashing the bottles of alcohol that were put on counters and tables, while Gunter scrambled off the bed, followed him and tried to protest. Artisius was having none of it. His face was set in a determined grimace.

"You are not going to throw the Corporation away just because of some alcohol! I will not have you wallowing in self pity!" Artisius bellowed. Gunter cringed at the volume and held his ears.

"But...I'm usheless!" sobbed Gunter.

"Yes, yes you are!" said Artisius and just before he was about to smash the last bottle, Gunter lunged at him fists raised and hit Artisius in the back of the head. It was a clumsy blow that did not hit with much force.

Artisius turned and smashed the bottle on the ground face to face with his assailant. Before Edward could intervene, as it was obvious he approved of the removal of alcohol and had not stopped Artisius then, Artisius raised his right fist and punched Gunter squarely on the nose, quite hard.

Gunter whined and fell backwards onto his bed. "You, you hit me!? The CEO!" he bleated.

"No," Artisius replied, shaking his fist from the blow, "I hit a worm." And with that he stormed out of the room, crunching on broken glass, to the shouts and protests of the bruised ego that was Gunter.

Alfred was not exactly sure what a worm was, but he and Draz and Edward followed Artisius out of the room.

"Can you lock the doors from the outside?" Asked Artisius. He indicated the lock as they left.

Edward nodded dumbly; he had seen something he had never thought to see. He locked the CEO's room doors from the outside.

"Remember to feed him, now and then," said Artisius dismissively. "I guess you are in command of the ship now, First Officer Edward. Gunter is in no state to command."

They headed down the lift again, in silence.

When they reached the correct floor, they got out and Edward managed to say something. "I would prefer if you took control, sir."

"I...cannot yet. But thank you, I will keep the request in mind, for later." Artisius smiled to his friend. "And there's no need to 'sir' me."

"What will I say to the crew then?" said Edward.

"Tell them what they know, tell them the CEO is ill and that you have been given command temporarily. It's the truth after all..." Artisius said.

Alfred was silent through all of this. He had seen his CEO. He had seen his scumbag of a CEO drunk and refusing to take command. He felt like spitting, but did not want to foul the clean floor of the starship.

"It's amazing what happens to people under stress, isn't it?"

"Oh, not now..." said Alfred.

"What?" asked Draz. She had been silent and thinking too.

"Uh...nothing..." said Alfred. He had to be careful when he talked to his voice.

Artisius and Edward were in quiet and intense conversation. Alfred and Draz lagged behind as they walked through the corridors. Alfred was trying to keep the voice in his head from talking to him, and he could tell that Draz was concerned about him by the looks she periodically gave him.

"You seem...distracted?" asked Draz.

"Oh, it's nothing. Just my implant malfunctioning." Alfred was frank. He knew he did not have to be coy around Draz. They were good friends now. He did not want her to worry, but he saw no reason in lying to her.

"Oh..." Draz seemed lost for words at Alfred's candour.

"Relax...I'm fine. I'm on meds now," Alfred kept walking.

"I hope they work!" whispered Draz.

"So do I..." whispered Alfred.

"So, has a report been made to Neptune High Command about the debacle of Jupiter?" asked Artisius. Alfred and Draz overheard at a distance behind.

"Well, not exactly," said Edward. "We were waiting on-_"

"Gunter..." said Artisius with a sigh.

"Indeed," groaned Edward.

"Would you like me to table a report and give the information to Neptune High Command? I'll need your permission and assistance, but I can do it in place of Gunter," Artisius asked frankly as he walked.

"That would be good," said Edward. The relief was clear in his voice, "I had a sinking feeling that I would have to take the blame alone for this."

"No one is taking the blame except for Gunter. I'll slam him in the report. However, we must warn Neptune as soon as possible. They'll need all the time they've got to get ready," Artisius sounded resolute.

***

The four of them made their way to the bridge. Alfred noted that it was very similar to the command station on Europa or like a massive version of the *Green Dragon's* bridge with multiple tiers and walkways.

As they entered the bridge, Alfred noticed the solemnity and dour air that hung over the crew. Many turned to see who entered and then when they noticed that their CEO was nowhere to be seen, they turned back to their duties in silence. It was clear that everyone was depressed about what had happened around Jupiter and about the reaction of their CEO. Alfred assumed that they all knew where and what the CEO was doing.

Edward beckoned them over to a communications terminal and with the assistance of the Communications Officer, they established a link and direction of beaming for the message.

While Artisius and Edward compiled a report and sent it off to *Neptune Prime* with the assistance of the Communications Officer, Draz and Alfred stood a respectful distance behind and looked around the bridge.

"Wouldn't it be wonderful if all these people died?"

Alfred shook his head.

"Oh, come on, it would be beautiful. All you'd have to do is--"

"Shut! Up!" whispered Alfred shaking his head harder. "The meds are meant to fix you..." He sounded pleading.

"You're in pain?" asked Draz.

"No. Well, not exactly. I'd love to zet--"

"Psh..." Draz exclaimed rolling her eyes.

"--but this is not it," Alfred insisted. "I hear voices now. Well, one voice in particular. It tells me to do things."

"I know." Draz raised an eyebrow. "You hear voices, I know that already. Right..."

"Right?" Alfred mirrored but uneasily. He did not know what she thought. His memory had decayed enough to forget about Draz already knowing about the voices. He cursed himself silently. He was forgetting so much.

"Well...we just have to get that fixed won't we? I mean, when we go to Pluto for you to have surgery," Draz said, smiling.

"Hah." Alfred laughed. "So, we're going to Pluto now?"

"Well, isn't that what you wanted, eventually?" she asked.

"Yeah, I guess. But you don't have to come..." Alfred whispered.

"But I will. And you can't discourage me. We're in this together. I'm not giving up on you!" Draz sounded very resolute. She smiled at him.

"You can thank her any time, for wanting to kill me that is."

"Thanks." Alfred smiled. He did not know what to say. She was a devoted friend and that was clear. Whether she felt more was up to her, but Alfred valued her as a friend at the moment. She and Artisius were good friends in hard times. Alfred had never really had such true friends, and it made him feel good that they existed, but anxious that they could disappear in an instant.

After a while the message was compiled and sent and Edward and Artisius turned back to Draz and Alfred.

"There, it's done," said Artisius. "*Neptune Prime* should be warned of the disaster."

"Did you say who caused it?" asked Draz. It was clear who she meant.

"We said that Gunter was...ill, and that he was mistaken in reading the combat zone and as such he lost the battle," said Edward.

"Too bloody nice if you ask me," spat Draz.

"We can't just say that he's incompetent and remove him?" insisted Edward, shifting nervously on his feet. "I can't believe we've basically mutinied and removed him from command of his flagship. If we sent that to Neptune High Command on *Neptune Prime* we would be arrested as soon as we arrived."

"Hrm," Draz huffed.

Artisius pulled Edward over to one side, but still within earshot of Draz and Alfred. "Now I have a favour to ask. I have some...cargo, that I believe should be removed from my ship."

"Cargo?" Edward raised an eyebrow.

"Yes, some cargo left over from my smuggling days; before this war. I have a number of...slaves left that I believe should be unloaded from my ship and reintroduced to the world from their cryo-pods," Artisius said.

"I see..." said Edward. "And why can't you do that?"

"Because," sighed Artisius, "they were picked up, by me, on their way to Venus one time, quite some time ago. It would be very odd for them to find out it was quite a few years later and they were in the middle of a war zone..."

"Right. I'll get some of my people on to that. At least you're coming clean about that. We won't have to arrest you right this moment for slave trading in Solar Solutions space. You may be still of some use to the war effort. If you obey the commands of the Solar Solutions Command," said Edward a little too forcefully for Alfred's liking. Did he not know this was a good man? Edward and Artisius were supposed to be friends.

"And what does the Solar Solutions Command, command?" asked Artisius.

"As I'm acting commander, it's up to me," said Edward.

"And what do you command?" Artisius was obviously losing his patience.

"We'll need someone to run rear guard. Someone to spy on the Collective Zone and gather information. I think we could overlook your slave trading if you undertook such a task..." Edward looked down his nose at Artisius.

"But that's suicide," said Draz.

Alfred nodded.

"It is."

Artisius held up his hand. "My ship can do it. And I will do it. Send me the orders and I'll follow them."

"Good," said Edward and headed off.

"And he was your friend?" asked Alfred, rather perturbed.

"Yeah..." sighed Artisius. "Oh well, I guess I had it coming." Artisius smiled to them both. "He always was a stickler for the rules. Did you see his reaction to my attack on Gunter? Hah! Even if he is my friend he has a point about slaves."

"Do you want our help?" asked Draz.

"No, I can do this alone, with my ship. I don't want to worry about...others...friends." He smiled again.

"You're sure?" asked Alfred. He felt like they should help somehow. "What do we do here?" He looked around the bridge.

"Survive," said Artisius. "Don't worry about me. I'll be fine. Take care of yourselves. I'll be back before you know it. We will see each other again. I'm off to get my ship ready. Take care you two," and with that he exited the bridge and left Alfred and Draz in their own company.

"And what about your...insurance. Aren't you going to hand that over? You said you would!" Draz rushed after Artisius and stopped him.

"No...not now. I believe you're right; it is too dangerous. Given the state of the Solar Solutions command, I will deal with it," and with that Artisius left.

Alfred looked after Artisius who had departed quickly. He hoped he would see him again, but he understood the danger of the action Artisius was undertaking.

The pair stood oddly in the bridge before looking to find Edward and something that they could help with; and what quarters they could be assigned on the capital ship.

Chapter 25

CEO Uxus had made the short trip from his command ship the *Old Monarch* to the *Iron Bastion* in order to make sure his orders were being carried out. He stood bolt upright on the bridge with his Black Guard standing nearby.

Fleet Commander Boltha stood in front of him. She was at attention, but it was clear that she had little respect for her CEO.

They had been discussing the results from the assault on Jupiter.

"You are displeased?" hissed Uxus. He stood with his hands behind his back and looked down his nose at his most able commander.

"Yes, CEO," said Boltha, eyes fixed straight ahead. "You know my displeasure at letting the Solar Solutions fleet escape from my trap in order to commit...questionable...actions."

The rest of the bridge was silent and looking on while trying to look like they were not observing the conversation. It was a great honour for the CEO to board the ship, and it was plain to Uxus that many were waiting with bated breath for his reply to this rather insolent response from his chief commander in the field.

"I see." Uxus began to pace back and forth. He looked at the floor and then back at Boltha. "So you don't believe in punishing those who resist?"

"I don't believe in punishing those who should not have to resist. Our fight is with the Solar Solutions military, not the people." Boltha was resolute in her argument.

"So you would disobey your CEO?" Uxus paused in pacing and looked out the window of the bridge behind him. The bulk of Jupiter sat and occupied most of the space across the windows but there were the glittering lights of the Collective Zone fleet that had formed up in pursuit formation. The fleet was ready to follow the Solar Solutions fleet back to their home planet, all it required was his order.

"CEO Sir, I fail to see how pursuing the enemy fleet and vanquishing them is disobeying your orders. We should be following them now! Our ships may be slower, but we should put all the pressure on them that we can muster," Boltha sighed with exasperation. She ran a hand over her short cut stubble haircut.

"Don't presume to give me orders, commander." The last word was spat with such vitriol that Uxus thought that he saw Boltha shrink a little. His black guard almost reached for their weapons. He sensed them move in the corners of his vision. He began pacing again.

"No, CEO," Boltha said.

"I have great knowledge in tactical matters, Boltha. Even though I look younger, as you know I've undergone longevity surgery. I am not as young as I appear. Remember that. I have studied tactics for a long time, and now it is my chance to crush the Solar Solutions Corporation once and for all." Uxus stopped walking. He had clenched his right fist in a ball and brandished it in the air.

"And I've had a lifetime and a half in service to the military, Uxus," she said his name with anger. "I've had longevity surgery twice. Don't parade lifespan as a badge of honour. Unless you've had combat experience, you have no right telling me what is great knowledge in tactical matters. A good CEO would listen to his tactical advisor," she finished her attack and fell silent.

Uxus paused. He had rarely been talked to like that, and those who had had rarely lived. "I saw the last war, you know?" Uxus said through gritted teeth.

"And I fought in it, CEO. You watched as a Collective Zone citizen," retorted Boltha, just as coldly.

Uxus knew she was the best commander he had, and not even Acting Commander Tyyz could replace her. He knew that he needed her. And he knew when to back down, he had made his point, any more would be unnecessary.

"We've finished the attack on Europa now, it is no more," Uxus said in a conciliatory tone. "Now I need you to take the fleet and pursue the Solar Solutions ships."

"And I have full command?" snapped Boltha.

"You have command," replied Uxus, intentionally leaving off the 'full'.

"Now if you please, CEO Sir, I need my ship back and I need to continue my actions. The Solar Solutions ships are faster and have a large head start. We will be unable to catch them, but we should arrive at Neptune a few months behind them. I just hope they have not had time to regroup. They will have sent a message to Neptune to be ready for us." Boltha finished by spinning on her heel and dismissing herself from her CEO's sight.

Uxus stood, rather lost for words, on the bridge. He had been shown up. He felt angry. He felt like taking his anger out on something or someone, but he could not without looking like a petulant fool. He smiled.

"Well played, Boltha," he whispered so that no one heard.

Snapping his fingers his Black Guard formed up around him and Uxus left the bridge of the *Iron Bastion* and headed back to the *Old Monarch* in his shuttle. He would be interested to see what Boltha used as tactics in the coming engagement. But first, there was the two or more years travel they would have to endure. He hoped his cryo-pod did not fail on the way.

***

Alfred had found the cryo-pod he was looking for with the help of a tech-slave guide. He sat in front of it. Inside was the man who had destroyed so much of his life. Inside was Virtus. He had been placed back into cryo-sleep for storage and transport by First Officer Edward's orders. Virtus had gone willingly.

"It would be so easy to shut it off."

"No, I can't do that...can I?" whispered Alfred to himself. He was alone in the cargo bay except for the occasional tech-slave or robot. They paid him no heed as they went about their unknown duties.

"Why not? I mean, it's just pressing a few buttons. Think of how many he killed on Florida Station."

"Yes but...I'm better than him," Alfred whispered.

"Are you? Your zetting powers war machines."

"Yes, but I haven't blown up a station!" This time a bit louder than a whisper. Alfred looked around to see if anyone heard. There was no one.

"Ah, right, so it's morality by the comparative method then."

"What else is there? I mean, if we don't compare ourselves to others, how else to we judge ourselves?"

"Possibly true, but you want to shut it off. I can tell."

"Of course, I do. He destroyed everything I had." Alfred was getting frustrated with the voice inside his head. It was not supposed to hold a conversation.

"Oh? Why not? I'm in you. I am you. I can converse with you as easily as you with someone else."

"Shut up!" Alfred cursed.

"No."

Alfred fell silent for a while and stared at the pod. He wanted to shut it off so badly. To say that it was a malfunction. But he knew that he was better than that. He knew Virtus had to stand trial for treason and mass murder, only then would the ghosts of the past be laid to rest.

"That's what you think."

Alfred shook his head again. Was it time for his next injection? He had lost track of time. It must have been. He carried the medication on himself now, as the *Green Dragon* had departed. Dr Antonia had left him with enough medication and syringes for a long time.

He used the tourniquet and spiked the vein with the needle. He felt the rush of the medication through his body and brain. The voice fell silent, for the moment. Alfred breathed a sigh.

The medication did not give him any feeling of pleasure, like an illicit drug, but it did make him feel somewhat calmer and more in control of his mind when he used it. It brought his mind back to reality.

He got up and stared long and hard into the porthole in the front of the pod. "You will be tried and convicted!" he said and headed out of the cargo bay and back to the bridge.

***

Alfred entered the bridge. He looked around for Draz. She was not there. He was about to leave when he was accosted by First Officer Edward.

"Ah, Alfred, good. You're an experienced zetter?" Edward took Alfred by the arm.

"Uh, yes...but..." Alfred stuttered.

"Good, could you please zet our system?" Edward ushered him towards the terminal.

"But, don't you have military zetters?" Alfred asked. He was torn. He wanted to zet more than anything, but he knew that it would damage him.

"Yes, but due to the combat with the Collective Zone some of them burnt out and the rest are off duty."

"Oh," is all Alfred could say. 'Burnt out' meant dead, he knew. The feedback from the strain on the systems during combat had fried their brains. "And we're not in combat now..." Alfred paused.

"No, we're not in combat. So the danger is low. Please, Alfred." Edward looked at him with a sympathetic expression.

Alfred thought for a moment, and then gave in. "All right..." he said.

"Excellent!" said the First Officer, clapping his hands. "You should be finished by the time Artisius gets back."

Alfred sat in the chair. He pressed the boot up buttons and initiated start-up procedure with automated ease. He knew exactly what he was doing.

After a short time, he picked up the needle and asked with time-honoured precision, "Permission to log in?"

"Permission granted," snapped the First Officer with a smile.

Alfred inserted the needle into his implant and the world dissolved into colour and light. It was the same as every other time, except for one thing. This time, he had a companion. He had the voice in his head.

"YEESSSSS."

Alfred felt a jab of pain in his head. The interface across his vision was malfunctioning too. There were artefacts across it. He zetted as best he could, but he was hounded by the voice in his head. It kept up a constant chatter with him. Some of it was intelligible; some of it was simply gibberish. He knew something was wrong, but he could not stop now. He had to see this through. He had to survive.

"We will be such friendsss."

Alfred screamed.

Chapter 26

Artisius strode back down the docking tube from the *Green Dragon*. He had completed his rear guard action to protect the straggling parts of the Solar Solutions fleet that had been damaged in the combat. The *Green Dragon* had ducked in and out of cloaking to avoid the Collective Zone scanners and prevent an overload of the cloaking system. He had also been spying on the communications of the Collective Zone fleet and had some interesting things to tell the First Officer Edward of the *Silver Ark*.

He was greeted by a couple of guards as he exited the airlock into the *Silver Ark*. They nodded their respect and then escorted him to the command deck and the bridge.

As Artisius entered the bridge he was met by First Officer Edward. "What did you find out?" Edward asked with anticipation.

"Well...Our fleet is spread out over a large area, and I tried to save as many ships as I could; but we lost another two to engine failure and they have been captured by the Collective Zone." Artisius paused as Edward grimaced. "It gets a bit better," Artisius continued. "The command of the Collective Zone fleet seems to be split. They are commanded by CEO Uxus on the *Old Monarch*, that we know from his past open broadcasts, he's basically their motivating guidance, but their tactical brain is Fleet Commander Boltha on the *Iron Bastion*. I overheard and decrypted what they thought were secure radio messages between the two ships where they were arguing over the tactical strategies for the upcoming assault on Neptune. And Boltha was complaining about bombing Europa. She wanted to pursue us, but Uxus ordered the retaliation and bombing. Boltha was livid."

Edward listened intently and did not interrupt as Artisius explained the situation. After Artisius fell silent, he asked. "What were their plans for attacking Neptune?"

"That's the interesting part. They don't exactly know how to do it. They know we've sent a message back, and they know it will be heavily guarded, but they just hope to bludgeon their way in and use firepower to their advantage. They seem to think Gunter is still in charge; most of our fleet still thinks that too; and the Collective Zone are relying on his incompetence." Artisius finished and stood awaiting a response.

"...Gunter still in command..." whispered Edward. He paced up and down while looking at the floor. "What would you recommend regarding Gunter?" Edward stopped pacing in front of Artisius and looked him squarely in the face.

"I recommend we keep him locked up for now, then when we cryo-sleep he can cryo-sleep with the fleet. If we unthaw him before the final battle it will look like he's still in control and the Collective Zone might become careless..." Artisius paused, thinking.

"But who will command?" asked Edward. "I mean for real?"

"You?" Artisius pointed.

"No...no...I can't; I can command a ship, not a fleet." The First Officer shook his head. "Could you?"

Artisius looked a little shocked. He had never thought he could command a fleet. "Wouldn't I be better running defence from my ship?"

"You can do that, but command from your ship. Its speed will be an advantage; you can see the whole battlescape from where you are. The *Green Dragon* can accommodate the command of the fleet? It has the capacity?" the First Officer asked.

"So, you want me to manage the defence of Neptune and run attack runs?" Artisius laughed. "You don't have small ambitions for me."

"Look Artisius." Edward looked candidly at him, "I know your ship has some kind of blanking mechanism that prevents it from being seen by the Collective Zone. It's how you escaped Europa and ran that rear guard action I asked you to do. I was testing you. I don't know what it is your ship has, and I don't want to know, but you can use that, can't you?" He finished still staring at the captain.

Artisius thought for a bit and then answered simply. "Yes...I think I can do that."

"You'll have to, if any of us are to survive," said Edward tapping his friend on the shoulder.

"It's a cloaking device," said Artisius coolly.

"I see," replied Edward, just as coolly. "And how did you get it?"

"That I cannot say, but I can say that the Collective Zone wants it...and would kill for it."

"Then you'll have to kill back," said Edward. "You sure you can't tell me more?"

Artisius shook his head. "When were you planning to cryo-sleep?" asked Artisius, changing the subject drastically.

"In the next few days," said Edward. It was clear he understood the change of topic, but he did not press the issue. "Then we'll wake up about 100,000 kilometres from *Neptune Prime* and organise a defence. Our engines are faster so we should have about a few months to prepare before the Collective Zone fleet hits." An aide came to Edward's side and asked him something. "Now if you'll excuse me, I have to manage this ship. Your friend finished

224

zetting an hour ago and went for a walk on the rear observation dome if you want to catch him. Good luck, my friend. March on." And with that Edward returned to commanding the *Silver Ark*.

Artisius stood for a moment. He felt the weight of responsibility weighing down on him. He had been given command of the whole Solar Solutions fleet and defence of *Neptune Prime*. He had never anticipated this. He hoped he could live up to the expectations of all those who were depending on him.

"March on," he said quietly, and left the bridge. He was worried about Alfred zetting again, but that was not his main concern right now.

***

Alfred stood, staring out into the space behind the *Silver Ark*. He was in the rear observation dome which had a great view behind the ship, but the bridge of the ship partially obscured the forward view.

"Interesting, isn't it?"

He had been here for about an hour. The voice was fully integrated into his consciousness now. He felt the pain in his head from the last zet. It had been a bad idea. He felt rotten. His implant burned. He had forgotten so much now that he had forgotten what he had forgotten. He did not know if he would survive until Pluto. One more zet might just kill him. He knew that, but it was all his body craved.

"Addiction's a funny thing."

"So is madness..." he whispered to himself.

"Indeed."

He heard the noise of footsteps behind him. He turned and saw Draz and Artisius approaching. The observation dome was rather large. They approached through a staircase in the middle of the floor.

"Alfred, how are you?" Draz asked as they approached. "You look..."

"Dreadful?" rasped Alfred.

"Well, you're no artwork," Artisius said with a laugh.

"I'm, not good, Artisius, Draz. I...don't feel well," Alfred said.

"Do we take you to the medical bay?" asked Draz.

"No, we'll be fine."

"No, we'll be fine..." Alfred parroted the voice.

"We?" said Draz raising an eyebrow.

"Uh...We, as in us..." Alfred said quickly indicating all three of them.

"Nice save."

"Shut up!" Alfred whispered.

Draz and Artisius looked at each other.

"Well, I have some news," Artisius broke the silence. "I've been put in command of the whole Solar Solutions fleet..."

"What!?" blurted Draz and Alfred together.

"Yeah. I know!" Artisius sounded nervous. It was the first time Alfred had heard the man sound truly nervous. He had been anxious before, yes, but Alfred could see that Artisius was stressed.

"Congrats! I think..." said Draz.

"Hrmm...no pressure though right?" said Artisius with a smirk.

They all fell silent and stood looking out at the stars. Jupiter had receded as the fleet broke the planet's gravity and headed into inter planetary space. Some of the Solar Solutions fleet could be seen scattered around them.

"I'd like to thank you both, for your friendship..." said Alfred, not quite knowing where he was going with the sentiment. Silence followed. Alfred continued. "I mean, we might not see each other together after this. Neptune might

226

be it...so I'd just like to thank you for being there when I needed you, both of you." He turned to smile at both of them.

"We've been good friends to each other," Draz said. "If it all ends I'll be proud to have called both of you friends. You helped me through some tough times. And if either of you get yourselves killed I'll never forgive you." She smiled.

Artisius laughed. "I'll be flying my ship in the Neptune engagement. You two can stay on the *Silver Ark*, it'll be safer. And yes, thank you both for showing me that I could take a side and be a better man."

"But don't think that it'll all be over, Alfred, we still have to get to Pluto and get your implant treated." Draz looked at the zetter with caring eyes.

"Yeah..." Alfred said absent-mindedly. He was staring out into space. He had forgotten most of what had happened to them all by now.

There was more silence. It was clear to Alfred that they all wanted to express what they meant to each other, but had no idea what to say. So they stood, silently, looking into space.

"Well, I need to get to my ship to prepare for cryo-sleep," said Artisius. "You two stay here. I can't have you two rattling around in my ship when I have to command a fleet."

Alfred and Draz looked a little hurt at this statement.

"Oh, don't look like that. You know you'll be safer on the *Silver Ark,* and we still have some time at Neptune before the Collective Zone will arrive," he paused.

Draz lunged at him and gave him a hug. It caught Artisius by surprise and nearly pushed him over, but he rallied and reciprocated with a tight embrace.

"All right, all right," he said untangling himself from Draz's arms. He turned to leave and said over his shoulder, "March on, both of you."

"March on!" Draz and Alfred repeated back to him. They knew he was right.

"Where did you hear that?" asked Alfred as Artisius was leaving.

"Edward said it to me a little while ago. I thought it was good and appropriate..." And he left without further protest.

Alfred and Draz were left on the observation platform. They stood for a while in silence, just watching the stars.

"We'd better get set up for cryo-sleep," said Alfred.

"Erch, I still hate it," said Draz.

"Come on." Alfred turned to go.

Draz waited a little longer and then followed Alfred down the stairs and towards the cryo-storage banks.

"How touching."

Chapter 27

The Solar Solutions fleet made its way back through the Solar System in a headlong retreat. They had out distanced the Collective Zone and because of this most of the crew could safely enter cryo-sleep.

Gunter himself, willingly went into his cryo-pod and slept away the shame of what had happened. He had agreed to be awake during the final battle, but not take any part in giving orders. He had been informed that Artisius was taking control of the fleet, and had welcomed that news in a melancholy way.

Cranmere had disappeared from the running of the ship. He had retreated from all positions of responsibility and simply taken to fawning over his CEO. When the incompetence and inability of Gunter had been exposed, Cranmere's position had become untenable. He was the second in command of the Solar Solutions Corporation, but he relied entirely on Gunter for his power. Now that Gunter was unseated, Cranmere's star had waned. The First Officer had taken over control of the *Silver Ark*, something Cranmere should have done, but did not; and many of the crew were thankful that Cranmere had run away after his lord, rather than take command.

It was still unclear what would happen to Gunter and Cranmere should the battle of Neptune go well for the Solar Solutions forces; if it went badly, the outcome was pretty self-evident.

Artisius stayed aboard his *Green Dragon* and ran some final defensive actions before, he too, gave in to the solar slumber.

Alfred and Draz remained on the *Silver Ark* and had their assigned quarters and cryo-pods. They were anxious as to what was going to happen around Neptune, because if the Solar Solutions Corporation was overthrown, there would be some very dark days ahead for the Solar System.

Alfred, of course, cared differently from Draz. He was a Solar Solutions citizen. It was his home and way of life that was under threat. Draz, on the other hand, was originally from the Collective Zone, but she had seen what her Collective could do and had definitely renounced all ties to it.

***

The Operations Deck of *Neptune Prime* had received the message from the Solar Solutions fleet about the debacle at Jupiter and the need for Neptune to prepare for the worst.

A Council of War was called, in the absence of the CEO Gunter and the COO Cranmere. They debated the necessary steps that had to be taken to defend their home.

The boardroom was full apart from the CEO and COO's chairs.

"We must initiate the final plan!" wheezed the Fleet Officer. "Our fleet must be so much stronger than the enemy's forces! I demand that the reserves be conscripted to build more ships!"

The room erupted into disagreement. After a minute, it calmed down again, and another voice was heard.

"No, no, no. We must use the conscripts to build and crew extra gun turrets on *Neptune Prime*. If we draw them in then annihilate them with firepower. Our ships will never stand up to the Collective Zone fleet. They've always had better ships!" yelled the Chief of *Neptune Prime's* Defences.

The room erupted into chaos and insults again, as it had a dozen times before as the board debated what to do and when to do it. It was a chaos of democracy. The board did not have their commanders and as such, there was no set hierarchy as to who should obey who.

"Ladies and gentlemen, please!" An icy voice cut through the chaos and everyone, almost instantaneously, fell silent. It was the voice of Chief Weapons Officer Michael. He had arrived unnoticed to the meeting and had remained silent until now. Everyone respected him. He was old, with at least one longevity surgery, but no one knew if there were more. He had sat in silence years earlier when Gunter had taken them to war; now was his time to speak. He walked with a walking stick and had a limp. "Ladies and gentlemen," he repeated calmly. "I believe we need to come to a decision so that we can prepare for the next approximately two years before the fleets arrive. We need to be ready."

Everyone nodded in agreement.

"Well then," Michael continued, "I believe if we strengthen our fleet, we have the better chance. We can also boost the defences of *Neptune Prime*, but if they get that far, we are rather in a problematic situation. We need to defend in depth. We need to lure them in and then hit them from the flanks. They will try to reach and bombard *Neptune Prime*, so we need to prevent them from doing that." He fell silent.

The boardroom members looked around at each other. They could not find fault in this argument and nodded their agreement.

"Will you take control of the defences?" said the Fleet Officer.

"I will, if the board room tasks me with this. I still have a few years left in me yet and should be able to muster our forces to meet our retreating brethren," the CWO said. His voice slicing through the layers of fat on the Fleet Officer and making the Fleet Officer shift uncomfortably in his seat.

"I think the board room agrees that you would be best suited for taking charge of our defences?" The Fleet Officer looked around. "With a show of hands?" And with that, the entire boardroom raised their right hands, and the motion was carried unanimously. The Chief Weapons Officer would muster the defences of *Neptune Prime* as he saw fit.

"Well, I think we all have our jobs to get on with. We know that in two years we must not be found wanting," said the CWO. The boardroom shifted uneasily again. And then the boardroom members filed out to put into place the plans that had to be done for the upcoming battle.

The CWO stood looking out of the boardroom windows when the others had left. "We will be ready. We will not be found wanting. We must prevail," he whispered to himself. He was not sure whether he was talking to some unknown force and asking for assistance, or just trying to convince himself of his own purpose. Whatever the case, he had his doubts. They had two years to prepare, but if the Collective Zone had been so successful at Jupiter, how would the Solar Solutions forces stand up to them here?

He sighed. He had hoped that he would not see war again, but humans forget, and they always seem to want to play soldiers.

He looked out across the surface of Neptune and out into space. "We must prevail," he said again, before turning smartly on his heel and limping, with the aid of his walking stick, out of the boardroom and down to his office where he would put into action the defence of *Neptune Prime*.

***

So, the years went by. The Solar Solutions ships crawled through space closely followed by the Collective Zone ships, which did not give up the chase.

Thanks to the orbits of the planets, Neptune was the closest planet to Jupiter and so the distance was closed in only two years.

As the years went by, the defences of *Neptune Prime* were bolstered and improved. Ships and fighters were churned out from the dockyards and new weapon emplacements were built on to the bulk of *Neptune Prime*.

The building of the defences was undertaken earnestly and well under the guidance of the Chief Weapons Officer. The defences were the best they would ever be, given the circumstances and the resources available in two years work.

The New Defence Fleet as it was known comprised of a new carrier, a few new cruisers and half a dozen destroyers combined with a full complement of fighters for the carrier. It was an impressive build given the limit of time. There were no ships the size of the *Silver Ark* though, which bothered the CWO, as in the report it said that both main battleships of the Collective Zone were on the way. The problem was another *Silver Ark* would have taken all the resources for the two years and then that would have been it.

Whatever the misgivings, the New Defence Fleet was ready, and it glittered in the cold light of the distant Sun. It hung around the newly bolstered *Neptune Prime* and waited to join the fight. It would be used as a last line of defence in the defence in depth. This meant that the Solar Solutions fleet would draw the enemy in and hammer them as they came and then give ground and do it again with the last line of defence as *Neptune Prime* itself.

After two years travel, the Solar Solutions fleet was nearly back at Neptune, and the final battle for their Corporation was going to commence. They still had a few months before the Collective Zone caught up with them. They began to bring their crews out of cryo-sleep and prepare for the upcoming engagement.

As the Solar Solutions fleet rearmed and repaired around Neptune and waited for the Collective Zone to catch up, Artisius kept the *Green Dragon* away from the prying eyes of the Solar Solutions command in an attempt to preserve the secrecy of his cloaking device.

The Solar Solutions board knew he was their new admiral and they let him keep his distance. They could always question him when time was less pressing.

Chapter 28

Artisius stood in his quarters. The room was cool and dimly lit. He had dressed in his full dress uniform. His medals were on show on his breast. His brace of pistols was on his belt. He stood in front of the window of his quarters that looked out over the hull of the *Green Dragon*, his ship. In the distance, he could see the lights of the Collective Zone fleet and closer he could see the glittering forms of the Solar Solutions ships that had been arrayed in a defensive pattern around *Neptune Prime*.

He breathed heavily. He tried to steady his breathing. He was...afraid. He realised he was truly afraid. Not necessarily for his own safety, but on him lay the fate of the Solar Solutions Corporation. If he failed in his duty this day, then the history of the Solar System would be written for the worse.

Artisius was not a religious man. He never had been. He did not believe in investing in the Corporation to save yourself. He did not think that the latest incarnation of religion in the Solar Solutions Corporation was the best way to inspire people. The Church was misguided in its application of faith. Faith, he thought, should be about hope, not profit. Even so, he looked out the window into the vastness of space beyond and he caught his mind playing on the thought that perhaps, just maybe, he should ask for help from something bigger than himself or any of the soldiers involved in the coming fight. Maybe, just maybe, something out there would listen. He shook his head, that was nonsense he knew; but he could not drive the thought entirely from his mind.

"Just a little help..." he said. "We're going to need it...Help me be a good man..."

Artisius moved to the mirror in his room. It was a full-length mirror that stretched from ceiling to floor. He checked his uniform in it. He checked his medals and braid. Everything was in order. The dress uniform was partially about vanity. It was partially about showing off, that was true. Artisius knew that he was a vain man. But it was also about status and show. He had to show his crew that he was the Supreme Commander. He had to act the part. War was part show and if he did not look the part then his crew would not be inspired to fight as hard as they had to. If he looked his best, they may be inspired to fight just that little bit harder.

"It's time..." he whispered and left his quarters and headed to the bridge.

As he walked along the corridors, he stroked his fingers across the walls. He moved from left wall to right wall and back again. He knew all too well that this might be the last day of his command of his ship.

He felt the vibrations of the engines and reactors through the wall and his fingertips. "Okay, Old Girl. I need you to perform this time."

He paused before the bridge doors. He adjusted his tunic. "Let's go," he said and stepped onto the bridge.

"Captain on the bridge!" snapped the First Officer.

Artisius mounted the command dais and stood as the First Officer reported on the situation.

"Sir, the battle lines are prepared. The ships have been arrayed in a defence in depth pattern with the *Silver Ark* in the centre. The Collective Zone will find it hard to break through to *Neptune Prime*. What are your orders?" The First Officer of the *Green Dragon* stood to attention in front of Artisius, who stood in a commanding position on his dais.

Artisius stood silently for a moment. He stood with legs apart and with his hands behind his back. He had his eyes closed and he breathed steadily. He knew this time would make him or break him. He had no idea whether he would see the end of the day or which side would win. But he knew that he would give it his all and he demanded that his crew and his fleet, yes his fleet, would give their all in the upcoming engagement.

"Sir, it's time. The Collective Zone ships have lit up our scanners. They're moving in," the First Officer spoke authoritatively.

A smile crossed Artisius' features. His eyes were still closed. "Prepare a communication channel for the fleet. I have something to say..."

***

Draz and Alfred stood on the main observation dome on the *Silver Ark*. It was empty of people except for them. The crew of the *Silver Ark* were all at their war stations. The dome was not the rear one that looked backwards and not the one that was part of the bridge, but the one that was in the centre of the dorsal part of the ship and had a good view out on the surrounding space.

"I think it's a little unfair that we're not on the *Green Dragon*...I wanted to be there in the fight! I don't want to just sit around and watch!" said Draz, sounding a little annoyed.

"I'm sure he has his reasons," said Alfred. He waved a hand to dismiss the thought.

"Yeah, true. He doesn't want us rattling around him as he's commanding," Draz said with a laugh.

Alfred chuckled too.

They fell silent quickly though, both aware of the gravity of the situation.

"I hope we win," said Alfred.

"I hope Solar Solutions wins too," said Draz, looking at Alfred.

"Sorry," Alfred said noting the different use of words, "I keep forgetting you're from the Collective Zone...I keep forgetting a lot these days..."

"That's all right," Draz said, smiling. "How is the memory?"

"Pretty shit. Now it's at the stage that I've forgotten what I've forgotten so I don't know how much I've forgotten...if that makes sense? The injections don't work so well since we got out of cryo-sleep." Alfred said, sounding annoyed.

"Yeah, it does," said Draz with worry in her voice. "Do you remember how we met?"

"Um...maybe?" Alfred said. "Somewhere on Earth? Shit..." he trailed off realising the extent of his memory problems.

Draz did not know whether to correct him or whether that would make things worse. "Close, the Earth Moon," she said after a time.

"Ah...right, of course," Alfred said. It was plain he could not picture it.

Draz regretted bringing up the memory problems. "Don't lose heart. We'll head to Pluto and have the problem fixed." After a short pause, she changed the subject. "The Collective Zone shouldn't be able to get through all this!" She waved her hands at the surrounding ships.

"I just hope we survive this day," said Alfred.

"So do I. So do I..." whispered Draz. "So do I..." They fell silent for a while and brooded on their own thoughts.

"Do you think it weird, that in all this, in all this majestic wonder," Alfred broke the silence and waved his hands to indicate the stars, "humans still insist on killing each other? I think that's weird."

Draz smiled at her friend. "Humans often can't see past their own noses." They fell silent again.

Draz noted that in the anxiousness of the upcoming battle and having nothing to do in it stoked the fires of her addiction again. It had been a while since she felt the pangs of withdrawal, but now she did. She bit her lower lip to try to ignore the pangs. It did not work. She looked back out into space; at the surrounding ships; and the incoming enemy fleet.

"What's wrong?" asked Alfred. He had turned his head to look at her.

"Oh, just withdrawal. The feeling is back. Don't worry about me. I'll be fine..." She smiled at him again.

"Oh...right..." Alfred said. It was unclear to Draz if he even knew what she was feeling withdrawal for. She did not press the issue.

They stood, staring out into space for a time. Then Artisius' voice was beamed throughout the fleet.

***

Artisius stood on the bridge of his ship and delivered the speech of his life. He knew he had to inspire the people who were fighting under him to do their utmost. He had thought through what he wanted to say earlier in his quarters, but, due to his repressed anxiety, the speech seemed spontaneous.

"People of Neptune. People of the Solar Solutions fleet. This day will forever determine the fate of our Solar System. For if we lose, then the Solar Solutions Corporation will be no more. Everything you know will change for the worse. I speak to you as leader of the Solar

Solutions fleet; as a guardian; as a comrade. This day your corporation needs you to fight. But fight, not for me, nor for your CEO. Fight for your friends; your family; for the person next to you. There is nowhere else to retreat to. This is it. Our home is a speck in the cosmos. But it is just that: home, and for it, we must be willing to give our all. Go forth this day to victory. Victory needs you to fight, and fight like demons!" Artisius fell silent. The speech had had the desired effect. He felt the electrification of the bridge as his words fell upon the ears of his soldiers. They had all stopped their tasks and turned to face him. In their faces he saw hope, and fear.

The communications were cut when Artisius indicated and there was silence on the bridge. Artisius spoke to the First Officer and another communications channel was opened to just the *Green Dragon* and its crew.

"Men and women of the *Green Dragon*, you just heard my speech to the whole fleet, but now I speak only to you. I know you will all do your duty, but there may come a time in this battle where I require you to go beyond duty; where I require everything from you; where I require your very lives. In that moment, and you will know when it is, I will need you to follow my orders to the letter instantly and without question. You know me; and I know you. We have flown for a long time together, and I know that you will follow me into the jaws of Hell and back. Be with me this day. We must prevail!" Artisius fell silent for a second time and the communications were cut. That speech had been improvised, but it had had the desired result.

Artisius surveyed his bridge. The crew had returned to their tasks. "Activate cloaking device!" snapped Artisius. The bridge went into red light and the *Green Dragon* disappeared from the scanners.

***

Draz pointed out towards the fleet. "The fleet is moving," it was apparent as the Solar Solutions fleet began to move towards the incoming Collective Zone.

Chapter 29

Fleet Commander Boltha paced the bridge of the *Iron Bastion*. She ran a hand through her stubbled hair. She paused mid bridge and looked out of the large bridge windows and then started pacing again.

"Ma'am?" asked the First Officer at her elbow.

Boltha kept pacing and watching out of the windows.

Arrayed around the *Iron Bastion* was the entire Collective Zone fleet. Many of the ships damaged at Jupiter had been repaired during the pursuit to Neptune and the fleet was almost at full strength again, bar the few losses during the last battle. They had even managed to capture and salvage some Solar Solutions ships and add them to the fleet. The *Old Monarch* was off to starboard. Ahead of them were the lights of the Solar Solutions fleet.

"We've burned most of our fuel in our reactors to try to catch up with their better engines. If we don't win this day, we'll never get home..." Boltha whispered to herself.

"Ma'am?" came the word again. It was a little more forceful and demanding this time.

Boltha stopped in front of the large central window of the bridge. Her piercing eyes shone.

"Ma'am, CEO Uxus wants to communicate." The voice of the First Officer was now rather exasperated.

Boltha waved her hand in acknowledgement and the communications link crackled to life.

"Boltha? Why are we waiting?" came Uxus' voice.

Boltha grimaced in annoyance. "We've been through this, CEO. Don't you trust me? We've got to be careful of our fuel, now that we've used most of it to keep up with the

Solar Solutions fleet." Boltha was tired of Uxus' undoing her command. Her voice was strained.

"Boltha, don't push me!" The voice was cold.

"CEO, I don't have time to wage war and assuage your ego at the same time. Let me do my job! Now I must address my soldiers." With that she indicated for the communications with Uxus to be cut and redirected to the entire fleet.

"Men and women of the Collective Zone fleet, begin the assault!" It was not a rousing speech, but Boltha was not one for speeches, as her soldiers knew. She found no need for them. They wasted time. War was time for action, and action demanded few words.

Boltha stood on the bridge and felt the engines of the *Iron Bastion* through the vibrations in her feet. The Collective Zone fleet began to move out in an assault pattern towards the Solar Solutions fleet.

There would be no traps or tricks this time. It would be a slog of fleet versus fleet. There would be no fancy tactics and no bluffs. The battle would play out faster than the battle for Jupiter, as both sides knew that this was it, and the Collective Zone would need to press the attack fast.

The Solar Solutions fleet was on home soil and well prepared. Boltha knew that the Collective Zone fleet would find it hard going. But she knew that she had the best soldiers in the Solar System under her control. They would always remember this day, for it would decide the fate of both the corporations. Both sides would be tested to the limits, and she hoped that her soldiers would not be found wanting.

As the fleets closed with each other they began to open fire. It was apparent that the distance was closed too fast for the Solar Solutions to deploy its bombers. Boltha had calculated that in to her plans. But soon enough fire burst across both fleets as guns and missile pods opened up and casualties soon began to mount. Reports came in from different ships of the damage that they had suffered. It was an endless chatter of reports from her aides.

Boltha believed absolutely in her soldiers and her skill. Yet this did not stop her from feeling nervous before the fight, due to the stakes involved. Once battle was joined however, she felt calm.

She barked orders to her crews while striding back and forth confidently on the bridge. "Go to it! Charge them. Break their defensive formations where our ships can take them on, one on one, where our guns are better! Smash them aside! Smash them to pieces!"

As the battle raged, Boltha's old heart stirred. She chuckled to herself. She loved war. It was a terrible thing; but she knew she loved war.

***

Uxus smarted from the slap in the face by Boltha's communication. Acting Commander Tyyz stood at his elbow. It was clear that she wanted command and it was clear that Uxus wanted to give Tyyz command. But Boltha was definitely the better and more able and experienced commander. Uxus knew this, so he endured the insolence of Boltha while he fumed.

He was still the head of the Collective Zone and without him then the Collective Zone would fall apart. He was technically the CEO, and they could easily appoint another, but no member of the board was even capable of commanding as much respect and obedience as he was. He knew this well. He had engineered it to be that way.

His crews still worshiped him; he could detect that from the bridge crew of the *Old Monarch*. As he moved around the bridge, he noted the lowered eyes and the hush that preceded him. Uxus liked this reverence. It fuelled his ego.

Acting Commander Tyyz waited at his elbow and followed him around. "Orders, CEO Sir?"

"Stay close to the *Iron Bastion*. Keep the fleet together," Uxus paused. "Follow Boltha's lead." He knew what he was saying, that Boltha was the better tactician. He was the figurehead, and she was the military tactician. It burned him to admit this, but he wanted victory and so had to endure it. He would have plenty of time to give orders once the Solar Solutions fleet was broken. Then he would give his orders to destroy *Neptune Prime*.

"CEO Sir!" Tyyz replied with a salute and hurried off to relay the orders.

Uxus smiled as he watched out of the bridge windows at the growing battle. Today would be a good day, he thought. It would see the end of his foes.

"Today we see the end of the Solar Solutions Corporation." He smiled and urged his bridge crew on.

***

The Collective Zone fleet charged at the Solar Solutions ships hoping to break their defensive formation and split the ships apart so as to deal with them individually.

Artisius commanded from the cloaked *Green Dragon*. He stood on the command dais in the dull red light of low power mode. The Scanning Officer barked his reports to him of what was happening throughout the fleet. He barked back orders that were relayed to the rest of the fleet.

"Damn it! Don't split up," he said to himself. "I know what you're doing." He stared out the observation dome of the bridge and saw the two fleets clash in momentous action. "HOLD THE LINE!" he shouted. The command was beamed to the Solar Solutions ships.

Artisius cursed that the *Green Dragon* itself could not take part in the combat as the cloaking mechanism means that if he fired the guns he would be revealed. However, the ability to go unnoticed into the Collective Zone fleet and report on their movements outweighed this drawback; he hoped.

The Solar Solutions fleet was weathering the storm reasonably. It had started to bend at the outer limit. This was to be expected as it was facing the entire might of the Collective Zone warships, but the majority of the fleet was holding position.

Artisius looked back at *Neptune Prime* behind them through the observation dome. He hoped that his command and the guts of the Solar Solutions soldiers would be enough.

"Sir! We've lost a ship!" cried out the First Officer.

Artisius spun around to see a flash out to starboard and then a massive detonation as one of their ships' reactors went critical and overloaded. The nuclear fire blossomed across space in what was a beautiful but terrible blast. It signalled the death of many soldiers.

"Which one was it, Lothar?" Artisius' voice was muted and solemn. He thought of the dead.

The First Officer paused. The captain had never used his real name in combat before. It was apparent that he was taken aback by the honour.

"Lothar!?" yelled Artisius.

"Uh, it was the *Gleaming Spear*, sir!" The man was clearly stunned by his captain.

"Damn, that was a large cruiser..." said Artisius.

The bridge had fallen silent at the news of the destroyed cruiser. Artisius barked for them all to return to their duties and keep him informed of what was going on; chaos returned.

"Send us in deep into the enemy fleet. I want to see what they're doing there!" Artisius commanded.

The *Green Dragon* angled for the centre of the Collective Zone formation. After a time, it came to a halt near the *Old Monarch* and *Iron Bastion*. They filled the bridge's observation dome and hung menacingly in space; their great mouths of launching bays in the front.

"If only I could hear what you're saying. If only I could hear your orders..." Artisius said as he studied the massive craft.

"Sir, their communications are newly encrypted. We have no idea what they are relaying, and they don't know what we're saying, and it would take hours to break the encryption for both sides, and we would have to divert a large portion of the onboard computer away from combat duties. We listened in during the rear guard action, but they've changed their codes now, and so have we..." snapped the First Officer.

"Yes...I know..." said Artisius. "But wouldn't it be wonderful if we could hear them? The advantage would be enormous. If only we had hours..."

Artisius stared intently at the bulky ships at the centre of the Collective Zone formation. He knew that the *Green Dragon* and her crew could do nothing at this point in time about the two main capital ships in the Collective Zone forces. He would have to wait until they made their attack before he ordered any form of assault.

"Sir, our right flank is starting to fail!" yelled the First Officer.

This snapped Artisius from his reverie and pondering and brought him back to the moment.

"Divert three destroyers from the centre!" he bellowed. "I hope that will be enough. We can't start buckling now. We can't!" he whispered to himself.

"Yes, sir!" Lothar transmitted the order to the Communications Officer, who was frantically intercepting and relaying information to and from the *Green Dragon*.

"Take us to the centre of our line!" Artisius ordered. His order was obeyed without question or delay.

Soon, they were back at their battle line. It was a chaotic mess of auto-turret and missile fire from both sides combined with various little craft zipping around and fighting each other. The *Silver Ark* still had not yet committed to the fight yet; similarly, to the *Old Monarch* and *Iron Bastion*, it was biding its time.

The whole fleets had moved toward each other, but the main carriers of both sides had not engaged. Artisius had said that First Officer Edward only commit the *Silver Ark* on Artisius express orders. This had not gone down well with Edward, who, understandably, wanted to fight. But Artisius had his tactical plan, and he would stick to it. If he committed the *Silver Ark* too early, then there was the risk of it being destroyed and that would mean the end of the Solar Solutions Corporation.

At least Artisius hoped he knew what he was doing.

Suddenly another Solar Solutions ship went supernova. It was close this time. The blast just missed the *Green Dragon*, but the light from the explosion blinded everyone on the bridge for a moment, before the remains of the destroyed ship boiled away in the ether. There were no survivors.

"That was the--" began Lothar.

"--the *Great Wisdom*...I know..." Artisius finished the First Officer's sentence. It had been a large cruiser. The Collective Zone had now destroyed two ships to the none destroyed by the Solar Solutions. Sure there were damaged ships on both sides, but in this meat grinder and battle of attrition, the main thing was destroying ships.

248

Artisius did not like this sort of battle. Slogs of attrition wasted lives and ships. He preferred grand sweeping actions and tricks that preserved ships and soldiers' lives. This grind was brutal and visceral; and the Collective Zone was winning with its better warships.

There was another explosion. This time it was from a Collective Zone destroyer. It blew up a distance to port from the *Green Dragon*. The bridge crew, on seeing this, cheered for an instant before returning to their duties. Artisius did not chastise them for cheering. He too had welcomed the development. The bridge crew needed their victories, wherever they came from.

"That's one to two, now..." Artisius whispered. "Take us above the battlescape! I want an overhead view!" he yelled to his crew. They responded instantly, wheeling the *Green Dragon* up and above the disc of combat. The ship rolled over and paused, hung above the combat zone, which stretched for many kilometres in every direction.

The *Green Dragon* hung there for some time, watching, waiting. Artisius, from this perspective, could give orders to his fleet below with precision and not risk being hit by stray shots.

In the period of half an hour, there were another two ship explosions: one Solar Solutions and another Collective Zone.

The three ships sent to bolster the right flank had worked. They had stopped the collapse of that sector, for now.

"Sir! Our centre!" blurted Lothar.

Artisius' eyes snapped to the centre of the combat. The *Old Monarch* and *Iron Bastion* were on the move! They had ploughed into the combat with the Solar Solutions ships and were sweeping them aside like confetti.

"Send in the *Silver Ark* and her support ships!" ordered Artisius. He did not yell the order. He said it with solemn realisation. He knew that this was going to be the deciding action of the combat. He knew, he had ether just doomed the Solar Solutions Corporation, or saved it.

He saw the engines flare on the *Silver Ark* and her five support destroyers. They began to move.

Chapter 30

OE15 waited in the briefing room of the *Silver Ark*'s fighter squadron. Since they had been stationed around Neptune, the squadron had replenished its losses from the Jupiter engagement with fighters and pilots from *Neptune Prime*. They waited for their scramble order.

He still had not made any friends in the squadron. It was hard as he was normally a bomber pilot. The other fighter pilots viewed him as crude and unsophisticated. Even though he had shot down three enemy craft in the Jupiter engagement, the pilots of the squadron did not want to get close to him.

OE15 thought this was probably for the best, as many of them would likely die in the coming fight and as such maybe making friends was a bad thing. He knew that he had made friends with his co-pilot on in the bomber squadron, and when she had died, years ago, at Jupiter, he had wished that he had never gotten close to her.

"GDE78," he whispered her name to himself. He had never known her real name; obviously he had not gotten close enough; so, the assigned name would have to do.

He sat by himself in the squadron waiting room next to the hangar. It was below the briefing room. The pilots sat in their vacuum suits with their helmets off and positioned on their chairs with the oxygen canisters close by. They had to be ready for a moment's notice to scramble and intercept incoming enemies.

They waited. OE15 was bored. He hated the waiting. He just wanted to be in space and fighting. Why must there be all this waiting? He thought. Damn the Collective Zone just launch a fighter or drop ship attack or something. He cursed silently to himself. He knew that they had to wait until the enemy launched something because of the fighters' low fuel load. They could only be in the combat zone a short time; therefore, they could not mount patrols. So, they had to wait.

AA3 moved amongst his pilots. He was the only one who did not seem tense. He was also in his flight vacuum suit and carried his helmet in hand in an easy and nonchalant manner. OE15 could not believe that he could be that calm. He must be hiding something.

AA3 stopped by OE15 and asked him. "You all right, son?"

"Yes, sir," replied OE15 looking up at the man. He was lying. He just wanted to get into action. It was obvious that AA3 knew this, but he nodded, patted him on the shoulder and moved on without another word. They were all on edge. They all just wanted to get out there and fight.

They had been waiting for about an hour when suddenly the sirens went. The klaxon sounded and, like a startled animal, the pilots flinched in their seats and then with a word from their commander, they dashed for their fighters. As the pilots ran, they pulled on their helmets. They had their oxygen canisters slung across their backs.

OE15 reached his fighter and climbed awkwardly into the pilot's seat. He stashed his oxygen canister behind his seat and connected the tube to it while fixing on his helmet. He triggered the canopy close button and the angular canopy closed on him. He heard the thud as the canopy sealed.

He began the start up procedure as the other pilots began theirs. When all the pilots had climbed into their cockpits and had stashed their oxygen containers and attached their helmets to them, there was another siren for warning and then the oxygen was sucked from the hangar, and the gravity disengaged.

OE15 heard the rush of air leave the hanger and his fighter and then there was silence. He thumbed the engine start button and checked the instruments. The twin engines of his fighter came to life on his command, and he felt the rumble through his seat.

"We're after the boarding ships. That's our target," came the voice of AA3 over his radio headset. "Ignore anything else, the Collective Zone carriers have launched a bunch of boarding ships and they're headed for the *Silver Ark*. We need to stop them!"

OE15 replied, as did the other pilots, "Yes, sir!" and the fighter pilots increased their throttles and rocketed out of the hangar bay and into open space.

As OE15's fighter cleared the entrance of the docking bay, and emerged into open space, he took in the battle scene around him. There were auto-turret lasers arcing everywhere and missiles from missile pods roaring past silently and impacting with great explosions on other ships.

He saw the burning wrecks of some of the Solar Solutions ships too and he shuddered at the sight of the burning hulks as they careened through space out of control.

"Watch your scanners," came the voice of AA3. OE15 looked at his instrument panel while keeping the formation. There was nothing yet except the signatures of the larger craft around him and stretching off into the Collective Zone fleet. The smaller boarding craft would not appear until they got closer.

The fighters took up a defensive pattern around their host ship. They knew that they could not let the boarding ships through.

Soon a number of smaller blips appeared on the scanners. "Sir, targets quadrant 1!" came the cry from one of the fighters.

"I see them," replied AA3. "They're our targets. Let's go!"

The squadron banked and turned and angled itself towards the incoming boarding ships. In a few moments, they had cleared the protective cover of the capital ships.

Smaller, defensive auto-turret lasers tried to target them, as did the flak batteries from the Collective Zone ships. OE15 had a number of close calls when flak burst a little too close to him and he felt the impact of the small shards of metal impacting on his craft.

"Not again," he said. "Not now!"

"Target incoming ships," ordered AA3. "Launch missiles on my mark."

OE15 selected one of the enemy ships on his scanner and selected a missile. He waited for the locking tone. It sounded loud and clear in his headset.

"Mark!" cried AA3.

OE15 loosed his missile, as did all the other fighters. The 12 missiles streaked out from the flight and OE15 saw them corkscrew away as the formation of boarding ships broke up and took evasive action.

Some missiles hit home and there were some silent explosions in the distance. But only a few missiles did that, most seemed to have been deflected by countermeasures or evasive manoeuvres.

Then they were on the boarding craft. The fighters had closed the distance rapidly.

"Hunt and engage! We've broken their formation," was the order from AA3, and OE15 knew that he could now break formation and start searching for a target for his guns.

OE15 spiralled his craft around and locked onto another boarding ship on his scanner. It was now in front of him. He could see it in the distance. The missile tone sounded, and he loosed two missiles this time.

The craft ahead began to take evasive action and jettison countermeasures, which fooled one missile, but not the other. The second missile hit home, and the boarding craft blew up in a fiery conflagration and shards of wrecked metal.

OE15 let out a cry of delight, but checked himself when AA3 told him to maintain radio silence unless it was necessary to talk.

He had three missiles left and then his guns. OE15 looked for another target.

***

Trooper Althar and Lieutenant Vauz sat side by side in the boarding craft as it ducked and weaved through the hail of fire on their way to their target. They were headed for the *Silver Ark* again; and this time they would capture the bridge!

Althar cursed as the craft went into a tight turn and a new welding drill, this time with more armour on it, that sat bulkily in the middle aisle between the seats, shifted and put its full weight against his legs. He pushed it back into place in the middle of the craft. He hoped that there would be less use of the drill this time, but just in case they had stowed more drill bits than last time.

They all checked their weapons in a tense manner over and over. All the soldiers knew that they had loaded guns and that their munitions were stowed on their belts, but they checked them again and again anyway. Except for Vauz, he sat calmly with his one good eye closed and simply breathed hard. The mechanical eye cut through the gloom with its red glow.

They had their vacuum suits and helmets firmly fastened. As before, there would be no atmosphere when they drilled into the side of the *Silver Ark* and so they would need all the protection from space that they could get. Althar hoped that they would not have to drill through every door and so there would be some atmosphere further in to the craft. But he checked his helmet seal again, just in case.

"We're almost there!" yelled the pilot from the upper section. "Get ready!"

"Right, soldiers, you heard the pilot! On your feet!" bellowed Vauz as his good eye snapped open while unbuckling his harness and jumping to his feet at the head of the landing craft.

The other soldiers followed suit and Althar stood behind his commander. He grabbed one corner handle of the drill and three other soldiers grabbed the other corner handles. They would run it into place this time rather than pushing it along the ground.

Althar felt for his rifle slung across his right shoulder. It felt hard and bulky, even thought it was low calibre to prevent unnecessary hull ruptures. He knew soon that it would be hot from firing. This knowledge calmed him a little. But his stomach still churned with nerves.

"You'll be landing near the bridge this time!" yelled the pilot back into the craft. "Hopefully it will be an easier job to capture!" After a few more seconds he said, "Here we go!"

Althar felt the drill section on the front of the landing craft spin up as it was made ready to bore into the side wall of the *Silver Ark*, and then a few seconds later there was a loud crash and a screeching of metal on metal as the drill section bit deeply into the side of the hull of their target. The jolt threw many of the soldiers off balance, but Vauz

256

and Althar stood firm and held on to the side of the landing craft with their free hands.

The welding drill in Althar's hand nearly careened down the aisle of the landing craft with the jolt but the press of soldiers kept it in place. Althar heard some cursing as thighs were bruised as the drill shifted in the movement.

After a few seconds, the boarding craft's front drill had cut through the side of the *Silver Ark*, the ramp at the front of the landing craft snapped down and with a rush, the atmosphere was sucked away.

This was it! With a surge of bodies and a cry of war, the soldiers from the landing craft rushed out of the mouth of their craft and into the corridors of the *Silver Ark*. There were a number of other landing barges that had landed in the same area and the soldiers from those were streaming into the rooms and corridors that had been breached.

Vauz ran in first. The loss of atmosphere had taken the *Silver Ark* crew in the area by surprise and a number were dead from loss of oxygen and exposure to space. But the emergency bulkheads had already closed, and the sirens had sounded, or so could be told by the flashing red lights on the walls. They would have company from the Solar Solutions soldiers soon.

With practiced precision, Althar hefted the welding drill into position on one of the bulkheads without having to be told what to do. He began to drill away with the assistance of a number of other soldiers.

"Where are we?" Althar asked while moving the drill. His voice sounded strained.

"Near the bridge! The pilot got it right," said Vauz, scanning for enemies.

"Excellent," cried Althar. "Excellent..." he whispered. He focused on his task.

Suddenly the door he was cutting through opened, and a hail of fire burst across the Collective Zone soldiers' positions. A number of Collective Zone soldiers fell.

"What the...?" blurted Althar as the drill cut out when it had nothing to bite into. "Are they making it easier for us?"

"Forward!" bellowed Vauz. Without another word, the platoon surged through the open door and forced the Solar Solutions soldiers back. The boarding teams bit down on their stim-units and energy flooded their systems.

As the platoon crossed through into the room beyond the bulkhead that had opened on its own. The soldiers brought the welding drill through and then Vauz triggered the bulkhead controls and it shut behind them. With a rush the atmosphere returned to the section of the ship.

With the sudden return of air, there was the sudden return of sound. The din of battle caught Althar off guard. But, as a trained soldier, he raised his rifle and let out short bursts of fire into the defended positions of the Solar Solutions forces.

"Bring up the drill, we might need it!" cried Vauz. "Take the fight to them!" It was hard to hear him over the din of the fighting.

The Solar Solutions soldiers had taken up a position in front of what looked like the bridge's doors, which were sealed, and they were firing upon the invaders from that position through the two open bulkheads that led up to the bridge.

There was little cover for the Collective Zone, and many soldiers fell trying to get into cover at the edges of the open bulkheads.

Vauz was on one side of the nearest bulkhead and Althar was on the other. They had left the drill in the passageway, as it was impossible to take cover with it.

"We'll have to clear them away from the bridge door and then bring the drill up!" yelled Vauz.

Althar had a headache from all the sound of gunfire. He nodded within his helmet.

They did not need their helmets but none of the soldiers dared take them off in case the sector depressurised again.

"Is that the bridge?" yelled Althar.

"Looks like it!" bellowed Vauz. "Come on soldiers, after me!" And with that, he aimed his pistol around the edge of the bulkhead and loosed off shot after shot as he ran down the corridor towards the cover of the next bulkhead.

Althar shook his head in disbelief, but followed his leader without question; loosing shot after shot as he followed. The rest of the remaining platoon followed them down the corridor in a press of bodies. Many fell to the concentrated fire of the Solar Solutions weapons.

The Collective Zone platoon managed to fight its way to the bulkhead before the doors to the bridge. They took cover behind the edges of the bulkhead that protruded from the walls of the doorway.

The Solar Solutions soldiers were putting up a desperate defence behind hastily constructed barricades of crates in front of the bridge doors that looked locked tightly shut.

Vauz hefted a grenade and smiled to Althar. "Be ready to run back and get that drill..." He primed it and threw it into the group of enemy soldiers.

There was a scrabble and a halt in firing for an instant and then a deafening explosion as the grenade went off.

The Collective Zone soldiers surged forward and inspected the damage, guns blazing. All the Solar Solutions soldiers in the section were dead.

"Now, that drill," said Vauz calmly, while he tapped on the bridge doorway.

Althar sighed and with three other soldiers ran back and hefted the drill to the bridge door. He was breathing hard as he approached.

Althar brought the drill up to the surface of the bridge door and turned it on. It made a horrid, high pitched, whining noise, which he had never heard in a vacuum. He began to drill through the door.

"This one's for Grox," he whispered to himself as the drill bit deeply into the metallic surface.

Suddenly there was a burst of gunfire as more Solar Solutions soldiers came in as reinforcements to the fallen bridge defenders. The Collective Zone soldiers took up a defensive position around the drill. They could not fail this time!

Chapter 31

Draz and Alfred watched the battle unfolding around the *Silver Ark*. They saw large explosions ripple across its surface as barrages of missiles and auto-turrets scarred and pock marked its surface. The beast of a ship was hurt but definitely not crippled.

The *Silver Ark* gave as good as it got, they observed. It fired its main batteries and missile launchers at the enemy ships that were ahead of it. The battle was a slogging match.

"We can't just stand here..." Draz said. She moved anxiously on her feet.

"Why not? We're not soldiers..." said Alfred.

"You mean you just want to sit this out?" Draz snapped incredulously. "We've been watching the fight for some time now. I want to get in there. I need to do something!"

The pair fell silent again and watched some bulky boarding craft duck and weave between the defensive lasers and flak and bury themselves in the hull of the ship not far from where they were standing.

Suddenly an alarm sounded. It was a warning klaxon. It was followed by an automated warning, "Warning! Hull breach! Warning! Bridge under attack!" It wailed a few times and then cut off.

"The bridge!? That's near here. We have to help!" Draz grabbed Alfred by the arm and hauled him out of the observation dome towards the bridge.

After a few steps Alfred shook free of his persuader and announced. "All right, all right." Draz looked at him as if he was a child.

"Look, regardless of your memory and implant damage, you can still fight. This is the fight of our generation. Every hand is needed. What do you reckon Artisius would think if he knew you were not pulling your weight?" Draz lectured Alfred.

"I said all right!" Alfred snapped.

They ran down the few dozen corridors to where the firefight was taking place in front of the bridge doors. They heard the combat from a long way off and it became deafening as shells were being exchanged in cramped metal corridors.

Draz and Alfred rounded a corner and came face to face with the muzzle of a raised Solar Solutions rifle.

"Whoa! We're friends," Draz blurted out to the officer and he lowered his gun.

Draz pulled Alfred down behind an upturned crate that was being used as a barricade at the side edge of the landing that stretched out in front of the bridge. There were a number of Collective Zone soldiers operating a crude drill that was trying to force open the bridge door. They were under constant fire from both sides and were taking cover by the drill.

"What's going on?" barked Draz to the officer.

Alfred peeked over the barricade to see what was going on.

"They're trying to break into the bridge!" snapped the officer.

The troopers near him started to return fire to the drill crew on the landing.

"We've got them pinned down," the officer continued, "but we're also pinned down from their support fire. The bridge blast doors are closed but they won't hold forever. That drill looks nasty and it's armour plated, unlike last time. We can't take it out with guns or grenades."

"Do you need us to do anything? We can help!" Draz asked.

The officer looked from Draz, to Alfred, and back to Draz, who nodded grimly.

"You?" the officer chuckled.

"Told you we should keep out of it..." sighed Alfred.

Draz was incensed. "I've not come all the damn way across the Solar System," she paused to grab a rifle off a nearby wounded soldier, "lost my Collective, my mind, and my profession, been imprisoned, and aided your stinking little Corporation," she turned to the officer, "just to be laughed at!" She stood up and braved the flying bullets and snapped of a few sharp shots at the swarming Collective Zone taking cover near the bulkheads, felling three of them. She ducked back into cover. "Now...you were saying?"

Alfred looked stunned.

"What?" Draz asked Alfred.

Alfred held up his hands in mock surrender and in actual fear.

The officer smiled and began to laugh. "All right, you can fight with us. You already have a gun now. How about your friend?" The officer indicated Alfred.

"Give him something...like a pistol. He can shoot that," Draz looked over the barricade again while the officer gave Alfred a pistol that he had an awkward time holding. The drill was still going with a high-pitched noise. "How long do you think the bridge has before it's breached?"

"Thirty to sixty minutes...maybe. It's the thickest bulkhead bar the hanger doors. We learnt from some captured soldier named Grox that the Collective Zone wanted to capture the bridge, so we were able to close the blast door in time when the enemy soldiers landed," responded the officer. "What's your name, fighter?"

263

Draz was a little taken aback by the question, but she answered. "Draz, and this is Alfred," she indicated the man on the floor next to them. Who are you?"

"Pleased to meet you, Draz, Alfred." He nodded to both of them. "Name's GammaOmega897, GO897 for short."

"I think we're past assigned names now, GO897...what do your friends call you?" asked Draz peeking over the barricade and ducking down as a hail of bullets snapped past her head.

GO897 was silent for a minute, then responded. "Mark...name's Mark."

"Nice to meek you, Mark. Now, I have a plan. I just need Alfred and me here to outflank their position and we can come up behind them. At the same time, I will need your troops to push from both sides of the bridge doors and we should be able to trap them where they are." Draz nodded towards Mark.

"We tried that, and they fought us off. But you're welcome to try yourself." Mark grimaced.

"We have to try. Otherwise, what else is there?" Draz snapped a salute to the officer, grabbed Alfred, and scuttled away with him down the corridor in a direction that should lead them to a junction behind the Collective Zone soldiers.

After a few seconds of scrabbling out of the way of bullets, Draz and Alfred got up and ran as fast as they could down a parallel passageway to the one the Collective Zone soldiers were stuck in. They came to the junction where it joined the other passageway and they slowed to a crawl so as not to alert the Collective Zone troopers.

Draz and Alfred were breathing hard from the exertion and the stress of nerves. Alfred held his pistol awkwardly; Draz gripped her rifle determinedly. They looked around a corner and saw a number of Collective Zone guarding the rear approach to their column. They were clearly alert and were prepared to be ambushed.

Draz held up a hand with fingers outstretched and began to count down from five. Alfred indicated he knew what this meant with a nod. He readied his pistol and gripped the trigger.

Draz's hand reached zero fingers and both of them poked their guns around the corner with as little of them exposed as possible and let fly with bullets.

The noise was deafening. The effect was spectacular. Five or six soldiers fell before they were able to mount any form of defence. Alfred and Draz ducked back behind the corner when bullets began to fly their way. They had begun the counter attack.

Draz's ears were ringing, and she assumed Alfred's were too as he kept trying to drill out his ears with his fingers while stretching his jaw open and swallowing hard.

She smiled at him. "Fun, huh?" she mouthed.

He looked at her sceptically. "Shut up," he tried to say. Yes, he was deaf.

They tried again: ducking out from behind the corner and letting fly. Three more soldiers fell this time. But this time it looked as though they were sending soldiers to deal with the small counter attack.

Draz's hearing began to return, and she heard the heavy booted footsteps of some soldiers approaching on their position.

"Time to move," she said. She grabbed Alfred and they rushed off down the corridor again in an attempt to find another junction to attack from.

They found another one further down the corridor that was further away from the Collective Zone soldiers. They rounded the corner and let fly with bullets just as the small squad reached their old ambush point. They were taken by surprise, and all fell wounded and screaming.

"This is getting too easy..." said Draz.

Draz spied a few large objects being man handled up the corridor. They had large warnings on them and looked like explosives. She was not able to see that easily, but she reasoned that they were heading for the bulkhead of the bridge in order to blow it open.

"They're willing to sacrifice themselves to blow up the bridge." She clicked her fingers. "The bridge is the only thing that matters."

"What?" shouted Alfred. He was obviously still deaf. Draz cupped a hand over his mouth, silencing him from alerting the Collective Zone soldiers.

"We need to get back. They'll blow the door and everything around it into space if those bombs get there!" Draz mouthed.

It was apparent that Alfred did not really understand, but he nodded. They ran back up the parallel corridor and back to the barricade and Officer Mark.

"Well?" Mark asked.

"We killed some, maybe five or eight; but they're man handling explosives up the corridor. They'll blow the whole bridge into space. The drill doesn't matter. They're planning to blow themselves up and the bridge as well," Draz said.

Mark nodded while Alfred took cover and looked distracted as if he was hearing someone speak. "Then we need to stop those explosives." Mark said.

"Do you have enough firepower?" asked Draz.

"It seems," Mark looked at her carefully, "we do now."

Draz smiled. "Just give the word and we'll attack!"

"No. No. This is a job for us soldiers. You've done enough. You give us covering fire." And he barked a few orders to his surrounding soldiers.

Draz and Alfred nodded. He could hear again. They prepared to give covering fire for the Solar Solutions counter attack.

Draz's pulse raced. She had lost all cravings for her drug of choice. She smiled and laughed. She was born for this. She gripped her rifle tightly. She was ready. They launched the attack.

Chapter 32

"It's no good," whispered Artisius to himself. He could see that the Collective Zone fleet was bludgeoning its way through the Solar Solutions fleet. "It's impossible..."

"Sir," snapped First Officer Lothar. "Our centre is giving way. The *Silver Ark* cannot hold everything!" The man sounded panicked and exhausted. They had been zipping around the fleets unnoticed and giving orders for hours now.

Artisius did not envy Lothar's position; he had to obey all orders and take the stress of them failing at the same time. He was not in the position of command, yet he took the risks of failure.

Artisius focused his gaze on the centre of the battle line. He saw the *Silver Ark* being pummelled by auto-turret and missile fire. And he saw that landing barges had buried themselves into the area just near the bridge. Things were not good. Things were not good at all.

"How's our right flank?" Artisius snapped. He flinched as an auto-turret laser scored a path almost through their bridge. They were still cloaked he had to remind himself. He had to be careful where he positioned his ship.

"Holding, but battered, sir!" came the reply from the Scanning Officer. He sounded ragged and tired too.

They had all been working like demons and were stressed beyond anything that they had ever done before. Nevertheless, Artisius knew that his crew could take the punishment. He trusted them absolutely; and he felt proud to be in this position with them. He knew they would not let him down. He knew that they would not let themselves down. Artisius smiled at the thoughts. This was what he lived for.

"Send the two cruisers there to the centre line!" he snapped. "Leave the remaining battleship where it is along with the destroyers. We can't have them lapping around our flanks. But we cannot lose the centre." He paused and then whispered, "We can't lose..."

The crew jumped on this latest order and radioed frantic messages to the two cruisers that Artisius had ordered into the centre. Artisius saw the two ships, after a moment's delay, begin to turn and set a course to rendezvous with the *Silver Ark* in the centre of the battle line.

Artisius watched the Collective Zone battle line trying to respond to the latest development. He grimaced as the Collective Zone ships in the centre were also reinforced by ships from the depleted flank.

Artisius cursed the skill of Commander Boltha. He knew it was not Uxus that was in command. Uxus was the figurehead; he did not have the tactical genius to command this situation.

Artisius watched the *Iron Bastion* and the *Old Monarch* surging through the centre of the Solar Solutions' battle line. They were pressing the attack. He swallowed hard. If only he knew which one Uxus was on, he thought. Uxus would be on one, but he had no idea which one for this battle. Uxus had been on the *Old Monarch* when he had run rear guard actions around Jupiter, but he could have changed position, and Artisius knew that he could not fight off both main carrier battleships.

He saw the central battle line beginning to fail again.

"Where are our reserves?" roared Artisius. He had not come this far to lose now.

"There's none, sir," said First Officer Lothar from the centre of the bridge.

269

The bridge seemed to go silent for an instant as the realisation of what that meant sank in. Artisius' stomach churned. They were losing. They were losing and there was nothing he could do.

There was a flash from the centre of the Solar Solutions battle line that lit up the surrounding space and flickered across the faces of the *Green Dragon's* bridge crew. The *Silver Ark* had been hit with an auto-turret in its auxiliary fuel tanks and they had burst into the open space and ignited on the oxygen that leaked from the dozen gashes in its flanks. There was a colossal but silent blast and then the damage reports began to come in to the *Green Dragon's* command about what had just happened. The *Silver Ark* was wounded, but not out of the fight yet.

"Sir?" Lothar asked quietly standing in the centre of the chaos.

"We're not done yet!" shouted Artisius. "Bring us near the *Iron Bastion* and *Old Monarch*!"

***

CEO Uxus smiled. From the bridge of the *Old Monarch,* he could see the carnage and, even to his untrained tactical eye, he could see that Boltha was winning the day for him.

He strode up and down the bridge. The *Old Monarch* was on the starboard flank and slightly behind the *Iron Bastion*. Most of the enemy fire was concentrated on the *Iron Bastion* and his flagship was left well enough alone. He smiled wider.

Acting Commander Tyyz was always at his side, ready to relay orders from him to the ship's crew. However, that was unnecessary as Uxus, against his own will, had restricted himself from giving orders and given the full tactical command to Boltha. He knew that this undermined his command, but it also meant that they would win. He could claim the glory later.

"CEO Sir!" snapped Tyyz. "The Solar Solutions forces are on the ropes!" She sounded delighted.

"I see it, Tyyz," Uxus snapped. He had an idea. "Open a communication channel to all the Solar Solutions ships in this area; all of them, unencrypted. I want them to see my benevolence.

"Yes, sir!" Tyyz ran over to the Communications Officer and then signalled to Uxus that he was live.

"Members of Solar Solutions, you have lost. Do not prolong your suffering. I offer you a peace deal. Surrender; lay down your arms, and I will let you go. All I want is control of your space. I can find no fault with those who know they are beaten and give in to save themselves. They are the sensible ones. Please, end your suffering; surrender and you will be given clemency. Resist further and I will destroy every single one of you. I leave this decision up to you and your commanders. We will continue to press the attack until either you stop fighting, or we destroy you. Your CEO Uxus out!" Uxus terminated the message. He felt magnificent. He had just ended the unnecessary bloodshed. They would surely see reason and stop fighting.

"CEO Uxus?" crackled the communications. It was Boltha. "I see what you are doing, but was that a totally unencrypted signal?"

"Yes, Boltha. I needed to speak to all the Solar Solutions people." Uxus sounded annoyed at the pestering.

"Well, CEO, you just gave away that you were on your ship. You see, if the message was unencrypted, they can trace it straight back to where it came from. You have now become a target." Uxus could hear the smile in Boltha's voice as she instructed her leader.

Uxus' pulse quickened with a twinge of anxiety. He realised what he had done. Suddenly the shots that were aimed at the *Iron Bastion* were now impacting on his ship.

"Well, this ship can take it, they have nothing left to fight with anyway!" snapped Uxus and the communications went dead.

Uxus snarled. He felt embarrassed. He had not thought of that problem. But he brushed it aside. The Solar Solutions forces would surrender as their ships were broken and swept aside.

***

Fleet Commander Boltha smiled to herself. She noticed some of her crew smiling too. Even though they were in the heat of battle and stressed, her little victory over Uxus had buoyed her spirits. Also, it was nice that the fire from the Solar Solutions ships was impacting on his ship not hers now. Nevertheless, Uxus was right, there was no chance that amount of fire was a threat to either of the two carrier battleships. They simply brushed it aside and forged on, slowly but surely.

"Port batteries, target that destroyer!" Boltha indicated out the port window on the bridge.

In an instant, the port batteries flashed, and the destroyer was engulfed in missiles and auto-turret lasers as the shots hit home. The destroyer rolled with the impacts, and it was clear that it was rendered out of action. It was dead in space. The *Iron Bastion* bridge crew let out a cry of delight at the sight, before settling back down into the rigours of combat.

Boltha did not chastise them for lack of discipline. They had earned a little celebration at every victory. Soon the Solar Solutions home planet would be in range and then the Solar Solutions forces would most definitely surrender. They could not keep fighting with nothing left.

"How many ships have we knocked out of action?" Boltha spun to face her First Officer.

"Thirteen, ma'am. With another six damaged," the First Officer responded.

"And our losses?" Boltha asked calmly.

"Nine ships, but most of those are light cruisers, destroyers, or frigates. Only one battleship is destroyed with another two heavily damaged. And our two flagships are only lightly damaged," the First Officer replied with precision.

"Good. Carry on," Boltha replied.

Even though the carnage was on both sides, the Collective Zone ships were prevailing. Boltha moved to the front window of the bridge, which had a good outlook on all aspects of the battle. She saw the *Silver Ark*, and beyond that, the target: *Neptune Prime*. She smiled to herself again. This was a good day.

Chapter 33

Gunter watched the battle out of the window of his private room. He had tried the doors time after time; they were still locked. Cranmere had been waiting on him and attending to him while he had been imprisoned in his own ship. Cranmere had been bringing him food and drink; non-alcoholic drinks, Gunter resented, but he welcomed the attention from one that he had previously written off as a lackey.

Cranmere was still loyal to his leader even when all others had deserted him. The guards at the entrance to his room, who let only Cranmere in and out, mocked him as he passed between the doors. But Cranmere was loyal, and he paid them no heed.

If Gunter got out of this situation he would have to decide what to do. He could clearly not continue as CEO of Solar Solutions, if Solar Solutions continued to exist after this day. If Solar Solutions won, he would have to resign and take up some business job somewhere. He could employ Cranmere, he laughed. If Solar Solutions lost, he knew he would meet a far grislier end at the hands of the Collective Zone. He did not like to think of Cranmere's fate in those circumstances.

Cranmere was not in the room. He had just delivered some food and water and made a humble retreat.

Gunter had at least thanked them for letting him cryo-sleep through the long journey to Neptune. He had no idea what he would have done if they had kept him awake and locked up over the two-year journey. He had been escorted to and from his special pod by guards.

Gunter had felt the impacts and explosions on the *Silver Ark* through the floor and walls of his suite that was now his cell.

He paced back and forth in front of the large window. His mechanical leg protested under him as it changed direction. It needed maintenance but that was out of the question at a time like this.

He was dressed in one of his business suits. It was a bit shabby; the tie was not quite done up correctly; and his shirt was untucked. But he did not care. Who else would care? Cranmere seemed to look at his leader wistfully and mournfully every time he came in. Maybe he should tidy up for him? Gunter laughed at the thought. His one true follower and now one true friend was a man who Gunter himself had dismissed as a...as a what?

A large explosion on the hull of the *Silver Ark* shattered his reverie and Gunter snapped back to the window. He craned his neck around and saw a large plume of debris blasted out from the side of the ship. It was near his quarters, but it did not threaten the integrity of his room's atmosphere. In fact, Gunter's private quarters had their own atmosphere generators and bulkhead doors to seal off in case anything nearby was breached. Only a direct hit could harm him. He almost hoped for a direct hit.

As Gunter watched the breach further down the hull, he saw a number of Solar Solutions soldiers sucked out into space from the hole before the flow of atmosphere was halted by various blast doors deploying and sealing off the damaged area. He saw them writhe around and cough their last as their bodies were ripped of all oxygen and their blood boiled in the zero pressure of space. They writhed and silently screamed for a few seconds, and then their unprotected bodies froze and stopped moving.

The bodies of the soldiers drifted past Gunter's window, close enough for him to see their frozen, agonised expressions forever set on their faces. They drifted past; and Gunter shuddered. Maybe he did not want a direct hit on his quarters after all.

Then Gunter heard his opposition CEO's ultimatum. It crackled over every communication network throughout the fleet. Gunter listened despairingly. It was evident that whatever happened after the battle, win or lose, he was finished. He had lost his corporation.

He turned from the window and walked over and sat on his large bed. He sat there a little time before reaching under the bed, which stood on legs about ten centimetres off the floor. He pressed a few secret buttons that only he knew about and then there was a small click as a compartment under the bed was released.

Gunter stretched his arm under the bed and reached inside the compartment and pulled out a small pistol. It was loaded, he checked. It held six bullets in a small antique revolver way. It was ornate and coloured bright silver. It had detailed inlay and carvings in its surface. It had been his father's.

Gunter rolled the pistol around in his hands. He gripped it tightly and then softly. He did not want to do this. He felt he had no choice.

He raised the pistol to his head. He waited. He knew that the longer he waited, the less likely he was to do it. He waited. He wondered whether he wanted to. The speech by Uxus came back to him. He tightened his grip. He waited.

After a few tense minutes of staring out the window from the edge of his bed he lowered the pistol. He could not do it. He waited too long. He put the pistol on the nightstand by his bed. He had let his corporation down utterly, but he could not give up on it. He knew he could not abandon his people and his life entirely. He had to face what he had wrought; it would be a coward's way out if he ended it now.

He stashed the pistol under the bed again. He reasoned that he might need it later, and he did not want Cranmere or the guards to know about it.

He stood up again, and while eating the meal Cranmere had brought in earlier, he watched as his corporation fell apart through the portal on the wall of his room.

**

OE15 spiralled after an enemy fighter. He had used all his missiles and so was left with guns. He squeezed the trigger as the fighter moved under his crosshairs. His tracer bullets indicated that he missed his target as it screamed out of the path of the projectiles.

"Shit!" he swore and followed the fighter around in a fight turn. It was just out of his crosshairs. "Damn it, damn it!"

The pair of duelling combatants roared over the hull of a nearby Solar Solutions cruiser. OE15 had been so focussed on his target that he had broken formation with the other *Silver Ark* fighters and gone off course. But a number had done that already. It was difficult to keep formation in such a mess of swirling ships and combat.

The target in front of him consumed his attention. So much so, that OE15 did not, at first, notice the burst of tracer fire over his canopy. It took a second to realise that he, in following this enemy fighter, was now being followed by another enemy and was under attack himself!

OE15 broke off the pursuit of his target and jammed the control column into his stomach. He tore out of the line of bullets that whipped past him and performed a loop. But there was no enemy where he thought there would be: at the base of the loop.

Again, tracer flew past his canopy, and he felt it impact the aft of his fighter. He felt the smashing of large projectiles as they ripped through the metal. The enemy had followed him around in the loop and was still behind him. OE15 desperately tried to out manoeuvre the Collective Zone fighter.

He radioed for help. "This is OE15, I'm hit! I need assistance!"

"I see you on my scanner, break left, and I'll get him!" it was AA3's voice. OE15 never heard a more welcome sound. He followed the instruction.

Suddenly AA3's fighter roared out of the mess and blew the Collective Zone fighter to pieces.

OE15's celebrations were short lived. He noted that his left engine had lost power and his right was failing. His controls had been hit by the flypast too.

"Sir, I have to return to base, I've been shot up!" he radioed. He began to panic as his controls responded sluggishly.

"Permission granted; you fought well today!" AA3's voice echoed in his headset.

OE15 cursed as he flew towards the *Silver Ark*. He was damaged and a sitting target. He hoped he was not noticed by the Collective Zone.

It was just like the flight back from the Jupiter bombing raid. OE15 was tense. He managed to hold his failing fighter on course and line up with the docking bay on the underside of the *Silver Ark*.

As he passed into the hangar bay, he felt the tug of gravity as he lowered his landing gear and crashed into the floor of the landing bay. The landing gear collapsed and as his remaining engine failed, he skidded to a halt on the metal floor.

He saw tech-slaves running up to his craft in an effort to extricate him from the wreck of his fighter.

The hangar was still in vacuum and as he was prised out of his cockpit, he lifted out the oxygen canister from behind his seat. He staggered out of the craft with the aid of the tech-slaves. He turned and saw the wrecked machine still smoking on the landing bay. It had been a good machine. Now it was inoperable. The landing gear had gone, and one engine was riddled with holes.

The tech-slaves were working in the cockpit. They were busy shutting the craft down and making sure it was safe. They then had the unenviable task of moving it out of the way of less damaged craft that had to land to refuel and rearm.

The tech-slaves ushered him away.

When he got past the airlock into atmosphere, he was assessed by some medical personnel. He shook them off. "I'm fine," he insisted.

He got to the debriefing room and harassed an orderly who was doing some menial task. "I need a new ship! Where is one?"

"We have no spares, sir," the orderly replied. "We have no more reserves."

OE15 sat down in a chair heavily. He was out of the fight. They had no more fighters, and he had just lost his.

"Any chance of a bomber sortie?" he asked.

"No, sir. We can't risk filling the hangar with bombers and bombs while the fighting is so close and the fighters come back now and then to refuel and rearm," the orderly replied, and then went back to filling out some forms.

"And so, I'm out of the fight..." OE15 breathed a sigh of disappointment. He felt tired. He felt so, so tired. He had been racing on adrenaline for hours. He felt like he had abandoned his commander.

So, he sat, and waited, while listening to the explosions that burst upon his parent ship.

Chapter 34

Captain Artisius observed the battle. The *Green Dragon* hung in space a good dozen kilometres above the melee. He could see that the Solar Solutions forces were losing. They were being brushed aside by the inexorable advance of the Collective Zone forces. There was the *Old Monarch* and there was the *Iron Bastion*, both forming a sledgehammer that was slowly smashing through any resistance put up by his soldiers.

His soldiers, he grimaced as the thought crossed his mind. It was his responsibility. The loss was his fault. His plans had been incomplete. His preparation had been imperfect. They all looked to him for hope and salvation and he had let them down.

There was the *Silver Ark*. It was battered, but resolute. It stood against the two Collective Zone carrier battleships like a rock in a stream. Nevertheless, even rocks are worn down by the waters that they hinder.

Artisius knew that Alfred and Draz were on that ship. He knew he would not; he could not, let them down.

The Solar Solutions fleet had fallen back and formed a last cordon around *Neptune Prime*. There was the *Silver Ark* and only a few other cruisers and destroyers with the last battleship, the *Voyage of Hope*. Artisius smiled grimly that that was the name of the last battleship that was still functional.

Most of the other Solar Solutions ships had been rendered inoperable through engine or reactor damage and been abandoned or worse, blown apart through combined fire from the Collective Zone onslaught.

The Collective Zone had sustained heavy losses too, but both the main capital ships were still functioning and there were half a dozen large ships with them along with a number of smaller ships. They just had the military edge over the Solar Solutions ships.

Artisius breathed hard. He tried to calm himself. He closed his eyes. His breathing slowed and his heart calmed itself. "I am ready," he said. He knew what he had to do.

Due to the unencrypted broadcast, Artisius knew that CEO Uxus was definitely on the *Old Monarch*; and if that ship were destroyed, the Solar Solutions forces had a chance to capitalise on the confusion. His little ship alone did not have the firepower to destroy such a large target. Artisius knew what he had to do.

"Sir?" It was the First Officer. As Artisius had opened his eyes, the First Officer had stood to attention in front of him.

"Do you trust me, Lothar?" asked Artisius.

"To fly through Hell itself, sir!" replied the First Officer without hesitation.

"Do the crew?" said Artisius.

"Without doubt! What do you have in mind?" Lothar looked sideways at his captain.

"All I ask is that the crew follow me without hesitation and with the utmost loyalty when I ask it of them..." Artisius trailed off.

"That they will do, sir. Your orders?"

"I need a communication link to the bridge of the *Silver Ark*," ordered Artisius.

"Achieved, sir!" said the Communications Officer after Lothar had carried the order.

"Edward?" Artisius said.

"Sir!" it was Edward's voice.

"I am going to do something, something unthinkable, but it will provide an opening for our ships to fight back. I will need you to lead the fleet. Carry the message to the fleet. They will need to respond to my signal. You'll know what it is." It was a short order, but clear.

"Lead the fleet? But, sir?" Edward sounded unsure. He then continued, "Yes...yes, sir!" It was clear that he knew not to question Artisius' plan; he simply obeyed. The communication ended.

"Now I need a direct link to Draz and Alfred..." Artisius' voice faltered a little. After a nod from the Communications Officer, Artisius continued. "Draz, Alfred?"

"Yes, we're here." It was Draz's voice; she sounded strained, and tired. "I'm just helping Alfred to the med bay on the *Silver Ark*. Relax," she cut in before Artisius could ask; "he took some shrapnel in the leg while we were defending the bridge, but he'll be fine."

"Yes, I'll be fine, ah shit it does hurt though," Alfred swore and Artisius laughed. It was a sad laugh.

"What's up? You coming back to us?" Draz sounded hopeful.

"I'm afraid that might not be possible. I have to do something. I have to end this. I have to make sure the Solar Solutions Corporation has a chance to survive. It's not looking good out here..." Artisius trailed off.

There was silence on the end for a bit. "You're not going to do something stupid?" Draz said, strangely resolved, as if she knew the answer already.

"I fear I have to..." said Artisius quietly.

Alfred's voice came over the line with Draz swearing in the background and cursing Artisius' name. "She's worried about you, she cares for you, we know you mean the best for us. What are you planning."

"I can't say in case the Collective Zone is somehow listening, this is encrypted, but it must be a surprise until the last moment, but remember this: I hope both of you live long, happy lives in peace, and that this stops the carnage. Alfred, I know you're suffering, but don't give up. Your condition can be treated. And Draz, you're stronger than you realise. You're one of the strongest people I know. Don't slip back into drugs. You know where that leads. Stay strong, stay safe. You can rely on each other." Artisius fell silent.

Silence greeted him for a while; even Draz had stopped calling him names. After a time Artisius heard, "Do what you must...I will remember you...What about the hard drive?" It was Draz's voice. She still had not forgotten. It sounded resolute, but mournful.

"I will take it with me. It's too dangerous to give to anyone. March on, both of you...look to the *Old Monarch*..." And with that, Artisius ended the connection. He had a tear in his eye that he quickly wiped away.

Lothar stood attentively for the next order, but at a respectful distance.

"Now I need a connection to the *Old Monarch*!" Artisius' jaw set and a different, vengeful air came over him.

"Uh...sir?" Lothar was confused.

"Just do it!" snapped Artisius.

"Artisius!" said Uxus' voice over the line as soon as the connection was established. "Come to make peace? Come to beg for your existence?"

"Not really," snapped Artisius. "I have some things to tell you, so shut up and listen. Have you wondered how I've evaded you thus far? I have a feeling you know, like when you detected us appearing and attacking a pirate base near Mars and then chased us. Well, it's because I have a cloaking device, stolen from Atraxa Prime on Earth. It's installed on my ship. It works wonderfully," With a swift motion, Artisius pulled the red hard drive from his breast pocket and regarded it carefully, "I have the plans right here on this hard drive..."

"Why you--" blurted Uxus.

"I said shut up! Now, I also know you're on the *Old Monarch* thanks to your last announcement. And I intend to kill you." Artisius paused.

"Oh? How do you intend to do that? Hand that drive over to me and I could find you a position of power in the Collective Zone...Fleet Commander perhaps?" The voice of Uxus sounded smug.

"I know that you built the cloaking device but had no chance to duplicate the plans. I overheard you saying so as I listened in earlier as I was spying on your fleet. So this is the only copy in the Solar System. I had to be sure of that," Artisius tossed the drive up and down in his hands. "Lothar," Artisius turned to his First Officer, "remember when you said you'd go through Hell for me? I need that now," Artisius said. Artisius' voice changed. "Accelerate to ramming speed! Helmsman, Lieutenant Orthox, aim for the engine block on the *Old Monarch*!" Artisius bellowed.

The *Green Dragon* lurched into movement in the direction of the Collective Zone capital ship in an instant. The Helmsman, Lieutenant Orthox, guided the craft expertly. The crew never hesitated.

Artisius' heart swelled with pride for his brave crew.

"You...WHAT?" yelled Uxus over the communications link.

"Goodbye, Uxus, perhaps you'd like to see your doom coming?" Artisius smiled. He knew that the uncloaked *Green Dragon* would not survive long in the fire arcs of the Collective Zone capital ship, but he did not need long. "De-cloak!"

With a whoosh the bridge returned to normal light and the instruments came back online. And Artisius cut the communications with Uxus.

Out the observation dome, Artisius saw the *Old Monarch* growing larger and approaching fast. He also saw the bursting of flak and missiles around him as his ship approached its target.

Artisius felt calm. He felt proud of his crew. "One last message, Lothar, to the crew." He smiled as Lothar nodded and indicated he was broadcasting to his ship.

"Crew of the *Green Dragon*, you have fought well, and now we are on a one way mission. We will ram the *Old Monarch*, killing CEO Uxus and hopefully saving the Solar Solutions Corporation. I feel tremendously proud to have been your commander. You have all done your duty. You have fought like demons! Captain Artisius, out..."

Now it was Lothar's turn to have a tear in his eye. He wiped it away quickly. Nevertheless, Artisius saw, and smiled.

Captain Artisius stood on his command dais. He adjusted his medals. He checked his epaulettes and braid. He looked out of the observation dome ahead of him at the rapidly increasing size of the *Old Monarch*. Missiles and defence lasers burst around him, but his ship stayed the course. It was as if it knew that this was it and it was not going to let him down.

"Disengage reactor coolant!" bellowed Artisius. His crew responded instantly. The klaxon sirens echoed throughout the ship as the reactor began to overheat and melt down. The *Green Dragon* was now a flying bomb. "March on!" Artisius called to his bridge.

As the bulk of the *Old Monarch* engulfed the observation dome Artisius whispered to himself, "I am a good man."

Artisius closed his eyes and gripped the hard drive tightly. He thought of the refugees in the docking tube on Europa. He thought of all the people he had tried to save. He thought of Alfred. He thought of all the women he had left behind in the Solar System. He offered them a silent apology. He thought of Draz.

***

The *Green Dragon* collided with the engine block of the *Old Monarch* just behind the bridge structure on the Collective Zone capital ship. At that moment, the reactor core of the *Green Dragon* overloaded and exploded, which caused the engines and core of the *Old Monarch* to go critical and detonate with the power of the Sun. Both ships were incinerated in the blast. There were no survivors.

Chapter 35

Through a window Alfred and Draz watched the bulk of the *Old Monarch* disappear in a nuclear flash as the newly appeared *Green Dragon* slammed into the capital ship near the bridge section. They were both stunned. They said nothing to each other for a while. Alfred even lost track of the pain in his leg where the pieces of shrapnel had hit him from a ricocheting bullet.

Alfred's voice in his head stayed silent. He wished it would say something, anything, to make sense of the situation. But it said nothing. For once in the past few years, his craziness said nothing. He longed for the silence to be filled with something, anything...

"He didn't...did he?" Draz whispered.

Draz looked at him. He looked at Draz.

"He did...he really did..." Alfred whispered.

They were not alone in the corridor. It was the main route from the bridge conflict down to the medical section of the ship and there was a steady stream of injured soldiers moving down to the medical bay and reinforcement soldiers moving up to the battle. They had all stopped. They were all watching the boiling fire that was what was left of the *Old Monarch* and the *Green Dragon*. It even sounded to them like the battle at the bridge had stopped. The sound of gunfire had ceased; but Alfred and Draz could not be sure of this.

"What now?" asked Alfred. His awareness of his leg injury had come back, and he winced. The injury was rather minor, only a few pieces of shrapnel in the calf muscle, but it hurt, and it bled a bit.

"I...I don't know," Draz's voice cracked and Alfred, while leaning against the wall where Draz had helped him stand, put a reassuring hand on her shoulder. She closed her eyes.

Alfred turned away and faced the window.

"He was good to us," Draz said. She looked at Alfred.

Alfred nodded; he could not speak.

"Look!" shouted a Solar Solutions soldier near them. She pointed into space near the explosion.

It was clear that the large blast had damaged the *Iron Bastion*. It seemed to be listing to one side and venting atmosphere in a dozen places. It was moving sluggishly. Furthermore, a number of Collective Zone ships that were around the two battleships that had been caught in the explosion were knocked out of action. Their engines were not operational, and they were drifting wildly out of control.

"The old fool may just have done it!" Alfred exclaimed.

"Oh shit!" shouted Draz and she stared out the window. "He may just have!"

They fell silent again in realisation that their friend, and saviour all those years ago, had given his life, and the lives of his crew, to bring them to this moment.

Suddenly down the corridor came a running Solar Solutions soldier. "The bridge invasion: it's over, the Collective Zone forces have surrendered!" he yelled over and over as he ran down the corridors.

Alfred and Draz looked at each other. The guns had fallen silent further up the corridor. They were not mistaken.

They looked out the windows of the corridor and noted that the guns on many of the Collective Zone ships had stopped, and that they were either drifting damaged in space, or milling around seemingly not knowing what to do.

"Have we won?" asked Draz, her voice sounded bemused.

"Maybe!" said Alfred. "Maybe...The enemy ships seem to be giving up. How about helping me to the med bay?" He grimaced.

"Oh sorry, I forgot..." Draz helped Alfred balance as they hobbled down the corridor.

"No problem, so had I..." Alfred replied with a twinge of sadness and also a hint of relief. Maybe it was all over, and he could head to Pluto for his surgery. He did not like to say that he had forgotten much of what he, Draz, and Artisius had done over the past few years. His implant was severely decayed and that it had wiped a lot of his memory. But he knew he had a long history with Artisius and Draz and that was enough to elicit an emotion from him. He knew what they had done was important, even if he did not know exactly what it was.

Alfred wondered if he could get a zet in before he had the surgery. It was a bad thought, but he had it anyway. He knew it was stupid.

"Stupid?"

They headed to the medical section of the ship, and said nothing to each other. They were absorbed in their own thoughts of one of the bravest men they ever knew.

***

"What the hell was that?" shouted Boltha as the explosion of the *Old Monarch* and the *Green Dragon* washed over the *Iron Bastion*, battering it in space as if it were some small insect.

"Ma'am...I...that was the *Old Monarch* going nova. The *Green Dragon* hit it...We're crippled..." gasped the First Officer. He was unsteady on his feet from the shock.

Boltha looked out the windows of the bridge. She saw the fleet around her had been severely damaged. She shook her head.

"Are there any survivors?" she said unsure of herself for the first time in a very, very long time.

"No ma'am, the scanners read none," said the First Officer.

"Shit!" is all Boltha could say for a few seconds. Uxus was dead. CEO Uxus, their master, their CEO, was dead. The ramifications began to sink in.

"Ma'am, other ships are reporting engine failures due to the electromagnetic pulse blast wave; it overloaded their circuits and systems. Many ships are dead in space; others cannot manoeuvre. And--"

"And?" Boltha's eyes flashed with a deadly gaze at the First Officer. She was enraged.

"And." He swallowed. "And some are reporting that...they don't want to fight now Uxus has...died. They're turning around and fleeing or surrendering..." he fell silent under Boltha's sight.

"Damn it! Where's our battle line?" yelled Boltha. "We had them!"

"Ma'am..." the First Officer was trying to get her to see something she did not want to see, "our line is broken. The remaining Solar Solutions ships are pushing back. We have lost."

"We haven't lost until I say so!" Boltha yelled, spinning on her heel and looking out the windows. "Full speed to *Neptune Prime*. It's right there! Bring the cruisers up and flank to the left with the remaining destroyers on their right!" She almost had them, Boltha knew, she almost had them.

"Ma'am, our engines are crippled. Our systems are fried. We are dead in space..." the words of the First

Officer cut deeply into Boltha's pride. She stopped for an instant.

The damaged *Silver Ark* and the remaining Solar Solutions ships in her view began to move out from their defensive cordon around *Neptune Prime* and cut a swathe through the Collective Zone fleet. Boltha saw many of her ships not even put up a fight and surrender on the spot. The Solar Solutions ships took them as prisoners; they captured them. They did not destroy them. There had been enough bloodshed already.

Boltha stood on the bridge of her crippled ship. She slumped as she stood. She was broken. She was defeated. She had lost. They had all lost. Due to one crazed move from a crazed man, they had lost all their advantage.

Boltha knew that morale was everything in war, and that the loss of their CEO had broken the will of the Collective Zone forces to fight.

Now not even she could fall as a soldier. She could not fight until she died. She had to surrender. Boltha knew this, and it cut her deeply. She had always imagined a warrior's death for herself.

"Not like this..." she said to herself.

"Ma'am...should I broadcast the surrender of this vessel?" The First Officer could see she was torn, and his words hurt his captain.

Boltha sighed. She walked over to a bridge window and leant against it. She was defeated. Her forces were in disarray. All because of one action.

"Well played," she whispered as she looked at her broken fleet. "Broadcast the surrender. We request terms. All Collective Zone forces are to stand down," she ordered her First Officer to transmit the message to the Solar Solutions command and her remaining forces.

Chapter 36

Days later, the Solar Solutions board held a great ceremony honouring the fallen from the war. The ceremony was held in the Great Square on *Neptune Prime* with the military forces that fought against the Collective Zone in positions of honour.

The Great Square was the central hub of the Government District on *Neptune Prime*. It was a vast space made of steel and stone imported from all over the Solar Solutions' corporate territory.

At the head of the square on a large pedestal stood and sat the board members of the Corporation. They faced outwards into the square and gave speeches of varying lengths and levels of interest.

In front of them, there were the bodies of a few very special soldiers who had died for the Corporation. The pride of place was reserved for an ornate coffin that bore Captain Artisius' name. His body was vaporised, of course, but this did not stop the Solar Solutions board from making him an honoured coffin.

Further back in the body of the square stood the ranks of soldiers who had fought in the war. There were ship crews and boarding crews and fighter and bomber crews from every ship set up in ranks. They numbered in their thousands.

Further back still, there were the civilian elements of the Corporation. Even after all their dealings with Artisius over the years, their role in defending the bridge of the *Silver Ark* and their devotion to bring the message of the danger of the Collective Zone to the Solar Solutions' notice; Draz and Alfred were stood back here.

Back here the words of the speeches were muffled and echoey, almost impossible to understand as the sound reverberated around the steel chamber.

Various members of the public strained and stretched to try to see what was going on many hundreds of metres away. Alfred did not strain; neither did Draz. They stood and watched blankly from their relegated position.

From what Alfred could understand, the board were expounding on the greatness of Captain Artisius. All Alfred could hear were the occasional words that did not quite bounce into oblivion in the speakers dotted around the space; words like 'martyr' and 'visionary' and 'sacrifice'.

When one of the board was giving a particularly rousing speech; something about how Artisius' martyrdom should inspire others to do the same if it was needed; Alfred scoffed at the sentiment. Other members of the public looked at him disdainfully and mumbled about some people not understanding greatness; Draz just looked at her friend. She smiled at him. He smiled at her. It was clear that she too, knew that what the board were stuffing themselves with was all rubbish.

Gunter's name was mentioned in another speech by some non-descript board member. It was mentioned how he heroically defended the *Silver Ark* with his soldiers until the battle was over. And now that he was resigning as he believed that a new CEO was needed to take control over the victorious Corporation. He could not run the Corporation after such a cataclysmic shift of power. New blood was needed to run the Corporation. The voice faded into numbness and static after this.

Then there was some great example of a Solar Solutions soldier by some name like OE15. He was a bomber pilot who volunteered to fight for the fighter pilots and gave his all in the battle shooting down a number of enemy craft. He was being presented with some medal or other.

Alfred began to laugh. He could not stop himself. He had forgotten much, but he could still remember the battle a few days ago, and what the board were saying was completely fanciful and wrong. It was simple propaganda.

"Did you expect any different?"

Alfred ignored the voice. It would be gone soon. He had booked a flight to Pluto as soon as the battle was over, and he had sent a message to the colony there that he requested surgery to remove a damaged zetting implant. He had stressed that it was urgent.

"Don't you like me?"

He ignored it again; and continued laughing. Some members of the public around him began telling him to be quiet. Draz put a hand on his shoulder. He stopped laughing and looked at her. She had understanding eyes. He smiled at her.

"Come on," she whispered. "Let's go." She cocked her head to indicate a side street that led off the square.

They left the adoring crowd to more of their talk of 'martyrs' and 'heroic saviours' and headed away from the square. The crowd pressed up against them as they forced their way away from the square. It was clear the population was completely enthralled by the rhetoric of the board. They bought every word; every syllable.

Alfred stopped in the street when they were away from the crush of people. He lent against the wall of a building. He was not laughing now. Draz waited and looked at him in a worried way.

"What's wrong?" she asked.

"I...I can't remember. I mean, I remember the words, but I don't remember the places..." he looked at her with pleading eyes.

"What do you mean?" Draz asked; her brow furrowed.

"I mean...I know I was on *Florida Station*...but I don't remember it. I mean, I remember we've been on adventures; but I don't remember them. I cannot remember important people in my past for the life of me!" Alfred sounded a little frantic. "I'd give almost anything to have my memory back and be back on *Florida Station* and zetting again."

"Ah..." Draz breathed. She put an arm around his shoulders. "We'll head to Pluto, and you can have the surgery. It'll be okay..." Draz reassured him.

"You...you're coming too?" Alfred stammered.

"Yes, I'm coming too. I can't leave you alone now can I?" She laughed.

Alfred felt reassured; and he really wanted to zet. He had not zetted in quite a while; but he knew that he could not risk it. Last time was almost fatal.

"Oh, go on...treat yourself..."

"Shut up!" said Alfred. "You're dead soon..."

"So are you."

Draz looked puzzled. Alfred explained it was the voice. She nodded, clearly not quite understanding the realness of the voice in his head. Alfred knew that no one could quite understand how real the voice was to him.

"Should we listen to more of the speeches?" Draz asked.

"No...It's all shit anyway. One more mention of 'martyrs' and I'll vomit. People only invoke martyrs when they want you to die for a cause that you're not quite convinced about or they're not quite convinced about," Alfred spat the words. "Artisius wasn't a martyr, he was a hero. He was a man who did what he believed was right. He was our friend. He would hate that his death is used as an example for others to follow. No death should be followed, it's life that should be followed, and used as an example..." Alfred trailed off.

"For someone with no memory, you're a good philosopher," Draz said with a smile. "Okay, no more speeches, let's get something to eat."

They headed off into the maze of streets on this level of *Neptune Prime*. Alfred's voice bothered him all the way.

Chapter 37

Alfred stood on the observation deck of the smallish shuttle ferry that was taking him to Pluto. It would take years; and he would have to cryo-sleep for a long time; but he felt calm. He knew that he was going to have the surgery that would fix things. He had the confirmation message a few months ago that his surgery was booked back when he was on *Neptune Prime*.

Alfred watched the stars, as the emptiness of space glided past.

There were not many people on the shuttle. It was rather empty. There was not much call to go to Pluto except for radical surgery and strange medical procedures, so the passengers on the shuttle kept to themselves. They did not want the disturbance of other people.

Alfred was alone on the observation deck. He felt he could watch the stars for ages. He liked it when he was alone.

"But you're not alone..."

"Soon..." Alfred whispered to himself.

"Don't you like me? Aren't we good friends? Why do you want to get rid of me?"

"You're not me!" Alfred said.

"Oh...but I am..."

"Oh, there you are!" Alfred's argument was broken by Draz approaching and calling out to him. He did not turn to face her. He kept watching the stars.

Draz moved to beside him. She too stood for a little while, in silence, while looking into space and then continued.

"I just caught the last news from *Neptune Prime*..." she paused, obviously waiting for a response. She got none. "The reports say that Trader Virtus is being put on trial for grand treason..."

"Virtus..." Alfred said. "I...don't remember..." his voice cracked.

"That's why you were exempt from the trial to give evidence. You couldn't remember," Draz paused. "Anyway, he's going to trial. We'll have to see what happens there..." She paused again before continuing. "Voting has begun to elect a new CEO for Solar Solutions. The process is rather secret so there's no obvious favourite at the moment. The process takes a while."

"Huh," Alfred scoffed. He still watched the stars.

Draz continued. "The fate of the Collective Zone Fleet Commander, Boltha was her name, is sealed. She is being tried for war crimes and it's almost certain that she'll be convicted and either sent to the Earth Moon for life or even executed. Good riddance I say. What with Mars and Europa and the war in general. How much blood did she spill!"

"But was it her, or was it Uxus?" Alfred asked quietly.

"Does it matter? Uxus is dead. She'll have to answer for what she did," Draz sounded perturbed. Draz continued with the news reports. "They sent the prisoners captured in the war back to their homes. Both sides exchanged prisoners. That's at least something. The Collective Zone prisoners captured invading the *Silver Ark* were also sent back. There were reports of a certain Collective Zone soldier who was taken prisoner, named Grox, who let us know about boarding tactics for the Collective Zone. His information helped us repel the attack on the bridge of the *Silver Ark*, so the propaganda reports say. He was returned along with the others." Draz paused for a moment and then continued. "I must say I don't envy him. All that interrogation..."

"I can't really remember anyway," Alfred said with a sigh.

Draz put a hand on Alfred's shoulder. He turned and looked at her. She smiled.

"Look, you'll be fixed soon--" she said.

"But my memory..." Alfred said. His face pained.

"We'll ask the doctors. It might be salvageable; once the implant is removed," she patted him on the shoulder. "Come on. It's cryo-sleep time," she shuddered. "I still hate the process."

Alfred followed Draz back down off the observation deck of the shuttle to the cryo-pods. A few were already in use.

"We'll sleep for years on the way there," said Draz while undressing.

Alfred muttered to himself as he undressed.

"Speak up, she can't hear you..."

"I said. I wonder if we'll dream?" Alfred replied.

Draz looked at him concerned again. "That was the voice wasn't it?"

They both stood there in their underwear and stashed their clothes and meagre belongings in the lockers near the pods.

"Yeah. It lives with me now. I just want it gone. I feel it. It burrows into my consciousness. It tells me things. It whispers things to me. It makes me believe things. I hate it!" Alfred said slowly.

"The doctors will fix it..." said Draz. She furrowed her brow in worry.

"I hope so!" Alfred said, getting into his pod.

"You'll never be rid of me. I am you..."

300

Draz entered her pod and they both fell into controlled sleep for the duration of the journey to Pluto.

***

As the shuttle slipped through the blackness of space to the farthest reaches of the Solar System, Alfred dreamed. Alfred dreamed of a young woman who jumped off some cooling stacks on a strange space station. He dreamed of a man who saved him from Earth, and he journeyed through the Solar System with him. He dreamed of a priest who seduced hundreds and killed thousands. He dreamed of a voice; a voice in his head; a voice that said it would never leave. He dreamed of a woman who cared for him. He knew this dream. It was Draz. He had not forgotten her. He dreamed of a strange ethereal shape that chased him down wires and networks while he zetted. He dreamed that it caught up with him and swallowed him whole. He dreamed in the deep sleep of the cryo-pod he saw things he had not seen in a very long time. He saw people and things he could not remember. He dreamed.

***

After years of travel, the shuttle docked at Pluto's main docking station. The station on the surface was small, but it stretched over the surface of the dwarf planet.

Alfred and Draz exited the shuttle in the landing bay. It was white; hospital white. The few passengers got off and were met by some tech-slaves and a number of people in white coats.

Alfred was approached by a man in a white coat. Draz stood nearby.

"Name?" said the man.

"Uh...Alfred..." said Alfred, a little unsure.

"Ah yes, zetting sickness and implant removal. Come this way please." The man proceeded to walk towards an airlock.

"Uh..." said Alfred.

Draz walked behind him and said reassuringly, "I'll be here."

After moving through the high tech airlock and walking down a number of bleached white hospital corridors with rooms and theatres on either side, the man turned to Draz and indicated that she could wait in the waiting room just off the corridor. Draz nodded and waited. One of the tech-slaves came over to her and started organising quarters for her to stay in and wait for Alfred.

Alfred turned to watch her sit in the waiting room. It was sterile and had grey carpet with grey chairs that seemed a little too uncomfortable to relax in. But soon the sight was stolen from him as he rounded a corner and proceeded into a room with a bed.

"This is your room, Alfred. Please undress and get into the hospital robes. We will be back shortly to prep you for surgery," the man ordered.

"How long will it take?" Alfred asked meekly.

"The surgery? About six hours. We want to get it started as soon as possible so the damage is minimised. You will be in Surgery 4." And with that, the man left.

Alfred looked around the sterile room. A robe was waiting on the bed. He obeyed and changed into it and waited by sitting on the bed.

After a short time, the man returned and beckoned for him to follow. Alfred did. The floor felt cold without his shoes on. He entered a room that had "Surgery 4" written on the door. It was a large room with a bed in the centre and machines all around that had wires and needles protruding from them.

Alfred froze. He did not like the look of the equipment.

"Relax. You'll be asleep. It looks worse than it is. Everyone always has your reaction," said the man.

302

"Ah..." said Alfred and climbed onto the operating bed in the centre of the room when the man indicated for him to do so.

"We'll just run through a start up procedure for the machine," said the man moving out of Alfred's sight behind him.

A woman entered the room and began prepping a needle for Alfred's arm. "This is just an anaesthetic," she said. "You won't feel a thing."

Soon the room began to spin, and words elongated and reverberated. Alfred slipped into unconsciousness as he heard the machine with the needles starting up.

"We had a good time, didn't we?"

Chapter 38

Alfred stood, in his old clothes, on one of the observation platforms that formed the upper level of the Pluto Medical Outpost. He watched the stars. He liked watching the stars. They stretched away into the sky as the dome of the observation deck towered above him. The stars made him feel calm. He wondered if anyone was out there watching back. He hoped so. He hoped there were other creatures experiencing life out there. He wondered if they fought wars and killed each other. He wondered many things.

The surgery had been successful, and the hard-wired implant had been thoroughly removed from all reaches of his brain. Alfred reached up and touched the side of his head gingerly. It was a cold metal plate that had to be inserted to fill the hole that was left. He winced as he touched it. The surgery was only a short time ago and the wound still felt raw; but the hospital had him up and about and thinking almost as soon as the surgery was over. They had insisted that he move around so that the remaining brain could grow and recover.

Alfred felt the scar on his arm through his sleeve where the injections to treat his condition used to go. Due to the repeated injections, there was a mark. He no longer needed medication since the surgery, but the scar on his arm would be silent testimony to his condition; that and the metal plate in his skull. He grimaced at the thought.

Alfred heard a noise behind him. He did not turn to see who it was. The person stopped by his left side.

"Good to see you up and about!" It was Draz's voice; he recognised it. She stopped by Alfred's left side and watched the stars with him for a little while.

Alfred said nothing. His head felt empty. With the removal of the implant, a large part of what he had been was removed.

"How are you feeling?" Draz tried again. It was clear to Alfred that she meant well and was concerned about him.

"All right. My head hurts a bit. I'm just standing here and thinking, I like watching the stars, they make me feel calm. I wonder what's out there. They make me think," Alfred said quietly and smiled.

"About what?" Draz asked.

"Well...After all that time...I miss it," Alfred said. Draz turned her head to face him and looked puzzled. "I miss the voice," Alfred said. "I miss the desire to zet. I miss not being able to zet..." he trailed off.

"But it was killing you--" Draz said.

"I know, I know," Alfred said. "It's for the best. But it's odd not feeling the craving for zetting. It's odd not having my companion voice that commented on everything that I did; running me down. Hah, I never thought I'd miss it like this..."

Draz looked relieved. "So, the voice has totally gone?"

"I think so. I mean, I haven't heard it since," Alfred looked at Draz. "You know the last thing it said to me before the surgery? 'We had a good time, didn't we?' I remember that..."

Draz scoffed. "That seems rather perverse."

"I know! But it's like it was saying goodbye and knew it was going. Weird huh!?" Alfred turned back to watch the stars. "The doctors say that the type of decay induced schizophrenia will slowly heal and the voice should not return. They also say that my memory should not deteriorate any more. My old memories may or may not return depending on their vividness. But I shouldn't get any sicker or any worse. The craving for zetting should be gone completely too."

"Well, that's good!" Draz said. Alfred heard the smile in her voice.

"How's your craving?" Alfred asked.

Draz stayed silent for a while, then answered slowly. "Well...It's still there, in the recesses of my head. It's been years now, due to the travel, since I've used. But the desire is still there. Artisius said it would never fully go. But I'm all right, thanks."

"Artisius...You won't use again, will you?" Alfred said.

"No...well, I can't honestly say, but I don't intend to give in. I have other things to fight for now; other things to occupy my mind." Draz paused and turned her head towards Alfred. "Want to hear some news?" Draz changed the topic dramatically.

"Sure." Alfred understood the change.

"I don't know if you remember Boltha? The Fleet Commander of the Collective Zone?" Draz asked and watched as Alfred nodded slowly. "Well, she was sentenced to life on the Earth Moon prison for war crimes."

"But right next to Earth would be easy for the Collective Zone to break her out and use her again?" Alfred said.

"Ah, but they condemned her too for letting CEO Uxus die. They also want her in prison. Even though it was Artisius who killed Uxus, she got some of the blame for not protecting him," Draz explained.

"I see...well, that's for the best, I suppose," Alfred said.

"Do you remember Virtus?" Draz continued.

"Partially. I remember he blew up *Florida Station*. That I cannot forget."

Draz nodded. "Well, he pleaded guilty to all the charges--"

"What!?" Alfred exclaimed, turning his head to look at Draz.

"It looked like he would get off, due to Artisius being dead and you not having a memory. The last two known survivors of the station. But Virtus pleaded guilty! He was sentenced to life imprisonment on the Earth Moon like Boltha. The sentence would have been death, but it was reduced to life imprisonment due to his guilty plea." Draz paused and looked at Alfred. "Want me to continue?"

Alfred nodded. "Yeah, go on."

"The corporations have appointed new CEOs. The Collective Zone appointed Maxtria, the Master of the Fleet, as their CEO. She is militaristic and tough, but cautious. She was head of the Great Fleet when it was around Earth. She's stern, but stable; so the news reports say." Draz paused to let the information sink in.

Alfred nodded

Draz continued, "And the Solar Solutions Corporation appointed their former Chief Weapons Officer Michael. He is well respected and a much more tactical and shrewd mind than Gunter, who resigned and now lives in a penthouse on *Neptune Prime*, by the way. The Chief Operating Officer, Cranmere, was found some out of the way place on the board of some company or other," Draz stopped.

"I see. So, things are returning to normal. Nothing really changes. The corporations go on and people live out their lives under the threat of war," Alfred said.

"I suppose, but the corporations have strengthened trade deals and opened dialogue which is different. There should be a greater peace this time..." Draz said.

"Now what do we do?" Alfred asked, still staring out the giant dome stretching away above him. "I'm not sure I want to remember. I'm not sure I want to..." He stopped before finishing.

"I can remember for you..." Draz said.

Alfred smiled. "That would be nice. But again, what do we do now?"

"Perhaps, we just have to live?" Draz sounded positive.

"I suppose." Alfred paused. He slipped his left hand into Draz's right hand as it was hanging by her side. He felt her stiffen a little and then she relaxed and squeezed his hand.

She looked at him, and smiled.

He looked at her, returning the smile.

Then they both looked out to the stars.

"I'm ready now," Alfred said quietly, but determinedly. "I am ready now."

***

End of Volume Three
You have reached the end of the *Broken Cosmos Trilogy*. Thanks for reading. I would be grateful if you would leave a review of each book (*Florida Station, Martian Flight, Neptune's War*) on the Amazon pages of the books.
***

Author details and sites:
Website: www.ikennedyauthor.com (mailing list link on website / contact email at bottom of website)
Amazon: www.amazon.com/author/ikennedy
Twitter: twitter.com/ikennedyauthor
Facebook: www.facebook.com/ikennedyauthor

www.ingramcontent.com/pod-product-compliance
Lightning Source LLC
Chambersburg PA
CBHW052017240626
47153CB00006B/1849